I0822343

THE WITCH OF TUT

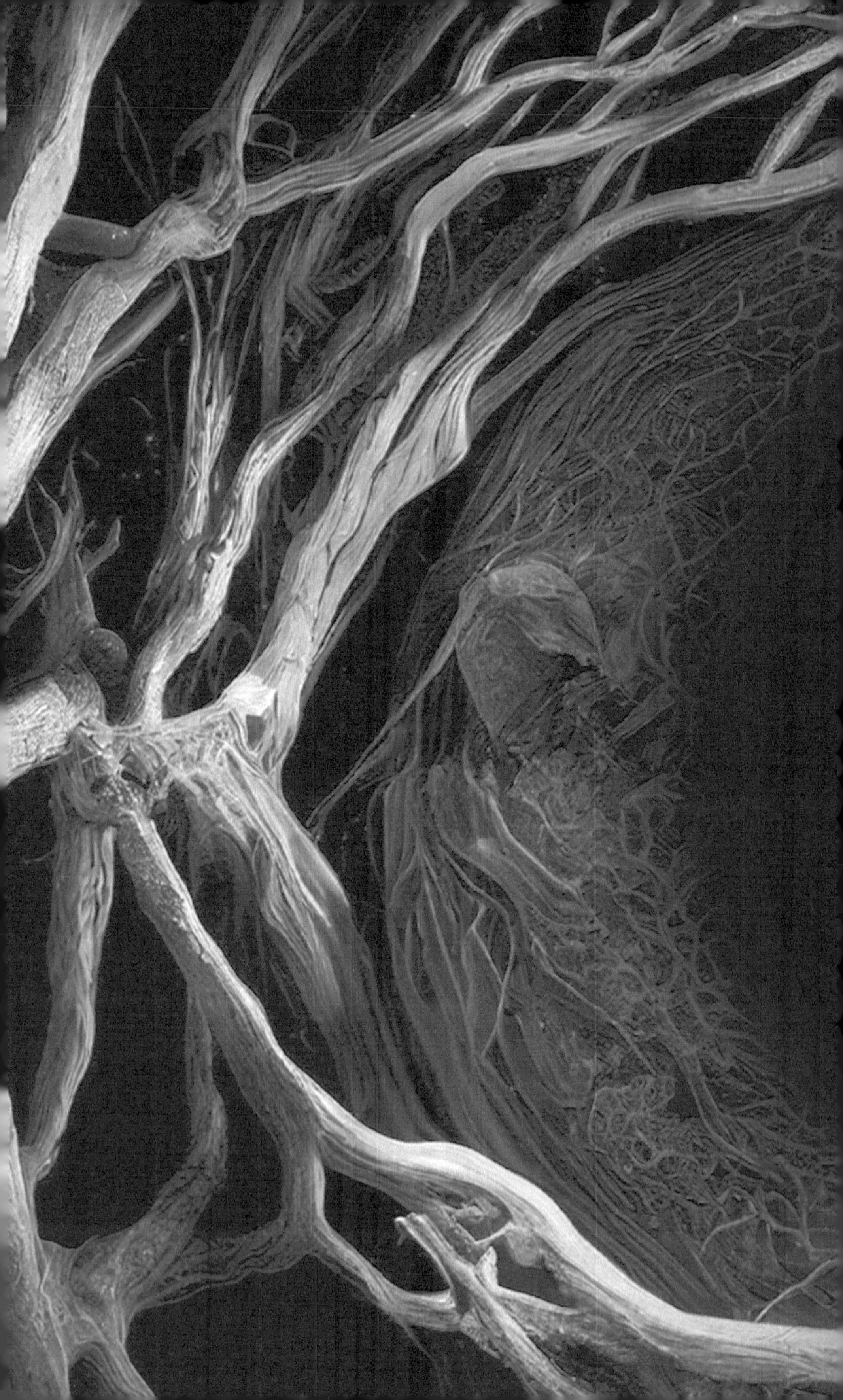

THE WITCH

OF TUT

D. A. SPRUZEN

The Witch of Tut

4 Horsemen Publications, Inc.
1497 Main St. Suite 169
Dunedin, FL 34698
4horsemenpublications.com
info@4horsemenpublications.com

Cover & Typesetting by Autumn Skye
Edited by Joseph Mistretta

Library of Congress Control Number: 2023938659

Paperback ISBN-13: 979-8-8232-0211-4
Hardcover ISBN-13: 979-8-8232-0213-8
Audiobook ISBN-13: 979-8-8232-0210-7
Ebook ISBN-13: 979-8-8232-0212-1

Table of Contents

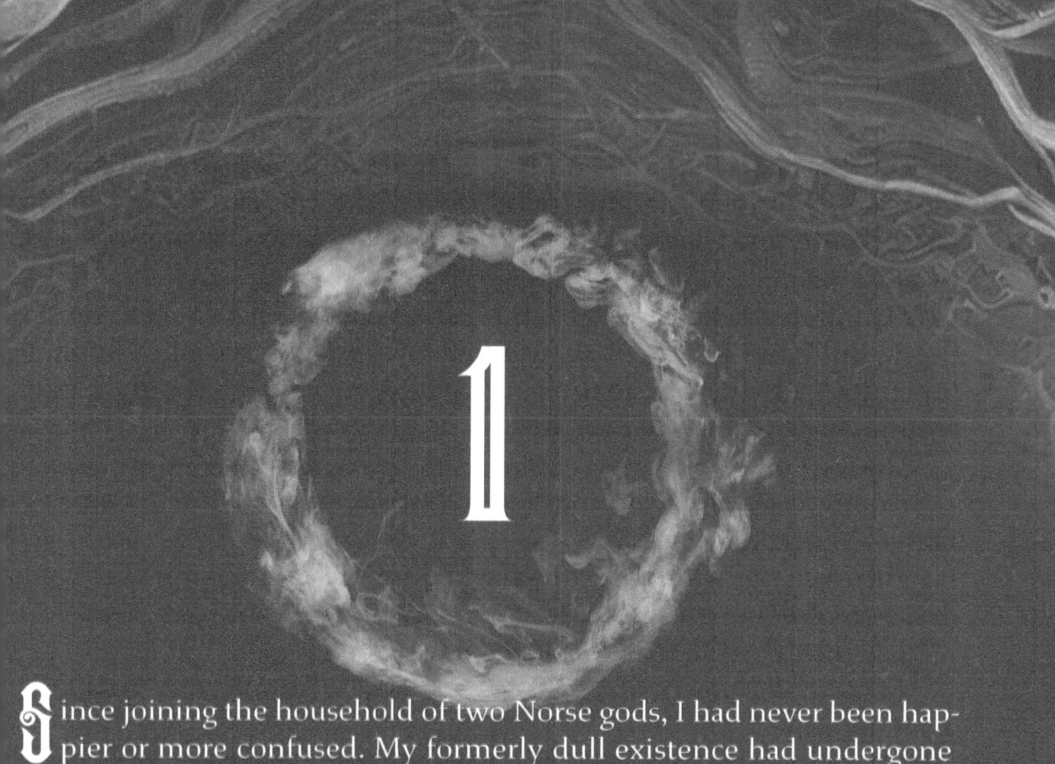

1

Since joining the household of two Norse gods, I had never been happier or more confused. My formerly dull existence had undergone a seismic shift: after being hired in September 2017 by Lin Thoren to ghostwrite her memoirs, I had fallen in love with her magnificent husband, the god Hoenir (now known as Hunter), and found myself pregnant. Lin didn't mind the situation. She enjoyed her own dalliances, and I had become integrated into the family in a very unorthodox manner. It's true, Hunter loved me, but he also loves Lin forever—which for them truly is. What I thought I knew, thought I believed, had been thoroughly upended, the hard questions remaining mostly repressed.

Hunter still didn't know we were writing Lin's memoirs. He thought that they were providing me with a haven while I wrote my novel, which I sort of am. He is terrified of being known for what he is, perhaps rightly so. People can lash out cruelly when they are fearful. Hunter believed I thought him a rather special man. Far from it—he's a god, all right. But that means that while I get older, he ages only one year to my ten. So unfair.

I hadn't seen much of their children, Sven and Margareta, because they were away at school. They proved friendly and welcoming when they came home for the holidays, although I didn't know what they'd make of having a new baby brother or sister. No, they wouldn't know it was a brother or sister. Just my kid.

The maid Dora, a former Greek wood nymph, was the only metaphorical fly in the proverbial ointment. I gathered she'd had a fling or two with Hunter in the past, so she was insanely jealous of me. She was a great cook, though.

The three of us had an idyllic vacation in the Caribbean that January. Lin was off with a mysterious friend most of the time (probably a lover), while Hunter and I enjoyed languid sessions sunbathing, swimming, and lovemaking.

My bump was beginning to show, and I knew I'd have to tell Auntie Peggy. But how? I thought about it for days. She often cooked Sunday lunch for us both, so I finally gathered up my courage during a visit around the beginning of February.

She took one look at my face and said, "Mary, whatever's the matter?"

"Auntie Peggy, I have something serious to tell you. It will come as rather a shock, I'm afraid."

She fixed her warm hazel eyes on mine. Her lips couldn't seem to decide whether to purse or twitch. "You mean about the baby, dear?"

"Uh, what?" Well, that knocked the wind out of me.

"Mary, I've known since Christmas. You were off your food and avoiding wine."

"I'm so sorry to disappoint you, Auntie, especially when you've been so kind. I'm going to keep it, you know."

"Well, I was surprised at first, but I've grown used to the idea. Now I'm actually quite excited, to be honest." Her smile scrunched up her face in a way that made her cute and lovable.

"Oh, Auntie." I rushed around to her end of the table, and we had a clumsy hug over her plate, resulting in a splotch of gravy on my cuff.

"Go and clean off your sleeve, dear. I'm not going to ask any awkward questions. Let's just enjoy the happy event. Will you continue working at the Thorens'?"

"Yes, they know, and Lin is quite looking forward to having a baby in the house."

"Well, that's nice, dear."

I couldn't believe how easy that was. Thank goodness Auntie didn't ask about the father. I'd worked out some explanation about having a little too much to drink at a party, but I'm not sure she would have swallowed it. If I'd been to a party, I would have told her all about it. She knew I hadn't made friends locally except through Lin and Hunter.

I spent the spring months putting the first volume together in book form. Lin wanted something publishable, although I wasn't allowed to submit it to publishers until they'd left the area. Probably many years in the future. She didn't know I was putting together my personal memoir in a separate document. I was so much a part of their lives by then, I wanted that just for me. I keep it locked away because if Lin knew, she'd get paranoid and make me destroy it.

2

We left for Italy in late April, as Lin had promised. About five months gone, I was still up for sightseeing. A trip to Italy was a dream come true. Rome first, then to an ancient monastery in Umbria, from where a car would take us sightseeing. Lin said we'd even go to Assisi.

I couldn't imagine Hunter enjoying sightseeing. As I expected, he spent most days lolling around and watching the stock market on his iPad or taking brisk walks I could not keep up with. His one stride required three of mine to match his pace. It seemed Lin had a special friend in a nearby town. Hunter didn't ask why we were never introduced to these friends in foreign places. I supposed they had a tacit agreement to let sleeping dogs lie.

Rome had me in a constant case of wonder. Every time I turned a corner, some ancient relic was tucked into a building or standing proudly in the center of a piazza. We stayed in a grand hotel full of carvings, massive paintings, and yards of velvet on the Via Venuto, an avenue of exclusive boutiques and a few larger, intimidating establishments. Lin sent me on bus tours every day that picked tourists up from the hotel. I lapped up my exposure to all this ancient and modern grandeur. She, meanwhile, went shopping incessantly and even dragged Hunter out to buy some new clothes.

On our last day in Rome, she took me out and bought me a few lovely tops and one dress, although they didn't fit very well. After the baby, they'd be fabulous. We found one top that would accommodate my expanding waistline, a glorious floral silk affair.

Chapter 2

Giancarlo, a manager from the monastery, came to pick us up from the hotel and stayed mostly silent, thank heavens, as I gazed out of the car windows in rapt attention for the several hours it took to get to Umbria. Lin and Hunter must have dozed off. The quaint old houses and fertile fields rolled by, vines marching in perfect lines, backed by misty hills and valleys, a panorama of unending beauty. It was the beginning of another love affair. In America, we are so proud of a building that's two hundred years old. Italy has buildings and ruins thousands of years old. And the food!

Giancarlo stopped around lunchtime in an alleyway next to a little old church, where he told us his parents had been married. He led us down the path to a door with a rooster painted on it. He strode in and kissed an elderly man and his wife with loud and enthusiastic greetings. The lady gestured toward a scrubbed wooden table, and we sat down.

I looked around at this simple room with only four tables and a few paintings, which on closer inspection, turned out to be mosaics. Pointing to the one next to our table, I said to Lin, "I wonder if that's from Orvieto."

The old lady poked her head through the hatch. "*Sì, sì, Orvieto!*" she called, before withdrawing into the kitchen like a shy tortoise.

"It will be a simple meal," our driver said. "Pasta with truffle sauce and a salad. Edmundo is picking the salad now, and the pasta will be ready in about twenty minutes."

Hunter opened his mouth to protest but yelped as Lin kicked him. He was more partial to huge slabs of half-cooked meat.

Soon the food arrived—a big bowl of pasta with a creamy sauce and another of very young leaves. I have never had a better meal, before or since. The truffles in the sauce were so tasty, like a cross between mushrooms and garlic. The salad was a fresh, crunchy delight with light olive oil and what I realized much later must have been a superb balsamic vinegar. I wondered if I'd be able to waddle as far as the car afterward.

But Giancarlo had other plans. He wanted to light a candle in the church. We said goodbye to the old couple, Lin and I conveying through Giancarlo how wonderful the food had been, while Hunter smiled broadly, keeping silent. He said he'd sit in the car while we visited the church.

The church was dark and damp, light seeping through begrimed stained glass. I collapsed into a pew and looked around while Giancarlo went to pick out his candle, make the donation, and pray. Lin disappeared into a side chapel.

When my eyes adjusted, I discovered murals depicting bible scenes on the plastered walls, some almost worn away. Plaster statues stood in niches, many missing various appendages. Generations must have been baptized, married, and memorialized in this church. Peace abounded.

Giancarlo strode to the side chapel and beckoned to Lin while I hauled myself up to follow them out. As dazzled as I was by the scenery, I think I fell asleep within five minutes, not waking until we pulled to a stop at the monastery.

We stepped out into a courtyard lined with pots of scarlet and pink flowers, most still in bud, and made our way up to the second floor of a former dormitory near the chapel. My room was next to a bathroom while Lin and Hunter's was *en suite*. I flopped down on the bed, only to suffer the shock of a rock-hard mattress. The driver had told us on the way that the monastery, now an art school, usually hosted groups of art students. The first batch would be arriving at the beginning of May, mostly adults for whom it was a vacation. I wished I had shown even a glimmer of talent in art classes at school. The best I can manage are warped stick figures.

Dinner was a little more to Hunter's liking, with plenty of grilled chicken in a basil-laden sauce, pasta again, and a mixture of grilled vegetables. He ignored the vegetables. That was about all I ate, still full from lunch.

I went to bed early, leaving Giancarlo, Lin, and Hunter drinking wine on the patio. I didn't envy them the wine. The very thought of it made me nauseous.

The next day, we enjoyed a spread of fruit, cheese, and fragrant bread for breakfast in the dining room off a surprisingly modest kitchen, followed by a short trip into Terni, the closest town. I wandered around with Lin as she looked at silk scarves. She bought at least a dozen as gifts for various people, including one apiece for Auntie Peggy, who had become a frequent dinner guest, and me. I had no idea what Hunter was up to. As soon as we got out of the car, he'd rushed off opposite us.

Back for lunch, another buffet spread, this time: stuffed zucchini flowers (a wondrous, to-die-for dish), fresh anchovies in vinegar, meat rolls made with ultra-thin slices of beef, and a few other tasty morsels, accompanied by carafes of red and white table wine.

Lin and Hunter said they were going to take a siesta. I decided to explore the property before taking a nap.

I started with the chapel. The ceiling was painted with religious scenes. Old oils adorned the walls, and the altar was surprisingly elaborate for a small monastery. Giancarlo had told us earlier that it had never been deconsecrated because the owners still held weddings and baptisms there. A dozen tables and chairs for students to paint were lined up in front of the altar, where pews should be. That not only seemed slightly disrespectful but looked downright odd. I wondered if the instructors opined from the pulpit.

I emerged from a different door into strong sunlight and found myself in an alley by a small house, which I guessed was inhabited by the school director. This led to a courtyard behind the dorms. A large, capped well occupied the center, and roses bloomed around the edge. A path led past a lookout with a stone wall. I stopped for a minute to admire distant, green hills and the misty, blue mountains far behind them before walking farther into a cool copse.

"*Buongiorno*!"

I whipped around but couldn't see anyone.

"Who's there?"

A disheveled figure stepped out from behind a prickly bush loaded with yellow flowers. He ambled toward me, his stained brown cotton jacket flapping and untied, cracked leather shoes squeaking.

"Pretty lady!"

Stale wine on his breath billowed into my face. His red-rimmed eyes looked slightly mad.

"I'm going back to the house now," I said.

"No, no, you have to be kind. Pietro is all alone."

My first maternal instinct kicked in—*he might hurt the baby*. I turned and ran.

It didn't take him more than a minute to grab me and push me to the ground, pulling at my clothes. I screamed for all I was worth, but that only seemed to excite him more. I fought as hard as I could but felt myself weakening.

Then he was off me and screaming. I opened my eyes and crawled onto my hands and knees to find Hunter holding Pietro over his head as he strode toward the lookout. Without hesitation, he threw the man over in a wide arc. You know those cartoons where characters fall off a cliff, and their voices gradually fade into the distance? I believe musicians call it a *smorzando*. In a cartoon, it would have been funny.

I was badly shaken not only by my lucky escape but by Hunter's ruthlessness, which I also found sexy. A year ago, Hunter's behavior would have horrified me. My moral compass truly pointed north now.

I got to my feet and tried to walk to Hunter but felt myself swaying a little. Hunter ran back and enveloped me in his arms.

"Hunter! It was so lucky you came by."

"I heard you," he said.

I merely nodded.

"You are not surprised?"

"I know you and Lin have unusually good hearing and are very strong, too."

"I see." His brow creased as I pulled back a little, and we looked at each other for a long few minutes. "You know, don't you?"

"Yes, I do. No mere man could be like you."

His face broke out into a sloppy grin, which suddenly switched off. "But no one must know. No one."

"Of course not, my love. I would never put you and Lin in any kind of jeopardy."

He picked me up and carried me upstairs to my room, laying me tenderly on my bed.

"Some wine, I think," he said, kissing my lips.

"No, no, I shouldn't drink wine. It's not good for the baby. I'd love some sparkling water, though."

He disappeared, and a little while later, it was Lin who brought me some lemonade.

"This is made with fresh lemons," she said. "Very healthy."

"That was a lucky escape," I said.

"Quite, and it won't happen again. We won't speak of it further."

I didn't let that incident spoil my holiday, although Pietro's terrified screams haunted my dreams at first and sometimes intruded during the day at the most unexpected moments. Those incidents subsided in a couple of weeks, although I still occasionally dream of that poor lost soul. The many new and wonderful experiences on that trip helped push aside the horror, and I emerged shockingly unmarked from the ordeal.

Hunter and I had plenty of time together while Lin was occupied with her friend. Sometimes Hunter even came along sightseeing with Giancarlo and me. I was particularly struck by a statue of St. Francis in front of the cathedral—before he was made a saint, as he rode into Assisi, exhausted by war. It was my first time in Europe, and the first time is always so special.

After we got back to Salton, we rested for a week to get over jet lag and for me to visit Auntie Peggy—who lived in the same Virginia suburb—present her with a silk scarf, and tell her about the trip. I skipped The Incident, of course.

Soon it was time for me to set up the recorder and for Lin to array herself on the couch on Monday morning and start talking again.

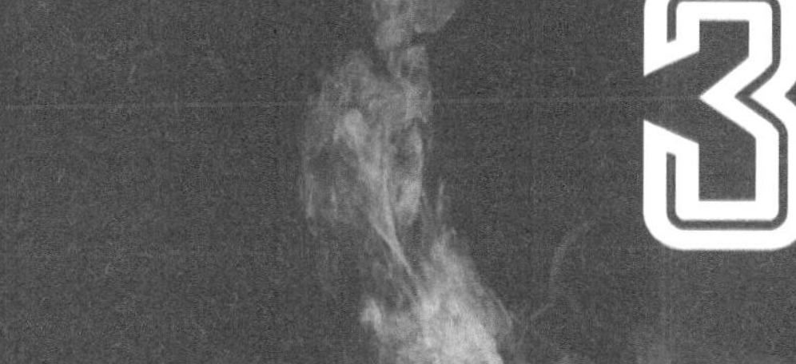

3

Lin wandered down at around ten, cradling a cup of something steaming. "Mmm, I love hot chocolate."

"Me, too. More in the winter, though," I said.

Lin sat in her usual spot on the sofa. I guess she didn't recline right away because of her drink. "Funny how I spent all my formative years without food or drink. I loved the aromas, though never thought to sample any of it."

"That is odd. I mean ... weren't the other gods all eating in front of you?"

"I suppose it was because we handmaidens were minor goddesses and assumed food and drink were only for our betters. We didn't think anything of it. At least, I didn't."

"I can see you really appreciate it now!"

"I certainly do. Hunter, of course, has always indulged. He was most amused when I first started eating when we got to Aetna. No, I drank first. Spring water. It felt so cool on my throat ... until I started to choke. I had never learned to swallow, you see. Hunter had to explain and show me."

"What about food?" I was fascinated. When my sister fed her baby daughter rice cereal for the first time, the poor tot didn't know what to do with it, so most spilled out of her mouth. She choked a little and cried. Lin must have felt like that.

"I started very slowly with food. Just a few berries at first. I didn't like their sour taste, so I left solids alone for a few days. Then I saw Hunter come back to our cave with some rabbits he'd trapped and killed. He did all the horrid things you must do to prepare the meat for cooking, which wasn't easy considering he didn't have a proper knife. I can't remember what he used—maybe a stone worn to a sharp edge. Then he had to do the cooking."

Lin couldn't continue; she was laughing so hard. "Oh, you should have seen him trying to light a fire! He'd always had someone to bring him his food. He'd never had to actually do the work." A little chocolate slopped over onto the carpet, barely missing her skirt. "Damn. Do you have any towels handy, Mary?"

I had a roll of paper towels in the little kitchenette in my basement apartment where I could make myself tea and a few easy things when I felt like it. I ran to get a couple of sheets and soon mopped it up.

"Sorry about that. Anyway, there he was, rubbing two sticks together until they broke. No sparks, no nothing. I could tell he was getting dangerously frustrated. I had an idea. I gathered some dry leaves and left them in the sunlight, which was really strong then. The dry leaves ought to catch fire, I reasoned. Well, they didn't. Then I remembered what Hunter told me when he went exploring our first day. At the top of the mountain, a great fire burned in a crater. He said even he could hardly get near the edge. I suggested we try up there."

"I've seen the pictures and read about it," I said. "That's a long way up. I don't see how even a god could get anywhere near that heat." Although they were both here, clearly intact.

"We were still ignorant of the world at that time. But Aetna wasn't nearly as big then as she is now. When we got up there, I was in awe of that white and orange heat. Smoke rose from her belly as if warning the world of her power. She threw up a few black boulders every now and then when she really got going and sent a steady stream of lava oozing from a cave on one side, which hissed and boiled when it reached the sea below. I could see at once what we must do."

"So dangerous!"

"Not if you're careful. I sent Hunter a little way down to a copse of young trees that could be easily stripped. He brought back a few branches. I helped him lay a few so the leafy ends hung off the rim. Quite soon, one caught fire. Once it was flaming, he ran down the slopes with it and set it among his own arrangement of kindling and logs. We soon had it roaring away and roasted the meat stuck on the end of sharp sticks from the same branch. But, as always, there were complications."

"Didn't you like the meat?"

"Oh, it tasted wonderful. The smell of searing meat actually made my mouth water for the first time—such a strange feeling. I did quite well with the chewing and swallowing, but after a while, my stomach started to feel odd. Queasy is how I would describe it now that I understand these things. You can imagine meat in a stomach that has never had to deal with it. In fact, it's remarkable that I even have a digestive system. Anyway, all of a sudden, I had this funny feeling in my backside. I got up and followed Hunter, who had already walked behind a large rock. When I saw what he was doing, I couldn't believe it. It was so disgusting. And then I suddenly did the same thing, but soiling myself because I didn't know to position myself right."

It was my turn to laugh. Lin half-laughed once, but her heart wasn't in it, and when tears started to roll down my cheeks, she frowned.

"You have to admit it's funny. Lin's first poop!"

"It's not that funny," she huffed. "I felt humiliated. Hunter thought it was funny, too."

I tried to pull myself together. Lin took a last gulp of her chocolate and set down the cup before arranging herself on the sofa as usual, looking like a marble effigy, preternaturally still.

"Let's get on with it," she said, her voice sharp as a splinter.

I switched on the tape recorder. Lin had explained when I first started work that she couldn't use electronics because her powers drained the batteries in seconds, hence the old technology. As long as I could obtain the tapes, we were fine.

Tape 1, Volume 2

We got yet another missing person case that took me to London. I remember it so well because it's where I met my friend Agna. You haven't met her yet, Mary, but she flies over once in a while. She's a charming witch. I didn't know any had survived until I met her. We had so much fun together.

My partner Lettie called me and said we had a new case. A Mr. and Mrs. Carmichael would be in the next morning at ten.

We arranged ourselves as usual: pens and pads on our desks, plain-Jane professional outfits, and the coffeepot newly replenished.

At about fifteen minutes past the hour, the door opened, and this large woman dressed head to foot in red strode in, followed by an equally large man in a suit whose buttons were suffering significant strain. Both foreheads were beaded with sweat.

The woman looked around and said, "The Thoren Agency, I assume?" She sniffed. "This is it?"

Presumably, she had read the sign on the door; otherwise, she wouldn't be here. "Indeed, this is it. Good morning. Mr. and Mrs. Carmichael, I assume? We've been expecting you."

She looked at me, perhaps wondering why I wasn't falling over myself to welcome her. I disliked her already.

"I'm sorry we're late," her husband said. He smiled at me kindly, so I smiled back.

"Yes, we're very busy people," his wife said. His smile dropped.

She sat down in the chair in front of my desk. Lettie helped him pull up another.

"It's our daughter, Dale. She's having a gap year between high school and college. She went to London for a few weeks to stay with a friend and look around. Then she was to fly to Paris to a language and finishing school in September. After the first ten days, she stopped calling us or writing. I spoke to the mother of the friend she was staying with yesterday. She said Dale moved out last week and has been spending time with a young man whom, I gather, neither she nor her daughter likes. He sounds most unsuitable. My husband is very worried. I'm sure the silly girl will turn up soon, but there you are." She patted her hair in place, although it hadn't moved a millimeter due to a heavy coat of spray. My godly sense of smell had picked up on the nasty odor at once, as well as that of man-strength deodorant.

"So you are not worried, Mrs. Carmichael?"

She pursed her lips, sensing a judgment. "Of course I am. It's just that I feel there is a simple explanation, and everything will be fine. But we do have our social standing to think about, you know. We can't have Dale carrying on with any Tom, Dick, or Harry."

I turned to her husband. "What would you like us to do, Mr. Carmichael?"

He opened his mouth, but his wife answered for him.

"He wants you to go to London, find her, and bring her home immediately."

"Well, it depends…"

"No Paris for her after causing all this trouble. Shocking waste of money."

Her husband looked upset. "But if there's a reasonable explanation…"

"She's had her chance," said his wife, almost snorting steam from her flaring nostrils.

"All right," I broke in. "I'll need a starting point. The friend's address and phone number. A recent photograph. Her passport number, flight information from London to Paris, and, of course, all your information. We will require an advance, of course."

"I brought a photo and a retainer," Mr. Carmichael said meekly, drawing both from his pocket.

"We never discussed that." His wife's tone suggested an evening of recriminations.

"It's to be expected, my dear. Is $10,000 all right to start?" he asked, turning to me. His wife looked fit to blow.

"Yes, that will be satisfactory," I said, taking it and putting it in the folder I had ready. "We will keep all receipts, of course, and meticulous records. My partner will discuss our daily rate and take down all your information. I'm afraid I have another appointment. Nice to have met you both."

I shook hands and left. He smiled, and she did not. Lettie handles money discussions better than I do. Besides, I'd had enough of that horrid woman. He seemed a caring father, albeit a weakling.

I went home, booked a flight to London for the following evening, and called a hotel I like in Bloomsbury. It's around the corner from the British Museum and within walking distance of Shaftesbury Avenue; I fancied visiting both locations. I wanted to see the Lewes Chessmen again. Fond memories! And there was always a good show or two in the West End.

When I told Hunter, I promised to make sure our maid Dora had enough food in the house—that is, meat. I'd go shopping in the morning. He didn't mind, as I knew he wouldn't. He had his own pursuits.

I traveled overnight to London, business class. It ate a lot of our retainer, but I was way past riding in back. One becomes spoiled very quickly. Once I got through immigration and customs, I hopped in a cab and was soon in my hotel room. Well, relatively soon, given London rush-hour traffic. It was still very early—I was lucky my room was ready.

After unpacking, it was time to look at the theatre listings and make my decisions. Also, time to enjoy an English breakfast before calling Dale's friend.

Only a few early birds sat in the dining room. I selected my breakfast and poured a cup of Earl Grey tea. Listening to the English voices, some more pleasing than others, I leaned back and closed my eyes. I always leave a little of my heart behind in London. Before long, the waiter arrived with my loaded plate. I surveyed the sausages (the British make the best), the eggs, mushrooms, beans, tomatoes, and toast with keen anticipation, the aroma filling my nostrils and brain in a way that was almost erotic.

After cleaning my plate, it was time to go to my room and make that call. A pleasant voice assured me she was Mrs. Melling, mother of Dale's friend Betsy, and I was welcome to come any time after eleven.

The taxi drew up in front of the Melling residence, which was large as English houses go. I asked the driver to wait, assuring him that, yes, I understood the clock would be running. Mrs. Melling, neat in her linen slacks and blouse, opened the door and greeted me amiably, asking me to "come through," a peculiarly British invitation. I spotted a couple of reception rooms with tall windows before being led to a kitchen that rivalled American ones in its size and shining splendor.

I sat at the counter while Mrs. Melling poured me some coffee.

"What can you tell me about Dale, Mrs. Melling? And where is your daughter?"

"I sent Betsy to a summer program at an art school in Cornwall," she said. "She didn't want to go, even though she loves art. There's probably some boy she didn't want to leave behind. But, to be honest, I wasn't happy with the way she was acting after Dale arrived."

"In what way?"

She hesitated.

"I'm very discreet, Mrs. Melling."

"They started staying out until all hours. One morning, I found a matchbook with the name of a pub in her jacket pocket. It's in a very unsavory part of London."

"Do you still have it?"

"Yes, I hid it away. She was really angry. I told her I didn't want her going to such places. She was downright rude. She demanded I give back the matchbook. I refused. She just shrugged and said there were plenty more where that came from."

"Was Dale around listening to this?"

"Oh, yes. She said nothing, just affected this silly little smirk. Finally, I told them both that this had to stop. I was taking Betsy to Cornwall, and Dale would have to find somewhere else to stay."

"Was she upset?"

"Dale?"

I nodded.

"She didn't seem to be. She said her boyfriend had asked her to move in with him, anyway. I saw him when he came to pick her up. We hadn't left yet, as I wasn't comfortable leaving her alone in the house. 'This is Eddie,' she said. He grunted, 'Mornin',' and nodded at me. Awful, low-class type of person. Betsy admitted she didn't think much of him, either. She said he's very bossy with Dale."

"How did Dale and Betsy meet? You were in America?"

"Yes, my husband was posted to Washington by his company for a couple of years, and we rented a house in Salton. They were in the same high school class."

"What does Mr. Melling think of all this?"

"Oh, he has no idea. He's been away for a month in South America on business. Typical. Never there when you need them!" Her face tightened and hardened.

I sensed a gripe session in the offing, so began the departure process. "You've been so helpful, Mrs. Melling. I can't thank you enough. Is it possible that I could call Betsy sometime? Girls often confide in each other more than they do in their mothers. And the matchbook?"

"I'll give you the school's number. I don't know how they feel about students receiving calls from anyone who isn't family. I tell you what. Give me your number, and I'll see if she can call you. I'll just pop upstairs and get that matchbook."

I wrote my name and room number on a hotel card (I'd stashed a few in my purse) and handed it over. In five minutes, I had the matchbook and was on my way back out to the waiting taxi.

I asked the driver to take me to the British Museum. The Lewes Chessmen called me. I'll tell you why I love them so much another time, Mary. Remind me. Right now, I'd better get on with the investigation part of the story.

I got back to the hotel after dinner in a Spanish restaurant in Soho to find a phone message from Betsy. She said I could call back before 9 p.m, and someone would fetch her. It was five minutes to, so I raced upstairs and placed the call. A breathless young woman answered.

"This is Betsy."

"Hello, Betsy. I'm Mrs. Thoren. I am a private investigator looking for Dale. Her parents are very worried about her because she hasn't been in touch for a couple of weeks, even before she moved out of your house. Can you help?"

"Are you going to send her back? She hates her mother, and she's ever so unhappy at home."

"Yes, I've met her mother, and I can well imagine. I won't force her to do anything. I just need to let her parents know she's safe. I won't even tell them where she is ... if she doesn't want me to."

"Well, she moved in with Eddie, her boyfriend. I've never been to his place, so I don't know where it is, just that it's not far from a pub we used to go to together. That's where they met."

"The Knight's Shield?"

"Yes, that's the one."

"Do you know anything about him? Job? Surname?"

"I'm not sure he does anything. Nothing honest, anyway. And I think his surname is Lester, or something like that."

"It doesn't sound as if you think much of him."

"No, he's a low type. I tried to tell her not to get involved, but she's in love with him, so she wouldn't listen. She thinks he's in love with her. I don't think he's the type to be in love with anyone."

"Did she tell you anything else?"

"Only that he buys her clothes sometimes. I've seen a couple of the outfits. They're awful. Not the type of things girls like us usually wear."

"How do you mean?"

"Well, sexy. But, you know, floozie sexy."

"Anything else?"

"Nothing I can think of. Just tell her good luck from me if you find her, would you? I'm really sorry things turned out like they did. She wasn't happy when we were at school, but she seemed to have it all together. Once she got over here, she went wild."

"I'll tell her, Betsy. You've been very helpful, thank you. You have my number if you think of anything else."

I didn't like the sound of the outfits Eddie was buying Dale. Introducing her to a new career? I'd find The Knight's Shield the next morning.

After a good night's sleep and another spectacular breakfast, I window-shopped for a couple of hours before hailing a taxi to take me to The Knight's Shield. Since it was close to lunchtime, I thought I might catch a meal at the pub. Most serve pretty good food these days.

The taxi driver was surprised when I told him where I wanted to go. "Have you been there before, love?"

I said I hadn't.

"Well, it's not in a very nice location for a lady like you. Are you sure?"

I told him I was a private investigator tracking a missing person. That impressed him, and we set off.

Gradually, tidy rows of houses and gardens gave way to iffy neighborhoods that gave way to nasty ones—grimy unkempt buildings converted into flats, equally grimy, sloppy young men hanging around the street corners, and a few murky shops with windows you could hardly see through.

We pulled up in front of The Knight's Shield, which at least had seen a coat of paint in recent years and the attention of a window cleaner. It was crowded, and customers spilled out into the street. I should have dressed down so as not to attract too much attention.

"Shall I come back for you?" asked the driver.

"No, thank you, I'll be fine."

He didn't look happy. I paid him and sauntered to the doorway, the drinkers parting like the Red Sea as I got closer.

Inside, the crowd seemed disinterested, although I caught a few surreptitious looks across the rims of pint mugs. I looked around for a table, but there wasn't one.

"Miss!" the barmaid called out, "the saloon bar's through there." She pointed to a door at the end of what must be the public bar.

It was quiet on the "posh" side, with only one couple sitting at a table eating lunch. What were they doing there, and why would this pub even bother with a saloon bar? I went up to the counter. The same barmaid appeared behind what must have been a continuation of the same counter.

"Do you serve food?" I asked her.

"Yeah, not much choice. Fish and chips or shepherd's pie."

"Fish and chips, please, and a half pint of lager and lime."

"Go and sit down, dear. I'll bring it over."

I chose a table where I could see out of the window and watch the locals. I had intended to eavesdrop on the conversation between the couple drinking at a nearby table, but they weren't talking, just gazing moodily into their pints. Eavesdropping sometimes proves most entertaining.

I smelled my lunch before I saw it. Golden chips (fries to you) and battered cod. Only it wasn't the barmaid; it was a man who brought it—a man with one eye that seemed normal and one that veered wildly off course.

He put the plate down in front of me and turned to face me.

"Will there be anything else?"

Neither eye was looking my way, but I had to assume he was addressing me.

"My lager and lime?"

This time, one eye focused on me. "Yeah, right. Coming right up."

When he returned with my drink, I asked him his name.

"Tom."

"Can I ask you something, Tom?"

"What?" The rogue eye swiveled back and forth as if looking for spies in every corner.

"I'm looking for a girl, the daughter of friends. She's American, and I know she used to come in here sometimes ... and recently. Pretty girl. Her parents are worried because they've lost touch. I think she's been seeing this young man, Eddie. Eddie Lester, my friend thought. Do you know him?" I watched him closely.

Eddie's name evoked a frown and pursed lips.

"Do you know Eddie? Do you know the girl, Dale?

"I might."

"I've got a very nice tip in mind. Say, twenty?"

"Thirty."

"All right, thirty." I dug into my handbag and brought out the cash. As he reached for it, I drew it close to my chest. "Tell me where to find him."

The eye started up again. "Don't you tell him I said anything. He's got a nasty temper, does Eddie."

"Mum's the word."

"He's got a flat a few streets away. There's a big block of flats on Davidson Road. He's in the last one at the back, building six, flat 2B."

"Thank you, Tom," I said. "You must have visited him, then."

"Once or twice, not for a while. I got a better deal ... never you mind."

"That's okay, I get the picture," I said, still hugging the money. "How do I get there?"

He told me. I handed over the money and turned my attention to my food, cool enough to eat now. It was surprisingly good, the fish fresh and the chips not made from frozen.

I got up and went to the bar, where I rang the bell for service. Another man had come in and stood next to me. Tom came around again, closely followed by the barmaid.

"Can I help you?"

The man next to me and I started to talk at once because Tom had managed to fix one eye on each of us. The newcomer stopped and, with a small bow and twitching lips, said, "After you, Miss."

I thanked him before turning to Tom.

"That was very good, thank you. How much do I owe you?"

"Ten will cover."

I paid and left.

The crowd didn't part this time but closed around me. When a hand snatched at my bag and the owner of its wrist screeched, I glared at the rest of them.

"Who's next?"

A real winner with a beer gut, a good couple of feet taller than me, loomed in front of my face. A blow to my cheek sent me flying because I wasn't expecting it.

I got careless and was so mad at myself that I lost my temper. The grinning ape who punched me had the compliment returned in spades. The beer gut got jabbed viciously, as did other locations.

The crowd thinned.

"Good afternoon, gentlemen," I said with a smile, sauntering away.

"She's a nutter!" I overheard with enormous satisfaction.

Was she a nutter? I suppose by human standards, she might have been, but I was not so quick to judge anymore. Different world, different mores.

4

I was surprised to find Lin and Hunter just starting their breakfast when I came up the next morning, as I'd slept late. I seemed to wake up very early, go to the bathroom, go back to bed, and not get up until at least 8:30 a.m.

They'd been murmuring to each other but clammed up when I entered the dining room.

"Good morning, Mary!" they chirped in unison.

They seemed very happy. Had they been making love? A stab of jealousy pierced me. I turned to help myself from the sideboard to hide my face. My feelings were unreasonable considering the situation, but feelings are not so easily denied. I put a little oatmeal in a bowl and added some cream and sugar before taking my place at the table.

"We had some good news from Sven last night," Lin said. "As you know, he will graduate next month and has won a big prize in mathematics. Not just mathematics but some special kind. I don't quite understand it. In high school, too."

"We are very proud of him," Hunter added, his face a portrait of delight.

"That's marvelous news!" I said, able to beam like the Cheshire cat. They were happy because they were proud of their son. I felt better. "When is graduation?"

"First week of June," Lin replied. "We'll go shopping this afternoon. I need a new outfit."

Lin didn't come down until around eleven. She almost bounced onto the sofa and gave a huge sigh before composing herself.

Tape 2, Volume 2

Once around the corner from the pub, I ran to Eddie Lester's flat. Remember, I run so fast humans can't see me. I hid in a stairwell and focused on shifting. I'd gotten really good at doing my old friend Gayle, so that's what I went for—dark, olive-skinned, and exotic. Once satisfied, I marched up to the door and rang the bell.

"Who's there?"

"I'm from the rental office. Is Eddie there?"

"No, he's out. I can't open the door, I'm afraid. I don't have a key."

"Who are you?"

"I'm a friend of his, Dale."

"Well, that's all right. I'll come back another day. Goodbye."

"Bye. Sorry."

So, he'd locked her in. Not good. Now I knew where I was, so I started running again. Moving through this dispirited part of the city, I suddenly yearned to see the pale regency houses and their small, locked park where I once lived so long ago, so I changed course.

I found Selway Terrace easily enough. There was the house—and with a "For Rent" sign. Should I? They probably wanted to rent it for a year at least, but I didn't mind paying for a few months, even though I couldn't stay that long. Maybe I could persuade Hunter to visit. Or at least put the children in a private school for the autumn term, although parents would have enrolled them in the good schools months ago.

The sign listed the same solicitor's office where I leased the house 75 years ago. Why didn't they use an estate agent like everyone else these days? I still wore my Gayle persona. Since the street appeared empty, I stood facing the front door and closed my eyes, concentrating until Lin appeared once more before ringing the bell. The door buzzed, which I took as an invitation.

An elderly lady with a blue-rinsed permed hairdo manned the reception desk.

"Good afternoon," she said. "How may we be of service?"

"I wish to enquire about the house you have for rent on Selway Terrace."

"You'll be wanting Mr. Hanberry," she said.

"Mr. Hanberry? But that's..."

"Yes?" her eyebrows rose.

"Oh yes, that's fine. Mr. Hanberry."

I could hardly tell her that was the name of the solicitor I'd rented the house from the first time.

She spoke quietly into the phone, presumably to the gentleman in question.

"He will see you now. Up the hallway, third door on your left."

When I got there, a chubby young man with sandy hair stood at the door.

"Come in, come in," he said in jocular tones as if this were a party.

We sat down in two small armchairs set at a round coffee table.

I explained that my grandmother lived in that house for a few years in the time of King Edward VII and had rented it from a Mr. Hanberry.

"Well, I never! That must have been my grandfather. Well, well."

His delighted chuckle went on for a fair bit. I put an end to it by saying that I was only over for a short time. Would they consider a three-month lease?

"We were hoping for a six-month lease but could certainly consider less. The previous owner died long ago. He was an archeologist in the Middle East and disappeared. No one ever saw him again. It stood empty for some years before being bought by a gentleman who has also passed. His two nieces, themselves elderly, inherited the property. They travel a good deal and are now going to Switzerland for a health spa experience."

"That sounds perfect. I will pay in advance for the three months, naturally. It's still furnished, I take it?"

"Oh, yes, nothing's changed ... except the sheets and towels."

We laughed politely.

After a delicate double cough, he said, "There is a small matter of references..."

"I don't have any over here, of course, but I would be happy to furnish the name of our lawyers in Washington. We own property in a Northern Virginia suburb."

"That will be very satisfactory."

I wrote down the name and number of our firm. I'd notify them when I got back to the hotel.

"When can I sign the lease?"

"Would tomorrow afternoon at 3 suit? You can move in any time after that. I'll get the cleaners in tomorrow morning."

"Excellent. I'll see you tomorrow." I was so happy to gain possession of that old house again. Misplaced nostalgia?

The next day, I checked out of my hotel and asked the driver to wait while I went through the leasing formalities. I'd taken note of the driver's name and number since he had all my baggage. He was nice enough to help me to the door with it all once we reached the house, so he received a generous tip.

I left my cases in the hall while I looked around. Everything was as I remembered. Hunter was an unruly toddler, having been reborn only two years before. I'd chosen this house for its sturdy furniture, which I felt even Hunter would be unlikely to damage too much. His strength has always been prodigious, even as a child. This was where we lived for so long with his wonderful nanny, the sweet girl who taught me all about celebrating Christmas. She was long dead, of course. I hadn't thought about her for years, but now her serious face, as she did her best to civilize Hunter, came to mind in all its English-rose loveliness.

I entered the library and saw the desk, remembering the hidden key. Was it still there? I sat down and felt around under its bottom drawer. The catch released, and the little drawer slid out, the key its only occupant. I closed the drawer again. There'd be time to explore another day.

I had been assured the phone was still working, so I called Hunter. We reminisced about our time in the house. I thought he might be annoyed, but he seemed quite content. Dora must have been taking good care of him.

"Take as long as you need, my dear."

I gave him the number and hung up.

In the taxi on my way there, I'd noticed a Greek restaurant a couple of blocks away and memorized their number. Yes, they delivered, so I enjoyed an excellent moussaka and a bottle of Greek white wine before bed.

That night I dreamed of Egypt. You remember how I loved Egypt, Mary? How precious my daughter Reema was to me? I didn't dream of her, just of this little boy with a big crown on his head who sat on a throne and kept pointing at me. I felt myself floating toward him until he reached out to touch me—or smite me?—with his scepter, which is when I awoke.

I went downstairs, hoping to find some tea bags. I could always go out to eat breakfast. For some reason, I'd completely overlooked the need to do grocery shopping. To my surprise, I found a fridge full of milk, butter, eggs, juice, sausages, and some sort of meat pie. The cupboard next to the fridge was equally well supplied with tea, coffee, sugar, and other provisions. I set to work producing a good breakfast that felt like a celebration.

Replete, I washed the dishes and boiled more water for tea. I took great pleasure in laying myself a tray, complete with teapot, sugar bowl, milk jug, and a pretty cup and saucer. I turned over the blue cornflower-patterned cup. Royal Albert. Only the best. I wondered how old it was. I carried it into the living room. Would there be a newspaper? I went to the front door and opened it to find two elderly ladies on the doorstep, one holding a newspaper and one with her finger almost at the doorbell.

"Oh, good gracious," twittered one. "We are so sorry to disturb you."

"We are the owners, you know."

"Anne and Margaret Fullington," the other chimed in.

"Oh. Mr. Hanberry told me you were in Switzerland," I said.

"I'm afraid the spa has been closed because of a fire."

"We didn't find out until we got there."

"Disgraceful," one tutted.

"Most disappointing." More tutting.

"You must think me very rude," I said, painfully aware that I was still in my pajamas. "Please, do come in."

They followed me through to the living room and perched next to each other on the sofa.

"Shall I put the kettle on? I'm sure you would like some tea."

"Oh, no, that's quite all right."

"Most kind, but we can make some later."

Later? Were they going to cancel my lease?

"You see, the thing is, we've got nowhere else to go."

"This is our home, you see."

"So we were wondering..."

"If we could stay here."

"It's a big house with lots of bedrooms."

"We'd refund your rent."

"And do the cooking."

"We promise not to be in the way."

"Oh!" I said, a little dizzy from turning from one to the other as if watching a ping-pong match.

Well, that certainly wasn't what I had in mind. But those two sweet old things, who'd been so long together they finished each other's thoughts—how could I turn them away?

"Of course," I said. "I'd be happy to oblige."

"Thank you, thank you."

"So very kind."

"We'll just go upstairs and powder our noses."

"Where's your luggage?" I just realized they'd walked in empty-handed.

"Oh, my goodness!"

"Goodness, gracious!"

"What's the matter?" I asked, bewildered.

"It's still outside where the driver left it."

"By the railings."

"I'll get it in for you," I said.

"But you're not dressed."

"Pajamas!"

"I'll be quick," I said. "You stay here. Maybe make some more tea."

I looked from one to the other, waiting for a chorused response, but they simply sat and looked at me expectantly, heads tilted slightly to one side and beaming wide-eyed.

I opened the front door, ran to snatch up their two small suitcases, and darted back inside before anyone could possibly have seen me. Back in the now-empty living room, I sat down again and opened the paper I'd left on the table. Soon, the ladies came back in with a tray bearing three cups and a larger teapot. Biscuits, too (cookies to you, Mary).

We had a pleasant chat while enjoying our tea. I told them what I was doing in London, and they were all agog to know the details.

"You must bring her back here, where she'll be safe."

"Yes, best place for her."

"Thank you, ladies. I might just have to do that before taking her home to America or off to Paris."

"Now I think we'll have a little nap before lunch."

"Yes, a nap would be nice. Traveling is so tiring."

"Simply exhausting."

"We can have that lamb pie for lunch."

"Yes, a lovely pie our cleaning lady makes for us."

"It was lovely to find the food left for me," I said. "Thank you." I forbore asking them just when they'd done that.

"Our pleasure."

"Oh, yes, our pleasure indeed, don't mention it."

They went upstairs, and I settled back in my chair with yet another cup of tea, albeit lukewarm, and the newspaper.

We ate lunch together, and the pie was indeed delicious, accompanied by new potatoes and peas cooked with mint.

"Thank you, ladies, that was delightful. Please excuse me. I must try to see this girl."

"Of course, my dear. Do be careful."

"Yes, careful, be very careful."

I went to my room to get ready, then left for Eddie's.

The same scenario happened as the day before. Eddie was not home, and Dale couldn't open the door.

"When do you think I can find him in?"

"Try tomorrow around four. Sorry. I can't help it." She sounded low in spirits.

"That's all right. I understand." I thought I understood only too well.

I got home just to find the sisters dressed to go out.

"Any luck, dear?"

"No, he wasn't home."

"We need a few things from Selfridges."

"Towels."

"Washing-up cloths."

"A petticoat for Margaret."

"You should get one, too, Anne."

The old biddies finally left the house for their safari to Selfridges with much clucking and several return trips to fetch umbrellas and handkerchiefs, reminding me each time that they would be back in time for dinner. They were like actors playing old spinsters, employing every cliché in the book. I appreciated their kindliness, so I felt guilty about how much they got on my nerves already.

Alone at last, I suddenly remembered the key. I wanted to explore the attic properly this time. After waiting ten minutes in case the sisters had forgotten something else, I retrieved the key from its hidey-hole in the study desk where I'd found it all those years ago. What horrible secret lay in that attic? From a distance, the smell was different this time—sweeter and stronger. Surely those old dears couldn't be involved in anything nefarious?

Tiptoeing up the stairs seemed silly, but I didn't feel alone in that house and hadn't during my first visit so many years before. My sixth sense had always served me well, and I'd learned to heed it.

The passage for the final flight of stairs was much narrower than the rest and would not have accommodated the plump sisters without a struggle. How had people moved those ancient artifacts up there, those sarcophagi I had seen and decided not to meddle with? The larger mummy case had certainly been wider and taller than I, although I didn't remember the passageway being so narrow or the ceiling so low back then. Or the attic door being quite so wide and high.

When I looked behind me, the stairs seemed to snake around in a spiral, descending into a rising mist.

I gently inserted the key into the lock. Turning it required enormous strength, even for me, and produced an unholy screech that set my teeth on edge. Although the sisters were out, I still sensed a presence close by. There was that sweet-rotten smell, too, stronger now that I stood closer to the source. The door had no handle, so I pushed. Silently, it glided open, and I stepped into the black interior, slipping up to my ankles in something wet and freezing. I moved no further into the void.

The door clicked shut behind me. How? It opened inward, and I'd only taken one step in.

The unpleasant odor gradually dissipated until the air felt fresh and clean, although it chilled my bones. A lemony sun slowly rose over the horizon and lit up an icy landscape littered with black lava boulders draped in snowdrifts. A pack of wolves howled in the distance. Their calls sounded alien, so I didn't reply. Massive paw prints led off to one side around the largest boulder and smelled of bear.

Some sort of ethereal form, a swirl of snow, started to drift toward me before fusing into the shape of a woman, who floated across the snow as I used to on my missions to Midgard. She passed through the boulders as if they were a mirage, which, of course, they were—if there is such a thing as a mirage in snow. She stood in front of me. Beautiful. With a shock, I realized she could have been my twin, except her hair was white rather than golden.

"Who are you?" I asked, forcing myself to sound confident.

"I am Margaret Anne," she said.

"Like the sisters?"

"I am the sisters."

I couldn't help gawping. Not my usual poised image.

"Oh, do come along, Margaret, you're always forgetting things. Don't nag so, Anne. I do my best." She mimicked their voices perfectly.

"All right, then," I said, "I suppose the real question is, what are you?"

She laughed, a musical trilling so high it raised my hackles. "I am a witch, one of the old ones. Like you, if I am not mistaken, Lin, handmaiden to Frigg."

"But our witches were seers, only looked into the future. They couldn't do things like this."

"Freya was my mistress. She needed more services than even Frigg's handmaidens could provide, so I widened my abilities. I consulted some of the ancient Norns, too. They knew more than any of us realized, not only matters of destiny. And don't forget, Freya herself was a witch."

"Then why did she need you to develop such powers?"

"She wanted to be queen of the Aesir, to take Frigg's place, so she helped me transform into the creature I am. Ragnarok ruined our plans, but I hid in one of the gnomes' treasure chests. Not the one you and Hoenir looted before you took off. The one you thought held only old cloaks and caps."

"That's outrageous! My lady Frigg was so good and true. How could Freya betray her so?"

She shrugged and pursed her lips in an annoying French kind of way. "For some, even gods, power has the pull of a magnet."

"Why are you here?"

"I ended up in Egypt and became one of Tutankhamun's favorites. I saved his life on several occasions. I know medicine, too, you see, and he was a sickly boy. But in the end, even I couldn't save him. I'll tell you more about him one day. For a few thousand years, I lived in a beautiful house near where he was buried so I could watch over him. Tomb robbers were always searching for his treasures. Many got too close. It never ended well for them."

She'd been looking me in the eye while she spoke, her eyes wide and innocent, unblinking—the sign of a liar. She bit her lip, and I thought I saw a tear turn to ice on her cheek. Her shoulders slumped a little.

"I was rejuvenating my spirit in the land of jungles and tigers when the man who bought me this house paid his pet archeologist to break into my lovely boy's tomb and steal the items he needed in the afterlife, disturbing his eternal sleep. The earl wasn't strong, and it didn't take much to poison his blood.

"I stole his body the night before the funeral and interred it in a mummy case I'd set aside. You could ship antiquities to Britain with impunity in those days. He only used this house on the rare occasions I was in London. He was a decent fellow on the whole, but he had crossed the line. I believe you saw a sarcophagus on your earlier visit when you opened the door to the attic?"

"Why did you want to take the body? It's not as if you loved him."

"No. I was quite fond of the old boy, but love? No. I took it because he had to be punished. He would not be buried in hallowed ground but instead spend eternity in an attic."

"I see." Interesting. She was not a Christian, yet she believed in their version of the afterlife. "I could smell the evil up here, so I left it alone. At that time in my life, I didn't want complications."

"Ah yes, little Hoenir. Well, it wasn't the same sarcophagus."

"What? Is this some kind of cemetery for people who cross your line?"

"No, that one you saw was a real mummy … thousands of years old. Nothing evil, just something long dead. It's still here, joined by the earl for eternity. But things turned out well after all. Now my boy is famous, admired wherever he goes, and his sarcophagus has traveled the world. I think he would be proud."

It was such a strange conversation. We both stood stock still and exchanged words with little inflection or gesture. My feet felt as though they were freezing off, but I suppressed the discomfort.

"I'm a little confused. Mr. Hanberry said an explorer owned the house, and he disappeared in the Middle East."

"Ah, yes, the earl used a false name and gave out that he was an explorer. He actually paid other people to do the exploring. It wasn't hard to forge a will and claim the inheritance, and it goes without saying he'd kept our love-nest a secret from his family. Different names down the years, of course."

"What are you going to do?" I asked.

"I will stay here with you until you leave. It will be pleasant to be close to someone who knows what I am."

"They all say that," was out of my mouth before I could think better of it.

"Who else said that?"

No holding back now. "Loki and Eir. They also survived and traveled down the millennia together."

"Loki should endure the torments of Hel."

"Agreed," I said. "Eir has left him and will move close to us. She had been keeping him young with potions she concocted—he's not a full-blooded immortal, as you know. When she met me, she decided to follow a more righteous path and stopped administering it, rendering him old and ill, practically bedridden. He escaped with a nurse and has vowed to wreak vengeance on us all, including my children."

"You said you were here to search for a missing girl. Is that the truth?"

"Oh, yes. I'm a private detective now. I wanted to earn my own money. Hoenir is rather stingy because he's afraid of drawing attention to us. I've changed, you know. Not the saintly little virgin you probably remember."

"Glad to hear it. Leave now. Dinner will be on the table at 7."

"What about the body?"

"He has completely decomposed. You only smell it because of your godly qualities. No one else can."

Night fell as if the stage's safety curtain had snapped down. I turned to find the door open to a well-lit, wide flight of stairs.

I took a hot bath with a good dash of lavender salts I found in the medicine cabinet. Another one who escaped. Who else? Was this witch a danger to us? What did she want?

Dinner turned out to be a delightful affair, reminding me of the dinner Eir served me while I was still imprisoned in her Manhattan house. All the favorites of the Aesir. I never ate in those days, but the feasts I attended to wait on my lady were sumptuous, and I remembered the aromas as if I tasted them. We reminisced. I told Margaret Anne about my life, the Syrian girls I saved, and my mortal children. She told me about her life journeying between Egypt and London.

"I don't have many friends in Egypt and only go out at night. I don't age, you see. I change servants often, except for one. Hassan knows what I am. He is a deaf-mute and loves me because I can talk to him through his mind. I know him as well as he does himself. I taught him to read, and that is how he spends his spare time. He's getting old, and I suppose he will die soon. I must find one like him before that happens."

"It's a lonely life," I said. "We have to disappear every forty years or so for the same reason. We never tell the children what we are, so we fake our deaths. We used to simply go away but realized that not knowing is too difficult for them. They do have strength greater than most humans but no other godly qualities. It's so hard to say goodbye. The only one I used to go back to visit in her sleep was my daughter Reema ... born in Cairo. My happiest memories lie there."

"It's funny how Egypt gets under your skin. Their old ones touch you, somehow."

"Yes." I felt sad for a few moments. Reema.

"Tell me about your case. Have you found her?"

"I think so. She seems to be living with a pimp who she thinks loves her. An old story."

"What are you going to do?" The witch looked at me intensely.

"I will visit tomorrow. See how the land lies. Try to talk to her. Her mother is absolutely dreadful, by the way, a *nouveau riche* bully who is impossibly snobbish, more concerned about what people will say than her daughter's welfare. The father is pleasant but weak. I don't blame her for leaving. But she's very young. Too young."

"Let me know if I can help."

"Thank you, I will. By the way, you never told me your real name."

"Agna."

"A real witch? There are really witches?"

"She's real, for sure, Mary. I don't know if any others survived. Some of the old gods had them, but I think they've all died out. Although, you never know who might have tucked themselves away, as I've discovered. They're not like your fairytale witches. Some good, some bad, but they were usually in some god's service."

I seemed to spend my life in a constant state of surprise ... and even shock. First, the stab of jealousy I suffered at the thought of Lin and Hunter making love. They were married, for heaven's sake—a really old married couple. Then the witch. A real witch that I might even meet one day. But I lived with gods, so why would the existence of a witch assault my sense of reality? I wondered if Agna knew any leprechauns. And what about vampires? Should I ask?

Lin came downstairs a little after ten, later than usual.

"I'm going shopping later, so let's get on with this."

"Lots to think about," I said. "I've been wondering..." I wasn't sure I should get into it.

"Come on, out with it," she said. "I know the idea of a witch bothered you. But all you humans ever hear about witches is how evil they are. Well, one or two were, but we soon got rid of them. Most are pretty normal and only use their powers for good."

"It wasn't really that," I said. "I mean, if witches are real, what about leprechauns and gnomes? Werewolves and vampires?"

"Well, I've told you about the rich gnomes that lived underground in our old world. They were all destroyed. There were never such things as werewolves. I suspect that myth started with Fenrir, Loki's son, who took part in the ravages of Ragnarok. Leprechauns? Never heard of one, but then they would have come after our time. Again, probably a myth that started with some little old man with the gift of the gab. Vampires? I don't think so, and I've never come up against one in all my days on Midgard.

I've heard the stories but never met anyone who has ever suffered a bite from such a creature."

"I thought Norse gods were only myths, too. Not to mention witches. You can't blame me for wondering what other creatures might be around."

"No, don't worry. You're safe here with us."

Until Loki resurrects himself again.

Tape 3,
Volume 2

The doorbell rang a different sound this time, as if the Hound of the Baskervilles prowled the hallway. It sounded silly rather than menacing in this grimy block of flats. I heard someone look through the peephole before opening the door a crack.

"What do you want?"

"I'm looking for Dale Carmichael. Is she home?"

"Who's asking?"

"A friend from home. I just want to say hello and tell her parents she's okay. They're worried."

"She don't want nuffink to do with her family."

"Frankly, I don't blame her. I won't tell them where she is. Only that she is well."

He opened the door a crack wider, so I barged in.

"Hey!" I ignored him as he clattered behind me up the hall.

A young lady I barely recognized from her photo stood nervously in a doorway at the end of the hall, bleached hair curling around her shoulders, cleavage on full display, and a green skirt that looked like a glorified belt.

"Dale?"

She paused for a moment, shaping her mouth to several replies. "Yes. Who are you?"

I walked toward her. "May I sit down?"

She led the way to a living room furnished with a dizzying assortment of purple and black velour seating arrangements. The man brushed past me, grabbed her arm, and pulled them both onto the sofa.

"You suddenly stopped communicating with your family, Dale. What happened?"

She didn't look at me, only at her hands, which seemed to be dry-washing each other. "I had to get away. I was supposed to be having a holiday here, then go to Paris to study French at a stupid finishing school. Then I met Eddie."

"You're Eddie?" I asked the man.

"Yeah."

I looked at him closely. Thick dark hair, none too clean, close-set eyes, and a thin, hard mouth over dark stubble. A shifty lad if ever I saw one. The way he clutched Dale's arm looked painful.

"Well, Dale, what shall I tell them?"

"Please don't tell them where I am. Please don't!" She looked at me desperately. "I love Eddie, and he loves me. They'll make me go back. I can't live like they want me to."

"Don't forget, Dale, I've met them. I wouldn't dream of trying to make you go back. Why not write them a letter? At least let them know you are safe. I can arrange to have it mailed from another town. In fact, I have to take a quick trip up to Oxford tomorrow morning."

She turned to Eddie. "Can I?"

"Yeah, why not? Write it now. I want to read it, though. Then you can rest easy for our little party tomorrow."

"Party?" I asked.

"Yeah, few of my mates coming over to have a few beers, be introduced to my little girl here." Dale winced when he pinched her arm.

Introduced how?

"All right, let's get that letter written. I brought some plain paper and an envelope in case you don't have any. Be sure to date it."

Dale took the stationery and pen from me and went to a shiny black table in the corner. She started to write, reading aloud as she went, with Eddie looking over her shoulder.

"Dear Mom and Dad, I am writing to let you know that I am very happy in England and do not plan to return to the United States. I have met someone special, and we will be married soon. Please, do not try to find me. Dale."

She folded the letter, stuffed the envelope, sealed it, and addressed it.

"Dale, how will you find work if you don't have a visa?"

"She won't need no visa. I'll be taking care of her," Eddie growled.

Dale smiled, looking up at Eddie with that vacuous adoration only the incorrigibly naïve can feel.

"All right, then, Dale. I'll mail this in Oxford and let your parents know I met you, but you have since moved away. Okay?"

Dale seemed a little teary as I left. "Thank you for understanding. We're very grateful, aren't we, Eddie?" That look again.

"Yeah," grunted the erudite Eddie. "You're a bit of all right. In more ways than one." As I left, he leered at me with an unappetizing display of jumbled teeth and anemic gums.

Yes, tomorrow night the fun would start—for Eddie, that is.

I ran home, causing a little havoc along the way. Humans can't see me if I run fast enough, but of course, they sometimes get in the way, like that day when a bicyclist unexpectedly decided to mount the pavement—what they call sidewalks in England. His painful correction would have seemed to come out of nowhere. And my steps do make a faint buzz as they speed along, which young children and animals tend to pick up on. The children cock their heads in puzzlement, and the dogs try to give chase, sometimes pulling their owners to a sorry result. Cats look up and stare for a second before going back to whatever they were doing. I've often wondered if they actually see me.

I found Agna thumbing through British *Vogue* in the drawing room when I got home.

"Well, what happened?" It was amusing that Agna had been hanging around to find out.

"Did you stay up to find out?"

"Of course. We're going to save the girl and have some fun, too."

Agna started to laugh, so I cut in—I wasn't in the mood. "The man, Eddie, is a nasty piece of work, all right. She's besotted with him, thinks he's going to marry her and take care of her forever."

"How did you leave it?"

"She wrote a letter to her parents. I said I'd mail it from another town tomorrow and would not tell her parents where she is."

"Why?"

"Well, her mother is truly awful, so I don't blame her for not wanting to go back. Also, Eddie said he's having a few friends over to meet her tomorrow night. That might be her introduction to the life he's got planned for her."

Agna slammed her magazine on the table. "Well, I think that is our cue to show her what he's about and get rid of him once and for all … and his friends along with him."

"The girl's gullibility is infuriating. When you are an innocent from another culture, you often don't pick up on clues about background and so on. The way he talks, he's obviously totally uneducated, and he's exhibiting disturbingly controlling behavior, too. The little fool probably just puts it down to an English accent and being manly."

"We will take care of him."

"Agna, we can't have dead bodies all over the place. That might implicate Dale."

"I have witchy powers, don't forget. Remember Circe? What she did to Odysseus's men?"

That lifted my spirits. Agna, excited by her plan, started to laugh. It began with the little tinkly laugh I'd found so eerie when I first met her but rose into a multi-voiced peal, not unlike church bells, and soared to decibel heights I found almost unbearable. She looked completely mad, her arms held high as if invoking the devil's wrath.

She must have seen my horror-struck face and gradually ramped it down.

"Imagine the neighbors!" she said, spluttering. "A London apartment occupied by oinking pigs! The squeals when they panic—then maybe they'll turn on Eddie."

"The pratfalls when they try to climb up on the toilet," I chimed in, rolling around on the sofa, laughing now. "The stink! The neighbors will call the police, who'll come and chase the pigs 'round the apartment, trying to catch them, slipping and sliding in dung. Brilliant! I wish I could be there to see it."

"Oh, you will," said Agna, rubbing her hands together in glee.

I couldn't wait for the next bit.

"I missed you," he said, standing in my bedroom doorway.

I was so happy to see him, relieved he still loved me. "I was afraid you were getting tired of me. It's been a while." I said it with a smile on my face and opened my arms.

We enjoyed a delightful couple of hours together before he left. I couldn't help wondering if he would make love to Lin the same night. To my surprise, that didn't worry me as much as it had only a couple of days ago. He loved both of us. And I didn't see that changing. At least until I started to age.

I pressed that thought down with the belief that older people didn't feel desire. Even when they left, as they'd have to do in a few years, it would be different because their children and I would know who and what they are. There would be no need to hide from us. We would understand why they still looked so young. We would understand when they were reborn. It would be a relief for them, too.

Or would it? Because they would have to watch their children age and die. If, heaven forbid, one of the children was to contract a deadly disease, they'd have to watch that, too. My guess was that they'd make the break later rather than sooner. But it would be so tantalizing for them, knowing their children were still out there, still reachable, visible on social media, and maybe producing grandchildren.

A cruel dilemma, at best.

Lin and I walked downstairs together after breakfast the next day.

"I'm really looking forward to the next installment," I said. "I know it's going to be juicy."

"You have no idea." She laughed. "Such fun and games!"

It's a good thing I was so taken up with the story. It helped me to stop fantasizing about Hunter so much. But he still loved me, and he wasn't bored with me. That was enough for me.

Tape 4,
Volume 2

The next night, I ran to Eddie's apartment with Agna flying just behind. She had decided to render us invisible so we could slip inside once someone opened the door. That happened almost as soon as we got there.

Eddie opened the door a crack, checking this way and that, always acting guilty.

"Just going to the off-license," he called over his shoulder. "Back soon."

He jumped when the door flew wide open as if the wind had caught it. "What the fuck?" he muttered. He locked the door behind us.

We wandered around for a bit, then went to find Dale. She was in the bedroom, holding a dress up in front of her before the mirror.

"I don't know," she sighed. "But Eddie said I'll look gorgeous in it." She sighed again.

"She's having doubts. A good sign," I whispered to Agna, who dug an elbow into my ribs as Dale looked around her wildly.

"Who's here?" she said, her voice quaking. She locked the bedroom door, quickly threw on the trashy sequined dress the size of a cummerbund, and sat on the bed to put on spike-heeled silver shoes. She looked how Eddie wanted, but when she stood up and went back to the mirror, she looked sad. She stared at herself for a long time as she brushed her hair until static electricity haloed it into scarecrow territory. She darted into the bathroom to rinse her hands and smooth it out.

The front door opened. Agna and I heard it, but she didn't. Eddie banged around a bit, bottles clanking as he set them out. Dale finally realized he was home and unlocked the door. She went back to the bed and perched on the edge.

"Get on out here, girl!" Eddie yelled. "Let's have a look."

She rose and tottered out, clearly unused to such high heels. We followed.

"Very nice," he said. "Turn around."

She slowly circled, arms awkwardly stuck out like a penguin.

"Very tasty. My pals are going to love you. You be nice to them, mind."

"Of course I will, Eddie. Why wouldn't I be?"

"Well, some are a bit touchy-feely, you know. Just go along with it."

"They won't take liberties, will they? You wouldn't let them, would you?"

"Don't you bother your pretty little head about it, love."

When the doorbell rang, Dale gasped, raised her shoulders, and hugged her chest. *Beginning to see the light?*

I followed Eddie along the hall. He opened the door to two middle-aged men who didn't look as if they could possibly be part of Eddie's circle. They even wore ties, one a grey mix and the other white with red hearts down the front. Each placed an envelope in his outstretched palm, which slid into his pocket.

"Names?" he said.

"Jim."

"Tom. I've been here before, you know."

"Yeah, right."

I hoped there would be just the two of them. They went to the living room, where Eddie introduced them to Dale with uncharacteristic bonhomie. Dale greeted them warmly and said how glad she was to meet Eddie's friends.

"They paid him," I whispered in Agna's ear, not forgetting this time that while we might be invisible, our voices were still audible.

She scowled as her fists clenched and opened several times.

Tom, the chubby guy with the Valentine tie, sat on a loveseat close to Dale. "Tell me all about yourself," he said earnestly, leaning into her face as she flinched back. I could smell his breath, so I saw her point.

"Oh, there's not much to tell, I'm afraid. I haven't done much, you know. Not yet."

"Oh, you're American," said Jim, the nondescript, clerkish one with the grey tie, who had rather sulkily plonked into an armchair after being beaten to the loveseat by Tom. "That's a nice change."

"Change from what?" asked Dale.

"Well, Eddie's girls are usually..."

"Oh, she don't want to hear your stories, Tom. Let's have a nice drink. Loosen your ties. Take off your jackets. Make yourselves at home."

Eddie took orders and poured the drinks, asking Dale to take them to the guests. She was already looking uneasy.

When she went back to the loveseat, she wedged herself as far against the arm as she could. Tom edged up close again.

"How do you both know Eddie?" she asked.

"Oh, we met down the pub," Eddie quickly answered for them.

What I've heard referred to as a pregnant silence ensued.

"We're here to have a bit of fun," Tom finally said. "With you."

"What do you mean?" Dale sprang up, the situation beginning to dawn on her.

Eddie grabbed her arm and pulled her toward the bedroom. "Come on, you first," he told Tom.

Dale tried to fight him off, but Tom grabbed her other arm and helped steer her up the hall.

It was time. I looked over at Agna. Her eyes were closed, and she muttered and started to chant using several voices simultaneously, which stopped Tom and Eddie in their tracks. They let go of Dale and looked around for the source of the chorus.

The doorbell rang.

Agna stamped her foot. "Shit! Now I'll have to start again."

Eddie ran to the door, and I followed him. Two men in jeans and sweaters, two more envelopes.

"She's putting up a fight," he confided. "But don't worry, it's more fun that way." The new eager beavers entered the living room on his heels.

"Where's the bint?" asked one.

"Locked herself in the bedroom," said Tom. "I was looking forward to that. Here, give me back my money."

"No need for that," said Eddie, laughing. "All part of the fun. I've got another key." He opened a drawer in the drinks cabinet and drew one out, brandishing it aloft. "Hope you're feeling up to a feisty female, Tom!" He and Tom started up the hallway again, both having already forgotten the Norse chanting.

Agna stood silent, although her lips moved and her eyes remained scrunched shut. She suddenly roared as her arms shot above her head.

The men froze and paled. Their skin turned pink and started to bulge and break as they screamed and writhed. Their legs and arms squashed down as they fell on all fours. Mouths widened, and lips cracked, extra teeth poked through expanding gums as they ran in circles, tripping on strips of cloth from their ripped suits. The ties of the first two, which they'd loosened after they finished their first drinks, stayed ludicrously and chokingly in place.

Agna and I laughed ourselves silly as the swine raced around the flat, oinking and knocking over whatever lay in their path. One of them—Eddie, I think—shat an enormous pile in the middle of the living room. Nerves, I suppose.

I noticed the bit of jacket he still had hanging on his front leg showed a pocket. I approached him carefully and grabbed it, hoping it was the right one. Dale should have those envelopes. It was, and I put them in my pocket.

"For Dale," I told Agna, who had looked at me strangely.

Eddie charged me. I wasn't expecting it, so only just managed to jump over his head. The other four seemed to be circling. They could see us.

"Agna?"

"I can only work my magic for an hour or so. I'm not what I was."

Who was? "Now you tell me! We've got to get out of here. I'll get Dale."

A fight seemed to be breaking out between Eddie and Tom, who still sported the Valentine tie. I could understand why Tom felt peeved but wondered if this lower-middle class twerp—yes, I was acquainted with British class subdivisions—would fare against the likely product of a tenement. Quite well, it seemed. Blood spurted from Eddie's tail, and Jim rushed in to worry at his heels. Soon they were all after him, the noise deafening. At least they'd lost interest in us.

I rushed up the hallway to the bedroom, smashed in the door, and tucked Dale under my arm. She scarcely whimpered. We ran to the front door, out onto the corridor, down the stairs, and across the parking lot.

I stopped for a minute to let Agna catch up. She hadn't followed. Dale was in a state of shock, what with being offered for prostitution by the love of her life, then whisked off faster than light.

"Stay quiet and still," I told her. "Get behind that dustbin."

I ran back and found Agna chasing the swine out of the flat and down the stairs. Eddie fell down the last few and squealed a shockingly shrill protest. "Broke my fucking leg!"

Huh? I looked closer. The pig now had the head of a man, more or less. The others milled around the parking lot, swearing and squealing, while the railings above filled with gawkers. The pig men seemed to be in pain. They all had human faces now. Some had longer legs.

Agna came to stand beside me.

"What's happening?"

"The spell's wearing off."

"Can't you make us invisible again? I want to see how it ends."

"I think so. Just for a short while."

I went over to Eddie, who was looking more like himself, except for a mutilated curly tail and several bite marks. He showed no reaction when I waved my hand in front of his face.

Agna came over. "They're going to be themselves in five minutes or so. Starkers, of course."

I noticed a camera or two flash and heard police sirens. Let them explain this one! Once the police arrived, I ran back to Dale. "You have to see this!"

She edged out and watched the arrest of five naked men, all very much the worse for wear. Tom and Jim retained a curly little tail. One of the latecomers had big, piggy teeth that fought for room in his shrunken mouth, causing his lips to curl back. His pal's nose looked funny—not quite a snout, but not fully human. I spotted a trotter where Eddie's right foot should be, too, ensuring expensive custom shoes in his future. When he turned, I noticed he still had the little tail.

"Agna, they've still got little pig bits."

"Yes, I know. That often happens. I don't know why."

"It's going to put something of a dent in Eddie's style."

"At least he sort of matches front and back."

We both fell about laughing but stopped when Dale's weeping got louder.

"What..." she hiccupped.

"I'll explain when we get you home," I whispered.

I gathered her up, and off we went, Agna bringing up the rear, slower this time, probably worn out. I got back ten minutes before her.

We settled in the living room. Dale was still shaky—no surprise there—so I settled her on the sofa with a blanket across her lap and went off to make her a cup of tea, a panacea for any kind of trauma or catastrophe on British soil. I thought of mesmerizing her, but I was hungry and ready to relax. I wanted tea and biscuits, too. Definitely going native. It creeps up on you.

When I got back with the tray, Agna was sitting on one of the armchairs with her feet placed prissily on a footstool. They weren't speaking.

"What's up?" I asked.

"This lady won't answer my questions," said Dale, her voice a tad whiny. "I am so confused. Did I really see those men turn into pigs? Did Eddie put some kind of drug in my drink? Did you?"

The perfect out. "Yes, Dale," I said. "We hid in Eddie's flat because we knew he was up to no good. I asked around and found he has a bad reputation. I saw him slip something into your drink. You realize those men paid him so they could have sex with you, don't you?"

She burst into tears. "I really thought he loved me."

"You need to spend time getting to know a man really well before you trust him," I said. "Meet his friends and family, if possible. You can still make a mistake, of course, but keep your eyes open. Don't ignore red flags. We women let love blind us far too often. Don't you realize how controlling he was? Think about it."

Dale nodded miserably. "I know."

Agna looked at me, eyebrows slightly raised, clearly amused by my motherly advice that was about as original and inspiring as American white bread. Still, it was sensible and what she needed to hear. I just hoped none of the piggy antics made it to the newspapers.

"Now, we have to get you away."

"I don't want to go home!"

"I know, and I don't blame you. But you can't get a job here without a work visa. You have no experience to justify one, either. My advice is to go over to Paris and do that course. When does it start?"

"Day after tomorrow."

"Okay, I'll get you over there. I can report to your parents that you are safely there. You can think again when the course has finished. Maybe go back to the States ... but to another area? Do you have friends or anyone else you can stay with over there?"

"I could go to my grandparents in Boston. You see, I have to refer to her as mother, but she's my stepmother. My own mother died when I was ten. I hate that woman! And she runs rings around my dad. I don't think she'll mind as long as she can tell everyone that I've decided to go to college in Boston. Her social position is all she cares about. How she looks, what people think."

"All right, we leave tomorrow. We'll have a nice dinner, and then you must get a good night's sleep."

She said, "My suitcase is at Eddie's. He made me pack all my old clothes. I haven't got anything to wear. Except this. I can't go around like this!"

"No, you certainly can't. Okay, I'll go back and get it. We'll have to fly, so I'll try to book something later in the day. There are always loads of flights. Did Eddie take your passport?"

"Yes, I don't know where he put it. And I've got an open ticket to Paris from Heathrow. That's in the case."

I hoped that passport was still available. Had the police released Eddie? I'd have to go back that night.

We had a good dinner, and I left Agna to get Dale settled in bed. "Can't you cast a spell or something to make her sleep?"

"I haven't done that for years. I'll try."

"Don't you have that stuff written down?"

"Of course not. Almost no one wrote in Asgard, remember?"

"Oh, right. Well, maybe you should think about it."

I left her looking pensive. Maybe she'd never learned to write. She must have done to sign the lease, though.

The parking lot at Eddie's building lay silent in the night's shadows. Only one lamp still had working bulbs. A dark figure slipped down the stairs and clumped off toward the pub. I'd like to have visited myself to hear the gossip, but I might be recognized.

I ran up the stairs to the flat. The door was unlocked. I opened it quietly and slipped in. No lights were on, probably turned off by the police, because it was early evening when we left, and the living room had these chrome and enamel floor lamps that shone romantically dim; at least, I guess that was the idea. I didn't need light as there was enough moonlight for my godly eyesight peeking through the window. I stood still, listening for human breath to make sure the place was empty. Eddie's dung still scented the place.

I found Dale's suitcase in the wardrobe at once and set it by the front door. Now for the passport and ticket. I started with the drinks cabinet where Eddie kept the bedroom key, working fast to put some distance between myself and Eddie's contribution to the festivities. Nothing in or on top of cupboards, under mattresses (there were two bedrooms), in pillowcases, under carpets, in kitchen cabinets, or in the freezer. Nothing. I wished Eddie would come home so I could squeeze it out of him. I hoped he hadn't sold it. I had to admit defeat.

It occurred to me that although Dale told me she'd packed everything, that wouldn't include her toiletries, so I retrieved what was obviously her stuff from the bathroom and opened the case to see if I could fit it in. It was packed tightly, but I could push her hairbrush down the side, and toothbrush, too. I put her shampoo and cosmetics on the top since no baggage handlers were going to be throwing it around. I was curious to see what else she had in there and lifted a few things just enough to see what lay beneath. I caressed a cashmere sweater and felt something hard inside. The passport. I could have saved myself a lot of time and trouble if I had looked here first. How come she didn't mention it? Maybe Eddie thought it would be a good hiding place because she'd never think of looking somewhere so obvious. But what about the ticket? Time to empty the suitcase. Packing and, especially, unpacking are among my least favorite activities. No ticket. Eddie must have found it when he hid the passport and most likely sold it.

Eddie had been taught a lesson that evening, but I was in no mood to leave it there. That living room needed rearranging. If only I had a shovel. A kitchen knife would have to suffice. I carved avant-garde designs into the upholstery and decorated the gashes with broken glass. Maybe some scotch would add nicely to the aroma. Eddie's pile was on a fairly small rug in front of the loveseat. It wouldn't be hard to lift a corner and flip it onto the place where Dale's adventure with Tom had begun. I took a deep breath and heaved.

Standing back and admiring my handiwork, I felt proud of what my adolescent cravings for destruction had achieved. If only I'd had the stomach to leave it on the bed. If I were Eddie, I'd pick up a few necessities and skip town.

When I got home, I left Dale's case outside her bedroom. Agna was waiting downstairs and asked how it went.

"I got her case, as you saw. Believe it or not, I found the passport in it, but not before I turned the flat upside down looking for it!"

"I put champagne in the fridge. Let me get it. We've earned it."

We sipped and nibbled on the delicious little cocktail biscuits they sell in the U.K. I told her what I'd done to the flat. We had a good giggle while polishing off the bottle. I slept very well.

"You and Agna were a good team," I said. "I won't ever forget the mental image of pigs with human bits—or humans with pig bits—running around a parking lot!"

"Yes, we did very well, didn't we?" She rose in one fluid motion and sashayed upstairs.

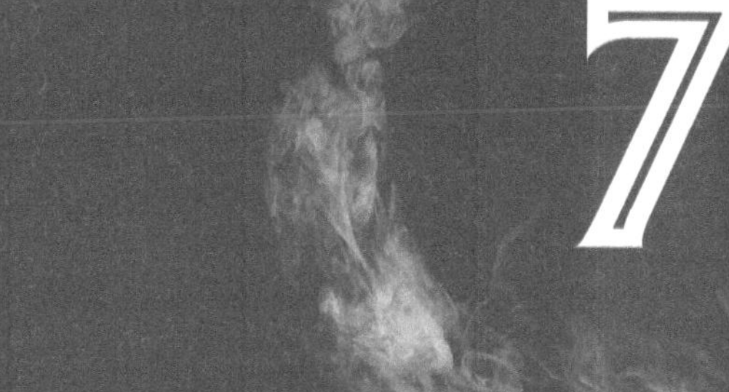

7

I wasn't really in the mood for Lin that morning, but I had no choice. She'd been out the night before with friends, so Hunter and I had spent a delightful evening enjoying dinner at a Turkish restaurant before retiring downstairs to gentle lovemaking. I didn't want to break the spell. But I'd been borrowing her husband, after all. Mustn't be ungrateful.

"Did you have a nice evening?" she asked when she came downstairs.

"Yes, I did. We went to a Turkish restaurant. I've never eaten Turkish food before."

"Did you like it?"

"Yes, delicious. I had some lentil soup and then stuffed flounder. They gave us complimentary dessert, too, but I was too full to eat it. I brought it home. It's upstairs in the fridge. It looks too sweet and sticky for me."

"Try their rice pudding next time. I love it. It's different."

"How about you? Did you have fun?" I asked. I always felt a little diffident about asking Lin about her time away from home.

"Oh, yes, thanks. Dinner with old friends."

She seemed to have an awful lot of old friends.

Tape 5, Volume 2

The next day, we caught an Air France flight from Heathrow to Orly that left just after noon. Once through customs and immigration, we took a taxi to the school, which turned out to be housed in two terrace houses in the 5th arrondissement. Dale wore more respectable clothes now, but not exactly chic. I hoped the school would sharpen her dress sense.

A young woman answered the door.

"*Oui?*"

"This is Miss Dale Carmichael. She is to be a student here. I called yesterday."

"Ah, yes, *bienvenue*!"

Both carrying suitcases, we followed her into a well-appointed salon with delicate upholstery and fine paintings. Dale stood awkwardly under the brilliant chandelier, which somehow made me think of the Sword of Damocles. Would she learn to fit in? Soon we were joined by an older woman, very chic in a well-tailored cream suit.

"Good afternoon," she said in barely accented English. "I am Madame Claire, the *directrice* of *l'école Claire*. You must be Dale." She extended her hand, which Dale met with a half-hearted shake, suddenly intimidated. Turning to me, she added, "And you are, Madame?"

"I am Mrs. Thoren, a family friend. I have been staying with friends in London, so her parents asked me to bring her over, which I was delighted to do."

"How nice." *Sarcasm?*

"To tell the truth, spending a few days in Paris is always welcome." I turned to Dale and handed her an envelope. "Open it later, dear. It is a small gift. Spend it wisely. You may wish to hand it over to Madame Claire for safekeeping. Madame, may I have a few private moments?"

"Of course. Nicole, please show Dale to her room."

I hugged the girl and whispered that she must call me if she needed anything. I felt tears on my neck. She looked back at me from the door, a look somewhere between despair and regret. She'd been through a lot, but I felt she would settle in if she tried.

"Madame Claire, I just handed Dale quite a lot of money, which you should probably hold on her behalf. Her clothes are serviceable but hardly chic. Do you advise your young ladies in such matters?"

"Of course. When she has been with us for a few weeks, and her French has improved, one of my staff will take her shopping. We enjoy the occasional social occasion, you know, so she needs some evening wear as well as outfits for daytime."

"Excellent. I was hoping so. Well, I must find a taxi to take me to my hotel."

"I will call one for you. Where are you staying?"

"The Georges Cinq."

She looked pleased, impressed with my good taste. I was actually staying at a small boutique hotel around the corner.

My hotel was simple, clean, and comfortable. To my surprise, the room had two beds. I unpacked my case and thought about where I should go for dinner.

"Where are we having dinner?"

I just about jumped out of my skin, although I knew at once it must be Agna. No one else could sneak up on me like that. "How did you get here? How did you know where I'd be?"

"First, I flew. On my own, you understand, not on a horrid tin can airplane. Second, I heard you make the reservation. When I got here, I told them there would be two of us, so they gave us this room. Easy!"

I was pleased to see her. I'd have more fun with her around.

"I'd love to see Paris. Is it as wonderful as I've heard?"

"Well, I don't know what you've heard, Mary, but it is very different. Settled in its antiquity, comfortable in its modernity. Sophisticated, splendid cuisine, even better *haute couture.* Parisians are less friendly than those in other parts of the country. Just like New Yorkers and the rest of the country here. We'll take you one day and show you everything."

So many dreams come true ... or about to. Would Hunter come again soon?

8

Lin came downstairs with a glass of sparkling water, which she bought by the case. She had given me a few bottles to keep in my little fridge. She wandered a little before gazing out of the sliding glass doors at the containers around the patio. The flowers looked as if they were swooning.

"I must speak with the gardener about those pots."

"They just need to be watered regularly. There's no hose down here, and it hasn't rained for ages."

"Well, he should have told me. And why didn't you?"

As if she hadn't been down here every day for the past week. She flounced onto the couch and arranged herself as usual.

"Her story was so compelling, I remember it almost word for word."

Once she had settled, I turned on the tape.

Tape 6, Volume 2

We had a great time in Paris for nearly a week, sightseeing and taking full advantage of the marvelous food and wine. I didn't keep in touch with home. I wanted to laugh and enjoy my new friend, free of responsibilities. I can't wait to go back again, hopefully with Agna.

The second night, we were sitting in a Chinese restaurant when I asked her about Tut. You may think it strange we went to a Chinese restaurant in Paris. I thought it very odd when Agna suggested it. She assured me she had been many times before, and the food was exquisite. She was right. Refined and tantalizing with fragrances and variety I've not seen in any other Chinese restaurant before or since.

When we had eaten our fill—and our fill astonished our waiter—we sat back to sip the rest of our second bottle of wine.

"Agna, you promised to tell me about King Tutankhamun."

"All right. I'm feeling happy enough at the moment to start. I'll do it in installments because it's too emotional. If I do it all at once, I'll become a blubbering wreck. I loved that boy with all my heart."

"I'm sorry. You don't have to."

"No, I want to."

She poured another glass and sat back.

She first saw that poor little boy after his father Akhenaten died, and he was taking part in the procession to the temple where the funerary rites would take place. He was an unattractive child—tall for his age but thin and sickly with front teeth that stuck out. He limped along with the aid of a cane because he had a twisted left foot with a special sandal tied onto it. He turned to look at Agna with the most beautiful almond-shaped eyes that held a frightened entreaty she could never forget. She knew at once he must fall under her protection.

What was remarkable about this encounter was that she had rendered herself invisible so that she could enter the inner sanctum of the temple—a divine place only the Pharaoh and the Priest of Maat might enter—because she wanted to witness the ceremony. Ay was the priest of Maat and Tutankhamun's cousin. Maat means harmony, justice, and truth—an important concept in Egypt at that time. Ay was a man of immense charisma who could bend most people to his will. Agna knew Tutankhamun had been moved to Ay's palace soon after his father's death and resolved to insert herself into the family. Ay's daughter, who had married General Horemheb the year before, also lived there. This was all common gossip, as were Ay's frequent dalliances with the dancers who performed at his feasts—boys and girls. The child needed someone by his side. He clearly had special powers, but perhaps not the kind of powers that would ward off evil directed his way.

Agna set about her dinner for another few minutes, staring at her plate as if analyzing its contents. I followed suit, reveling in the remaining juicy morsels of pork in a medley of vegetables. The secret of the wonder was, as always, in the sauce.

She put down her chopsticks with a clatter and sat back, holding her wineglass with one hand and tapping it absentmindedly with her thumb. She took a few sips before continuing.

The priests wore gold collars set with lapis lazuli and red jasper atop fine white linen robes, pleated at the skirt. Even their sandals were studded with precious stones. Ay wore malachite and turquoise on his extra wide collar, which stood out in the crowd—no doubt his aim. Agna rightly diagnosed him as seething with ambition.

The procession would have been enchanting but for the incongruity of a misshapen little prince dragging himself behind the bier and the old man who was Akhenaten's successor. The new pharaoh headed the procession, his worn joints bent and twisted by arthritis, which slowed everyone down, often resulting in the people at the back stepping on the heels of those in front of them. This led to whispered recriminations, glares, and vicious jabs. A pitiful show, indeed.

The crowd was unusually quiet. Akhenaten had not been popular, receiving only the minimal reverence due to a pharaoh. Most bowed their heads as the bier, with its burden of layered sarcophagi, passed.

The gold paint and jewels set in the outer sarcophagus dazzled the eye, even in the unusual absence of sun. She noticed several covetous gazes among the ominously sullen citizens. There was hardship in Egypt then. Akhenaten had neglected diplomatic relations with trading partners in other lands, as well as the careful husbandry of Egypt's resources. Egypt's finances were a mess, and the granaries had stood empty for too long. Many of the families lining the processional route looked thin and scruffy. Strangely, black clouds raced across the firmament as if the gods were angry and bent on punishment—maybe the sun god who had just lost his passionate adherent, or Amun, who had been set aside? The clouds opened just as the procession reached the temple gates. A bad omen.

The boy's father had been a controversial figure, and there were many who despised him, but none more than the priests of Amun. The Egyptians had worshiped other gods, with Amun billed as the top god—like Odin and Zeus—until Akhenaten, the new pharaoh, declared that there was only one god, and his name was Aten, the sun god. This meant that hundreds of priests lost power and riches. A few survived by refraining from protest, pledging their allegiance to Aten, and inventing new dogma—Ay among them. No one dared criticize a pharaoh openly, as he was considered divine. Akhenaten's death was said to be caused by a fever, which Agna found suspicious. Again, no one dared speak out.

She found it odd that Ay would take this boy under his wing, given the circumstances. Six-year-old Tut wasn't in line for the throne, as far as she knew. Ay walked in front of the boy and directly behind the new pharaoh. He looked remarkably pleased with himself. Agna wondered if she might need to seduce him. That would be one foot in the door, so to speak.

She could claim healing powers, too. Why not? She did have some knowledge of herbal medicines, and there were always a few spells she could fall back on to make the boy feel better ... if nothing else.

The rite in the inner temple turned out to be underwhelming. The new pharaoh fell while trying to kneel before the statue of Aten. When Ay finally hauled him up on his knees, he writhed in discomfort during the prayers offered up for his success. No knee replacements then. People don't know how lucky they are nowadays. Egypt's doctors were far more advanced than those in the rest of the world, but even they had their limitations.

Agna looked at her glass as if surprised to find it empty. She slowly poured out the last of the wine and gestured for the waiter to bring another bottle. He frowned but quickly reassumed his professional mask. Neither of us would become intoxicated. It made us feel good, but that was the extent of it. Once the waiter had brought the new bottle and completed the uncorking ritual, she sat back and sipped before taking a deep breath as if to brace herself.

"Are you all right?" I finally asked. "You don't have to go on if it's too much."

"Yes, I'm fine. I think it's good for me. I haven't ever talked to anyone about it. Who could I tell? At last, I have the right kind of friend."

She squeezed my hand. I felt emotional when she said and did that. When have I ever had a friend I could tell my secrets to? Frigg's other two handmaidens were like sisters to me, but none of us had any secrets in those days.

Agna took another sip and another deep breath.

Agna initially felt she stood on holy ground when she entered the sanctum. The statue loomed over them, its white stone glowing in the semi-darkness. Then the ambience was shattered by the old man's infirmity, not to mention his farts polluting the air as he struggled to regain his dignity. No relief from the god for him.

Agna said she never saw or felt any sign from those gods. Only the Sphinx possessed an inexorable power that grasped her mind as she stood under its regal beard years before when it was still half buried. She reached up and stroked its nose, broken long before the French arrived.

A voice in her head said, "My child, care for him."

"I will, always," she answered, without knowing the who or the why. She said her mind swirled as it let her go.

Ay muttered the prayers at breakneck speed, anointed the old man with special oil from an alabaster pot hidden behind the statue, and hustled him out.

"You do not show the proper respect," Pharaoh complained in a querulous voice. "You are hurting my arm." The ancient eyes looked straight at Agna. "You shouldn't be here. You know that."

Ay looked startled. "I am the priest of Maat. I must be here with you."

"Not you. Her." He jerked his head in Agna's direction. Alarmed, she held her hand up to Ay's face. He didn't flinch. Yes, still invisible—to most, at least.

While Pharaoh was still staring at Agna, Ay rolled his eyes and smirked, no doubt thinking the fellow senile. When Pharaoh turned back to him, he looked down at the bald pate and said, "Forgive me, divine Pharaoh, I wish merely to protect you from harm. We are at the entrance now. You must greet the crowd alone." Ay stepped back.

Pharaoh shot him a dirty look under recently trimmed eyebrows, pulled back his shoulders, and did his best to stride out. He didn't do too badly, only stumbling slightly once. Those citizens who had braved the storm raised a half-hearted cheer. The official mourners stared at the cobblestones, bedraggled and annoyed. It took a lot of work to get the pleats in those robes right.

He set his shoulders as straight as he could. "My fellow citizens, there is much to be done to increase Egypt's wealth and bring prosperity to all. I have taken the crown, and I will honor it." A gilded litter awaited Pharoah, and he was borne onto its throne. The bearers took him back along the procession route to the palace. The crowd seemed more enthusiastic now. The old man had spoken strongly. Perhaps he had felt some kind of transformation during the ceremony, after all. Had that statue blessed him in some way?

Agna waited a few weeks before presenting herself in Ay's flamboyant reception hall. He turned to speak to his scribe and found her standing before him when he turned back. She looked into his eyes, and he melted. The buzz in the hall dropped as everyone stared at this strange encounter. When she dropped her gaze, he pulled himself together and said, his voice raspy, "What are you doing here, girl?"

"I am Agna, a healer with special powers to help those who ail."

"There is nothing wrong with me or my family!" he said, throwing out his chest as if affronted.

"You are strong, my lord, but not all are so formidable. I would like to help the boy, Tutankhaten." That was the boy's name before he became Pharoah.

"How do I know you have these special powers? This is a matter for priests, is it not?" His face turned thunderous.

This was tricky. "Of course, special powers in the sense of what lies in the realm of the gods are properly bestowed on priests. My powers lie in my knowledge of herbs and other natural materials that grant the gift of healing to those who know how to use them."

His face relaxed. "Please seat yourself here, next to me." He flapped his hand at one of his advisers to move him off his cushion, and Agna sank down, grateful to have controlled the encounter. They chatted a little, although Ay was deeply involved in several conversations about national affairs. He behaved as if he were Pharaoh. Agna took the opportunity to admire the walls of his hall, so beautifully painted in bright shades of turquoise and carnelian by master craftsmen. There was a story to every panel, whether a hunt, a judgment, an encounter with a god, or a wedding. No funerals, she noticed, wondering if that kind of painting was thought to bring bad luck.

She was in. A minor official allotted her a chamber next to Tut's, and they got on very well. He was a sad little boy at first. No one had ever really loved or appreciated him, and he was often sick with malaria. Agna's herbal concoctions helped a lot, but earlier bouts had taken their toll. He tired easily, especially given the constant pain his foot caused him. Cuddles and hugs when he was tired or ill were their little secret.

But he wasn't stupid—far from it. They walked in the gardens one cool morning and settled under a pomegranate tree.

"The Pharaoh does not like Ay, you know," he blurted out. "Either Ay will go or he will."

Agna didn't dare comment one way or the other. Little boys can be indiscreet. But as he grew and studied astronomy, reading and writing, and mathematics with his tutor, it became clear that the child possessed precocious intelligence.

As you can imagine, this old pharaoh didn't last long. He appointed Ay Vizier of Upper Egypt at once, which increased the man's power almost limitlessly. Then came a fever, which progressed to death. Agna was often called upon to treat members of the household and the royal court, but not this time. Ay didn't want her anywhere near the sick man-god.

A new pharaoh ascended the throne, the younger brother of the old one, although not a whole lot younger. He was fit enough to be a lecherous old goat, though. His antics were notorious, as were the treatments doled out by his so-called doctors to enhance his virility. Tut went through another procession. Agna didn't bother with the inner sanctum this time, as it had proved disappointing, although she walked next to Tut, invisible. He knew she was there, and it comforted him.

Agna sipped and told me she was hungry again and would like dessert. I could eat another small thing, too. Our waiter couldn't hide his concern this time.

"It's all right," I said, trying not to laugh. "We are young ladies with large appetites. We are quite well."

He bustled away and brought back our crème brûlée, setting it down too carefully before retreating to watch us from a safe distance.

"I've had enough for one day," Agna whispered as she picked up her spoon.

"Food or the boy?" I asked.

She laughed as if easing her nerves and refilled her glass. "Well, just a little more. Until the bad bit."

She almost lost her young charge early on. Ay had decided to make Agna his mistress, at least for the time being. She knew she had little choice if she wanted to stay close to Tut. Agna told him in the morning that she would be with Ay that night. The boy was furious. He was only eight, not yet of an age to marry, so he was probably jealous of having someone else claiming her attention.

"You don't care about me at all. All you want is a man like all the other silly girls."

That hurt. "Tut, my dear, you know very well how much I love you. You also know very well that I cannot refuse Ay. He could separate us."

He knew that was true but still sulked all day. Agna gave him a soothing tonic before the evening meal as she was commanded to sup with Ay. He woke up calm and refreshed very early. When he burst into her chamber, there she was. He climbed into her bed, and they cuddled, dozing on and off for an hour or two. Crisis over.

Agna hated sex with Ay, although she feigned pleasure. He was thoughtless and brutal. She would have been covered in bruises were it not for her magic. He thought it was her potions. It wasn't more than once a week, and after a few months, he found a very young dancer, so they alternated. Agna expected his wife to hate her, but she was always pleasant. Perhaps she provided a welcome respite.

Only another year passed before the new pharaoh suffered a fall that broke a wrist and most likely fractured his skull. Agna had never been in his presence, so she only heard the details from Tut. He apparently suffered from terrible headaches, not to mention a wrist that swelled to three times its normal size with an angry red stripe that ran all the way up his arm. She probably could have saved him. Ay let him die. That much was clear.

They all waited to hear who the next pharaoh would be. One morning, while Tut was working with the palace astronomer, Ay's soldiers crashed into the room and stood to attention in a double column. Ay entered and strode between them to stand before Tut, who jumped up, fear radiating from his eyes.

"I salute you, Pharaoh Tutankhamun."

"What?" they chorused.

Ay turned to Agna. "You are in the presence of Pharaoh. Make your obeisance."

She dropped to the floor and prostrated herself.

"When we leave, you can gather your things and go. Pharaoh has no need of a nursemaid."

Agna's heart sank. Poor Tut. Ay would rule through him, and he would only last as long as it served Ay's purpose.

A clear, high voice commanded, "She will stay. Pharaoh has need of her counsel. Stand, Agna."

She rose and looked at Tut. He had drawn himself up and looked—well, regal. She turned to Ay, who looked as if he would like to slay her there and then. It only occurred to her later that Ay had changed the ending of Tut's name from -aten to -amun.

The crowds at the consecration ceremony were not impressed, given Akhenaten's unpopularity. Now, here was his son, maybe planning to wreck the country again. The ceremony in the inner sanctum was quite different. Agna felt the holy presence this time, as did Tut. When he knelt, she did, too, because she knew the god could see her. The statue shimmered silver, and she felt its vibration through her spine. She looked up at the child when he rose, reveled in his inner glow and the halo around his head. Ay didn't see it. The procession back to the palace felt different, too. The crowd saw his glow, although the halo had faded. They cheered and called out blessings. Agna sensed a new peace in her boy.

They moved into the palace. She loved it there, although no mortal was safe who had any influence over Tut. Tut made it clear that Ay was forbidden to bed Agna. Over the next few years, Ay tried to kill her several times but grew to fear her. The last time she cast a spell on his penis, rendering it non-responsive. She felt guilty after hearing how badly he'd beaten a young girl who failed to arouse him.

Agna cornered him one morning on his way out of the throne room.

"I hear you injured a young girl last night."

"What concern is it of yours?" He clenched and unclenched his fists.

"It wasn't her fault, you know."

"What do you mean, woman?"

"It was my fault. You remember what you tried to do to me three days ago? The asp in my bath?"

"That had nothing to do with me." He moved in close, looming over her.

"Oh yes, it did. I saw you empty it from a bag into the bath water after you sent away my maid. I'd heard your footsteps approach our wing of the palace, so I rendered myself invisible. I can finish you with my magic. Is that what you want?"

He stepped back. "Lies. You couldn't possibly hear anything that far away."

"Oh, I assure you, I can. If you ever try to harm me again, you will never again lie with a woman."

"Prove it, witch!"

She rendered herself invisible—quite a shock to his system if his sudden pallor was anything to go by—then started to fondle him. Nothing happened until she chanted the incantation loudly enough for him to hear. Soon, he felt the difference. She became visible once more. "Any more of your tricks, and it is gone forever." He almost ran from the palace.

Tut was credited officially with all kinds of reforms, but everyone at court understood it was Ay's work. Worship of the sun god had been abandoned for good, and Amun was brought back into favor. Religious monuments were restored, fruitful diplomatic alliances were strengthened, and food production and mining of precious stones were planned and controlled. In just four years, Egypt was prosperous once more. Crowds cheered heartily whenever Tut made himself shown, which rather turned his head.

"I am a great pharaoh," he declared one evening.

"Yes, one day you will make all the decisions yourself," Agna answered, more tartly than was tactful. He glanced at her and drew his mouth into a tight line.

"Ay said I must marry soon. I'm thirteen, after all."

"Yes, I suppose you must. Has he picked anyone?"

"I will pick who I marry. But he suggests Ankhesenamun."

"Your sister?"

"Half-sister."

"Ah, yes, I remember. A lovely young woman."

"The thing is..."

"What, my sweet?"

His face flushed the color of rubies. "You really shouldn't call me that. I am the great Pharaoh Tutankhamun." He peered at her under his eyebrows, expecting a put-down.

"You will always be my sweet."

He gave up and sighed. "The thing is, I don't really know anything about marriage. About what might be ... involved."

Agna was shocked. There was so much libidinous behavior going on at court; had he really not picked up anything? Never seen animals? "You don't know what a man and woman do together? You've never seen dogs mating?"

"Oh, I've seen dogs, but that's disgusting. That's for animals."

"People are like animals in that way, only more special. We get married to one mate, although often men stray. And people get pleasure from it."

"Did you get pleasure from Ay? I knew you had to lie with him. I just didn't know why."

"No, I didn't get pleasure, although I pretended to. He was rough and often hurt me. He is not a nice person. I did it because he would have sent me away from you if I hadn't."

"I know. Could you, er ... could you show me what to do?"

Agna was taken aback. This boy was like her own child. But, after all, these people married their siblings. What the heck. "We'll have a little cuddle tonight and see what happens."

Given Tut's general sickliness, Agna wasn't confident in his abilities in that arena. And that could prove an issue in itself.

Well, he rose to the occasion splendidly and found he rather liked it. She didn't mind much, although told me she didn't want to think about it too much off duty.

Ay put on a huge wedding feast of roast birds and game with all kinds of vegetables and other delicacies in piquant sauces, dancing girls and boys, musicians, acrobats, and so on. The little newlyweds clapped their hands in excitement and ate well. Ay made a big show of escorting them to the marital bed.

"You may leave us now, Ay. Thank you for the sumptuous celebration." He turned to Agna, who hovered in the doorway. "Agna, please help my wife disrobe." And to his wife, he added, "Do you know what happens in the marital bed?"

"Yes, my mother explained it all," she said. "And I've seen the dogs. It's sort of like that, but mostly face-to-face."

Agna found this situation unnerving. Tut sat on a stool and watched while she removed the girl's robe and brushed her hair. She motioned toward the bed, and the bride lay down on her back.

"You may leave us now, Agna."

"Good night," she said and scurried out. It all felt most awkward.

Those two loved each other, and Agna grew to love Ankhesenamun, too. She looked upon her as a substitute mother, coming to her for comfort as she first lost one baby and then a full-term child immediately after birth. They would never become parents. A tomb was prepared for the babes' mummified remains, with provision for Ankhesenamun when her turn came.

Over the next few years, Agna nursed Tut through a succession of illnesses, a few more bouts of malaria, and tried to bring some measure of ease to his tortured foot. Tut became more and more assertive, often clashing with Ay. She cautioned him many times because she knew how dangerous Ay could be.

One morning, Tut and his wife started to descend the steps of a temple in Karnak to walk up the avenue of sphinxes Tut had commissioned when they both tumbled down to the base platform. They told Agna later that someone must have spilled oil on the steps. Ankhesenamun only suffered bruises, but Tut sustained a badly broken leg. Agna treated him with an opiate to put him to sleep while the doctor splinted the leg and took care to keep the wounds clean and sterilized. He was always in pain. He demanded opiates for the pain, as it also helped relieve the club foot. Agna tried to resist, but he got so furious she gave in. She didn't want to lose him by being sent away, although she knew she might lose him to the poppy. She reasoned that the boy's life was miserable with pain, anyway, so what could be worse?

Tut and Ankhesenamun were so wrapped up in each other that Agna often found herself at loose ends, even with her healing duties. She started to think about her old home, which was no more. The Land of the Snows was still up north, though. She often used to visit it from her blue heaven. She craved to see the dark green pines, the lakes that look almost black against their snowbanks, and the tough but kindly people. She'd gone up there once before and couldn't tolerate the cold. She was determined to brave it this time.

She broached the subject with both of them after an evening of entertainment. "Please don't think I want to leave you or don't care for you.

You know I love you both like my own children. But I long to see my old home once more. Just for a visit. I will be home in a month."

"Can you really get there and back that fast?" asked Tut.

"Oh, yes, you know I have special powers."

"What special powers?" asked Ankhesenamun, puzzled.

"I can make myself invisible. I can move very quickly, too." She looked at Agna as if seeing her anew, like a woman rather than just a mother. Agna suddenly worried that she would wonder why she couldn't save Ankhesenamun's babies. The truth is, she sensed their severe deficiencies, so she didn't try.

"Yes, you deserve to go," Tut said. He looked downcast. "But please hurry back."

"Of course I will. I will miss you both so much."

So, off she went, feeling a little uneasy. She'd left strict instructions about Tut's medications with his doctor and Ankhesenamun. But there was Ay.

Agna said, her voice breaking, "I should have listened to my misgivings. I can never forgive myself."

Lin sat up.

"I think I've finished for the day, too. Fish pie for lunch."

"Good, I love Dora's fish pie."

"So do I. I hated it when they served it in that British boarding school in India. I don't know what kind of fish they used, but we spent more time picking out hundreds of tiny sharp bones than actually eating it."

"But tell me, will I get to meet Agna? I can't imagine what a real witch would be like."

"Yes, you will. If not here, in London. Or somewhere. She looks just like me, by the way—as if she's my sister, which is how I think of her. Only my hair is golden, and hers is so blonde it's almost white."

I really wanted to meet a witch.

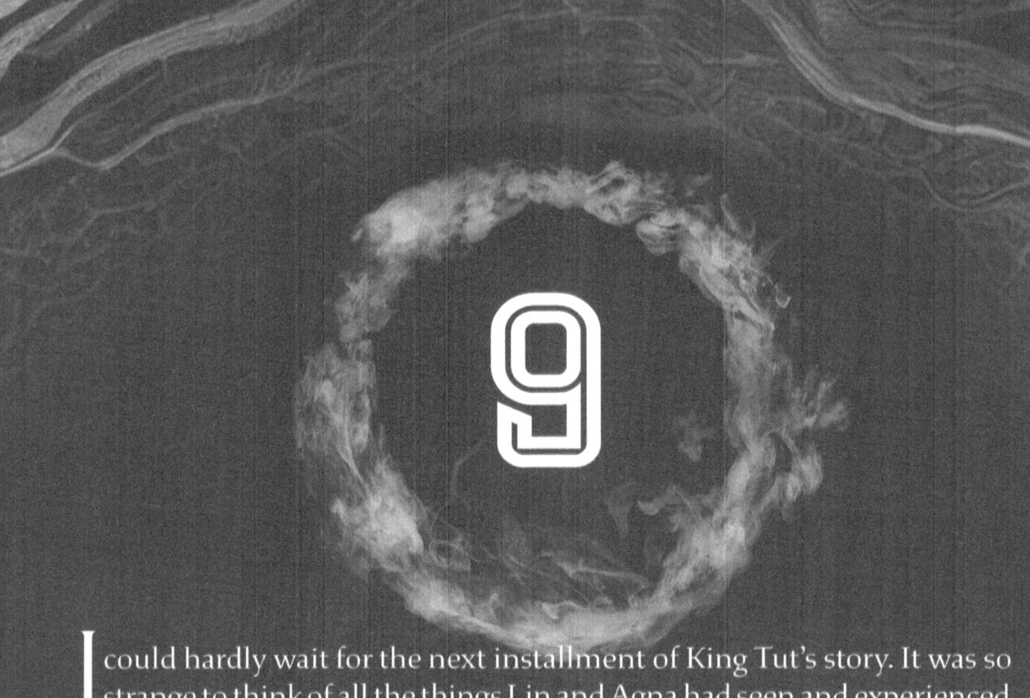

9

I could hardly wait for the next installment of King Tut's story. It was so strange to think of all the things Lin and Agna had seen and experienced. I couldn't help being envious; I hadn't seen or done much of anything.

Except that wasn't quite true. I was being paid to be a writer. I was privy to the life stories of gods—and now of a witch—and I was to bear the child of the glorious Hoenir. I lived in supreme comfort and was taken on holidays I could never have afforded if it weren't for the Thorens.

At breakfast after the King Tut revelation, Lin said she had a party to attend soon and wanted to shop for a dress. We'd go to the mall at ten, look for what she wanted, and have lunch afterwards at a Japanese restaurant she liked.

"Huh," was Hunter's response.

"Hunter doesn't like Japanese food. Not enough meat, that's all he likes," Lin told me with a dismissive hand wave. "Fish isn't robust enough for his manly tastes."

Hunter slapped down his knife and fork. "I am a big fellow. I have to keep up my strength. I do not know why you cannot understand that."

Sensing a fight in the offing, I asked, "I've never had Japanese food. What's it like?"

"Little bits of raw fish wrapped in seaweed," Hunter growled.

"Oh." Not to my taste, either.

"There's a lot more to it than sushi, as you know very well," Lin snapped. "Don't worry, Mary, you'll find dishes you'll like."

Chapter 9

The rest of the meal took place in heavy silence, only broken when Hunter strode out to his usual morning session in the study to check the stock market.

"So, you're not coming downstairs, then?" I asked.

"No, not today. I need a break. Besides, I need something nice for the party."

I was surprised because Hunter and Lin didn't usually socialize outside a small circle. "Is it a big party?" I asked.

"It's a fundraiser for the Salton Symphony next Saturday. Hunter doesn't want to go, but I really have to be supportive. Why don't you come? You might enjoy it. There's music, dinner, silent and live auctions, and even dancing. We'll get you a dress, too."

"Lin, don't feel you have to do that."

"I want to. Go and get ready. We'll leave in an hour."

A couple of days before I moved in here, Lin had invited me to a symphony concert in the theater she had been instrumental in establishing. That had been my first introduction to godly powers—when Lin frightened the bejesus out of a young pickpocket—and me. It was important for Lin to attend the fundraiser as a long-time member of the symphony board, which had switched from high school auditoriums to the theater she founded.

So many worries raced through my head. Hobnobbing with Salton's finest sounded nerve-wracking. I'd never learned how to do the sort of dancing they'd probably do, like waltzes and such. My social skills were subpar, for sure. I might make a fool of myself. But a new dress would feel wonderful, even though I had a big bump by now. And darn, I wanted to hear about Tut.

We didn't go to the usual mall, but a fancier one nearby.

"We'll start in my favorite boutique," said Lin.

The saleslady made a great fuss of us and held up myriad cocktail dresses for inspection.

"Ah, that's exactly you," she said when a pale green creation appeared.

I almost drooled; it was so gorgeous. It was essentially a caftan with jeweled applique around the low neckline and embroidered silver vines curling down to the hem. The saleslady took me to the dressing room and helped me put it on. I gasped when I saw myself in it.

When I emerged to show Lin, she grinned and said, "That'll slay them. That's the one. We'll get silver shoes and a bag to match." She held up a royal blue creation that even I could see was exquisitely tailored. Simple lines that would show off her perfect figure, and that shade of blue would look stunning with her hair. She tried it on. It was the perfect choice.

The saleslady was gushing about how we'd be the two most beautiful women in the room. I almost believed it—not that anyone could outshine Lin. I didn't ask about prices. I somehow understood that this wasn't the kind of place where one asked.

We tried on shoes next. I wasn't used to high heels, especially unwise now, so I chose pretty silver sandals with reasonable, two-inch heels. Lin bought Jimmy Choo stilettos, and her legs showed them off to perfection.

"Lin, you're spending too much money on me."

"Nonsense. Money is to be enjoyed. I loved the look on your face when you looked at yourself in the mirror in that dress. You looked beautiful. You know you did. I want you to feel beautiful. It's important at such a time. After the baby, I'll get you something sleeker."

I almost cried at her generosity, not only with money but with her spirit ... and her husband.

She said she wanted me to rest, as she had things to do the rest of the week. Why not go to Auntie Peggy for a couple of days? I would need to be back Friday night because we had appointments for hair and manicures on Saturday.

That night, Hunter came downstairs. I was really showing, so we didn't make love often because he was afraid of hurting the baby. He was heavy, after all. "Human women are fragile, he said. "And need protection." I loved him all the more for it. We lay on my bed and cuddled. I told him about my new dress and how much I loved it.

"Lin told me you looked beautiful in it. You look beautiful in anything. I will come with you both on Saturday, although I do not enjoy these affairs. But I have to see my girls in their finery."

"I hope you won't be disappointed," I whispered. "I'm not really beautiful; I mean, I can't compare to ... well, you know."

"Never compare yourself to a goddess, Mary. There is no point. You are a very beautiful woman. Has no one ever told you that?"

Well, no, they hadn't. Coming from Lin earlier and Hunter now, I began to feel maybe I was at least pretty.

After he kissed me tenderly and left, I changed into my pajamas and climbed under the duvet. The weather was unusually cool for June, so I was glad for the warmth. What kind people they were—but they could deliver swift and deadly justice if need be. I reminded myself never to forget that.

Chapter 9

The beauty salon was as elegant as could be, with its private cubicles—a thing of the past in most salons—and an ocean of marble. Lin told me to just leave everything to Alex. He would know best what style would flatter me most. I was happy to because I wouldn't have had a clue what to suggest.

Thank goodness I'd not cut my hair for a while because he accomplished a masterful updo. I was glad I'd showered that morning, so I wouldn't run the risk of messing it up. The shellac nail finish looked great, too—a soft, shiny peach that matched my pedicure.

Hunter whistled appreciatively as we came downstairs. "You will both outshine every other woman at the party," he said proudly.

The party was held in the ballroom of the huge house of one of the board members. She and her husband talked loudly about their new acquisition, showing various groups their wine cellar and the pool in the basement. I tagged along behind Lin. To a girl whose experience of basements had been a boiler and cobwebs, it was mind-blowing.

The buffet spread was sumptuous, with plates of shrimp that were attacked first. I did my part, too, thanks to Hunter, who brought me a plate stacked high. He made sure I had a chair and kept popping back to check on me. I chatted about god-knows-what to various people, mostly without knowing their names. I hadn't settled on a table, as some were reserved, and I assumed one of them would be for Lin's party. I was enjoying myself as much as I used to enjoy the circus. Was I a performer now rather than a mere onlooker?

"Hi, Mary. Nice to see you!" It was Joe, a local detective who now served on the board of the Salton Symphony. Lin told me he'd solved the case of a former board member who had turned out to be a serial killer. She and Hunter had become friends with him and his girlfriend, Helen.

"Hi, Joe, how are you? Where's Helen?"

"Oh, I think she's taking the guided tour. Having fun?"

"Sort of. Happy to see someone I know, though."

"I know what you mean. Where's Lin?"

"No idea—oh, there she is."

We watched as Lin threaded her way through the crowd.

"Hi, Joe, how's it going?" she said.

They exchanged pleasantries before Lin got down to business. "Joe, an old and unwelcome friend is here."

"What do you mean?" he asked, a small frown creasing his forehead.

"Remember the pickpocket at the first concert in September?"

"As you may remember, you sent him packing before I got to meet him."

"Yes, well, don't be huffy. He's here. A waiter. He hasn't seen me yet. Keep your eyes open."

"Who..." was all Joe got out before she disappeared.

"Let's just follow her and see what happens," I said.

"You should keep out of it in your condition."

"I'm pregnant, not sick. Come on."

I don't know when I became so bossy, but I suppose I knew nothing bad would happen to me while Lin was around. And Hunter, too. I looked around for him while pushing through Lin's path. There he was, sitting in a corner, a loaded plate in one hand, a glass of red wine on the table beside him. He was deep in conversation with a man in a pinstripe suit, gold-rimmed glasses, and a full head of white hair. The man might have had "banker" etched on his brow, but I couldn't swear to it.

I stopped suddenly when Lin braked beside a waiter sporting a wispy mustache and a recent crew cut.

Joe grabbed my arms so he wouldn't barge into me. "Sorry," he whispered.

The waiter must have seen Lin out of the corner of his eye, so he extended the tray of champagne in crystal flutes in her direction. "Champagne, madame?"

"Nice to see you again," she said.

The tray performed a backward dive over a bemused elderly couple, dousing them with bubbly. The young man made a run for it, but not fast enough. Lin moved like a snake and had his arms pinned behind him in seconds.

"I warned you," she hissed.

She dug in his pockets and brandished a wallet, a watch, and a necklace, which she passed to Joe as she fished them out.

People around us were emitting exclamations and little shrieks while the crowd pressed closer to witness the spectacle, which would be retold *ad nauseam* at Salton socials for months.

"You are under arrest. I will read you your rights as we leave," said Joe.

"Just you, not her," the boy said. "Keep her away from me!" His moustache, one side hanging loose now, quivered along with the rest of him.

Given what he'd gone through before, I almost sympathized with him.

Joe ignored him and turned to the crowd. "If any of you are missing these items, come to the front lobby now."

People took inventory—patting pockets, checking their wrists, and clutching pearls—and a couple of scowling guests straggled after the miscreant and his captors.

"Are you all right, Mary?" Hunter had come over to check the situation. "Joe, why don't you and I handle this and let the ladies get back to their festivities?" He made a small bow to our hostess, who stood on the edge of the crowd wringing her hands. "I'm sure our hostess needs to start the presentations and speeches."

"I'll have to get handcuffs from my car," said Joe.

"We'll walk him outside together. Can't you call for a car?" asked Hunter.

"Of course. But I'll have to go with him. I'll try to get back."

What a splendid charmer Hunter was. Suave and tactful. And, as I realized later, he would do anything to avoid sitting through speeches. He and Joe escorted the hapless crook to the front door and outside.

"Come on," said Lin as she guided me to a table near the podium. Helen, Joe's girlfriend, soon joined us. She realized something had happened but didn't know what.

Lin disappeared for a few minutes and came back with a waiter who carried a tray with a bottle of champagne and two flutes, plus Perrier for me. I nudged Lin when flashing blue lights filtered through a gap between the velvet drapes.

Helen frowned when she realized Joe had left.

"He said he'd be back soon," I told her.

"I hope so. You look beautiful, by the way." She looked at me curiously. She was wondering, but I didn't plan to elucidate. I felt good, though. Very good.

Ten minutes or so later, the presentations and speeches began. First, the hostess apologized for the unfortunate unpleasantness that had transpired earlier. Volunteers and donors were thanked, the silent auction (which I'd forgotten about) was formally closed, and the live auction began.

They must have raised thousands from NFL season tickets, resort vacations, and various decorative items gleaned from some of Salton's finest stores. The last one was a Labrador puppy, whose breeder cuddled him as she walked around the tables for all to admire.

"Damn," said Lin. "I really want him."

"Better not," I whispered.

Hunter joined us at that point.

"What did I miss?" he asked in a stage whisper.

"It's all over, bar the puppy," I said.

"Look at that sweet little thing," Lin whined. "How can you resist?"

"Not for us," he asserted loudly, glaring at her.

The pup sold for $5,000, and Lin sulked for the rest of the evening.

I wanted to know why Hunter was so against getting a dog.

Not long after, it was time to go. It was a fairly tiresome departure, as we had to wait for the valet parking guys to bring out the car.

The hostess was a little stiff as we said our farewells. “Such a dreadful scene,” she said. “Such a pity. But thank you.”

10

We lazed around all Sunday after the party. I'd felt so good in my new gown, so appreciated and part of a different world, a couple of worlds. After the *Washington Post* headlines, book reviews, and style section, I read a new mystery. I wasn't a political junkie, and this bare-bones approach suited me fine.

"How much longer before Sven's graduation?" I asked Lin.

"Next Friday," she said. "We leave on Wednesday."

"How come he's graduating before Margareta?" I asked. Sven's sister was older than he.

"She took a couple of years off to travel. We didn't mind too much, although we were relieved when she re-enrolled. She graduates next year."

Still in high school? "What's Sven going to do?"

"He wants to do some traveling with friends during the summer. He's been accepted to MIT. A PhD is his aim, then an academic career. He's a bright boy."

"He must be."

We all went to bed early.

I didn't see Lin and Hunter at breakfast the next morning, but when I got back downstairs, I found her waiting for me.

"Oh, good morning," I said. "I wasn't sure if you were coming."

"We ate early, as Hunter had a 9:00 appointment. I'm going to finish Agna's story this morning."

Tape 7,
Volume 2

Agna was gone only three weeks, as it happened. The Land of the Snows was still beautiful, but she was not willing to brave the cold for any longer. She could keep herself comfortable with potions and charms, she said, but it just wasn't her anymore. She wanted to feel warm air on her arms and warm breezes across her face. She wanted bright flowers in her rooms and spiced foods on her table.

Upon return, she went to bathe in her rooms but couldn't find the maids. She changed into a clean robe and walked along to Tut's apartments. They were empty. In fact, the whole palace seemed empty. The guards at the palace gates, who always stood to attention, said nothing. Agna's stomach clenched, so she went out and asked the younger of the two, "Do you know where everyone has gone? Where is Pharaoh?"

Tears filled the boy's eyes as he said, "Pharaoh is no more."

Agna said that her breath came in short bursts as the world reeled before her eyes. Somehow she stumbled back to her room and curled up on her bed, sleeping between crying jags. She wondered where Ankhesenamun was. She'd forgotten to ask.

The next morning, a courtier entered her room without knocking with a message from Ay: She had to leave. There was no place for her anymore.

She asked what happened, and the courtier told her.

"Pharaoh is dead," he said. "His broken leg got badly infected, and he couldn't be saved. His body is being prepared for the afterlife now. He will be placed in the tomb prepared for his two babies and his wife."

Agna asked, "Where is Ankhesenamun?"

She had returned to her family. There were no children, so she was not part of the dynasty.

Agna asked, "Who will be the next pharaoh?"

The man looked shifty and said, "No one knows." It would be Ay, of course.

Agna asked if she must leave at once and heard, "Yes, we will send a maid to serve you. She will accompany you to wherever you go."

No time to grieve, no time to adjust, no time to find another home. Calamity. But she had one more thing to do.

Ay was holding court in the palace audience hall as if he were already Pharaoh. He blanched when Agna materialized before him.

He almost growled at her, "I gave instructions that you were to leave."

"You are not Pharoah yet," she said in a clear voice that carried to all present. "I am not satisfied with the care the Pharaoh received in my absence. I hold you responsible."

"Seize her!" he commanded the guards, who had already begun to advance.

Agna turned, threw out her hands, and roared a spell. A gaggle of geese staggered around the hall, pecking at the marble floor. It wasn't long before a few furious ganders started chasing the dancing girls, whose practiced kicks knocked a few out.

Agna turned back to Ay, who shook like palms in a sandstorm, and said, "You forgot my powers, Ay. You forgot Maat. You will be plagued for the remainder of your days with carbuncles and rashes that will drive you half mad. Not a moment's peace will you know. You are forever impotent." She pointed at him and screeched, "The torment begins."

His face, which had been white with fear, turned angry red from the pustules that traversed far down his neck beneath the ornate collar. He tore at his cheeks before reaching back to his buttocks, bellowing with fear and rage.

Agna disappeared without another word.

Fortunately, she had gold coins that Tut had given her for her trip. Ay would have cast her out penniless. The new maid was barely polite, probably a spy. They packed Agna's clothes and other small possessions into chests, which a couple of soldiers came to lift onto a donkey-drawn cart.

Where would they go? Agna told the driver to take her to the tomb.

Both he and the maid looked startled. The driver protested, "No one is allowed close."

"Then take me to the nearest houses so I can find a place to live," said Agna.

The driver said, "There are only houses for the workers, nothing for a lady like you."

Agna said, "That will be fine." She could live simply as long as she could watch over her boy.

The maid said, "I cannot live in such a place."

"You are just a maid," Agna shouted. "No better than the workers."

They came to a row of houses. A family was straggling out of one house with bags and bundles. Agna asked the driver, "What's happening there?"

He said he'd ask and hopped off the cart to speak to them. A young girl was weeping, and a hard-faced older woman was shaking her head. The driver soon returned to report that the man of the family had died in an accident, and the family was returning to their village. They had told him whom to ask about renting the place.

The driver said, "I'll go and see to it now, lady."

Agna thanked him and asked his name.

"Adom," he said.

Adom negotiated with the landlord's man and carried Agna's possessions into the house. She thanked him and held out a coin, which he refused, saying he had been well paid by a man in the palace. His honesty touched her.

"No, take this, Adom, because I would like you to drive this maid back to the palace," Agna said. "I have no need of her."

The maid—whose name Agna hadn't bothered to ask, as she was such an unpleasant creature—looked elated.

Adom looked concerned. "But lady," he said, "the cleaning, the cooking, the washing..."

Agna suggested that he might help her find someone else. Adom agreed and drove away with the maid, leaving Agna alone with her grief.

Of course, it did not take her long to clean and arrange the house with a few incantations. A cousin of Adom's helped her furnish it, a few workmen built an addition onto the back, and she was comfortable there for many years.

After centuries passed, Agna's home was torn down. Hers had been the only house left standing in the row, but plans were afoot to build a new village, where she eventually lived. She moved several times but always stayed close until "those creatures," as she called them, broke all the way through into her boy's resting place.

She couldn't bear to stay after they took him away. Tomb robbers had found their way into the first chamber very early on and grabbed a few things, but after seeing Agna in ghostly form, they not only fled but spread the word.

She visited one of the early exhibitions in the Louvre once, intending to create a maelstrom and take Tut away to a safe place. She had already dealt with the aristocrat who bankrolled the expedition, as she related to me in London. And Carter, of course. He had to go.

But then she saw the lines waiting to see her boy. The excitement. Agna made herself invisible, walked in without queuing, and mingled in the crowd. People marveled in many languages, even expressing sorrow for this boy king. She knew then that this was for the best. He was in a glittering procession again, traveling the world, admired by all who saw him.

"So, Lin, there you have it," she said. "The story of me and Tutankhamun."

"I don't know much about ancient Egypt, but I doubt most people know any of these things," I said.

"Of course, they don't. History is retold and retold, often by men with their own agendas. Only the people who were there really know the truth. And they usually lie for one reason or another."

Lin was busy packing and making arrangements to leave for Sven's graduation. I couldn't help wondering why I hadn't heard about Margareta's time out from school. Was there more to it?

The Sunday evening they arrived back, Sven in tow, we had a lovely dinner at home with a champagne toast beforehand. I had bought Sven an antique copy of Euclid's *The Elements*. I was rather nervous because I had no idea if he would like it.

"Wow, Mary, this is fantastic!" He leafed through it almost reverently. "Thank you so much. I love it."

Both parents looked pleased and surprised.

Phew, I hit the jackpot.

Lin whispered to me later that she wouldn't be coming down for a couple of days. "It's so lovely to have Sven home. I don't want to spoil it. The next session isn't so happy."

We had a great few days going to the Kennedy Center to see a musical, the movies to see some ghastly action film—although parts of it were entertaining enough—and going out to dinner. What a life!

"Monday," Lin whispered to me again. "Sven's going to stay with a friend in Toronto on Sunday."

On Monday morning, Lin was not very happy, answering Hunter and me in monosyllables and snapping at Dora. I assumed it was because her boy had left, but she had mentioned she was coming to an unhappy subject.

Chapter 11

Soon after breakfast, she walked stiffly downstairs and lay on the chaise without saying a word. When she heard me snap on the recorder, she started.

Tape 8,
Volume 2

I fidgeted and fretted on the train as it sped southwest toward the small town of Brockenhurst. Agna dozed next to me, annoyingly unfazed. That note, that bastard.

We have your darling daughter, it said. *Come at once if you want to see her again. The three of us are in jolly old England, you know.*

I felt gut-roiling fear when I read that, a torture I have rarely endured. Although it was me he wanted to destroy, he wouldn't hesitate to harm Margareta.

Hunter had called the London house and left a message to say she hadn't come home from school. He'd asked Lettie to investigate while I was still in Paris. I cursed myself for being unable to use a cell phone and for not giving him Agna's number.

After we got home from Heathrow, I heard Hunter's chilling message, found the note pushed through the door, and called him immediately. Two days missing.

"Where were you?" he asked, sounding more anguished than angry.

I told him about delivering my charge to her finishing school. "I know Loki is involved. I knew it as soon as I got the note." I read it to him. "How did he know where I am?"

"I expect he got someone to trick the information out of one of the children," Hunter answered. "I'll let Lettie know."

"The note said I had to come at once. But it didn't say where."

"Call the cops if you have to. I'll come myself as soon as I get a flight."

"No, please don't leave Sven. Keep him close. I know he'll be very frightened for his sister, but I'm frightened for him, too. There's nothing you can do here that I can't."

"I suppose so. But call the cops if things get bad. Our daughter's safety is the most important thing."

I didn't call the cops because I knew I was the target and the little worm would get in touch. I had Agna, too, and we'd already talked it over.

"No way you're going through this alone. I'll stay with you through it all," she said. "We'll get her back."

The phone rang an hour so after I talked to Hunter. An American woman's voice, presumably the nurse who had helped Loki escape.

"Tomorrow morning, get a train from Waterloo to Brockenhurst at ten. It will get you there at about 12:30. You will find a taxi outside the station. Tell the driver to take you to The King's Forest Tavern in Burley. Sit in the garden and order a drink. I will pick you up there and take you to your daughter. No tricks, and come alone. If I don't return to my master in good time and good health, your daughter will die. Understood?"

"What a coward, taking revenge on a child."

"It is not wise to talk like that. We have the upper hand, remember? Show some respect."

My fury rose to dangerous heights, but I tamped it down when the wine glass in my left hand shattered, and a burgundy stain bloomed over Agna's white carpet. Margareta's well-being was all that mattered.

"Would you spell the name of those towns?"

She spelled both out. "It's in Hampshire, in the New Forest."

She hung up.

I told Agna what she'd said. "I'd like to kill Loki, but it's not that easy, even as decrepit as he is now. Thor gave him the gift of immortality. But even the great gods died at Ragnarok."

"Maybe we can figure out a way to at least make him worse off. I'll think about it. That woman has to go, though."

Indeed, she did.

I barely noticed the countryside we trundled through, stopping at dinky little stations with riotous flower beds that clamored for attention in front of the ticket halls. I'd bought a cell phone on the way to Waterloo and called Hunter with the number.

Finally, Brockenhurst. We got off—Agna had rendered herself invisible—and walked to the gate. I remembered to hand only one ticket to the collector before walking outside, where a couple of taxis stood. One of the drivers leant against his car, smoking. The other snored with gusto. His head dropped back against the headrest.

I approached the smoker. "The King's Forest Tavern, please."

"Very good, madame." He ground the stub under his heel before opening the door for me.

I let Agna slide in first. After about twenty minutes, the taxi pulled up outside a quaint little stone inn with a thatched roof and small cloudy windows. Strangely, a couple of horses wandered around the front garden. One went through the gate into the back.

"What on earth are those horses doing here?" I asked the driver.

"Eh, they be the New Forest ponies, madame. Wild, they are, and they have the right of way on all the roads in the New Forest. They go wherever it pleases them. That one's probably thirsty and gone looking for a pond."

"People don't mind?"

"Oh, no, it's part of life down here. There's a pub nearby where some of them line up to get the beer dregs. They love it. It's the malt, you see."

"And there are roads through the forest? Just how big is it?"

"Thousands of acres, but a lot of it be moorland. Enclosed by William the Conqueror for hunting. That's why it's called the New Forest."

Only in England.

I paid him and added a generous tip before following the pony into the back garden. I, too, was thirsty.

We sat at one of the tables in a corner of the garden, away from the few other couples enjoying a pub lunch. A fixed bench on either side of the table ensured we wouldn't have anyone try to push in Agna's chair.

"Why did you become invisible so soon?" I whispered. "You know how you get."

"I tried a special spell this time," Agna whispered back. "There might have been someone watching at the station."

"I didn't see anyone."

"No, but we didn't know that then. It's a good job you're wearing that dark wig. You look almost ordinary."

"Oh, shut up." *Me, ordinary?*

A big-boned woman came striding toward us, hair more or less swept up into a curly bleached ponytail. She doubled back when she noticed the pony worrying at some kind of grid on the pond, giving him a good whack on the rump and pushing him out of the gate before coming back to me.

"Do ponies often come in here?"

"All the time. That's why we have a grid over the pond. They'd suck up all the fish in their big mouths if we didn't. What'll it be?"

"A gin and tonic, please."

"Nothing to eat?"

"What's on offer?"

"We do a nice ploughman's lunch. Cheddar, Stilton, and Wensleydale with a good hunk of bread. We make the bread ourselves."

"That sounds good. Forget the g-and-t. I'll have a pint of bitter."

"Certainly."

After she'd disappeared back into the pub, Agna whispered, "A pint of bitter?"

"Easier to share," I replied. "The cheese will feed us both, too."

I'd managed to rally from my despair a little and figured food and drink might help. The waitress came back with my order after about ten minutes. It was only a matter of cutting and pouring, after all. It didn't take us much longer than another ten minutes to finish, alternating sips and bites. All hearty, fresh, and good.

I looked around, marveling at the lush display—roses flaunting themselves in numerous bushes, magnificent fuchsias posing in one corner, and a bed of various bright annuals along one hedge. The pony poked its head through the gate again, only to be violently pushed out of the way by a scary-looking woman who marched in and scanned the tables. She looked as if she belonged in a concentration camp—on the administrative side.

"That's her," I whispered to Agna. "Will you get in the car with me?"

"If I can do it unobtrusively. I can always fly if need be."

When the woman spotted me sitting alone, she continued her march and sat on the bench opposite me. Agna must have moved in time because I felt the draft as she slipped in next to me.

"Lin, I assume."

"You assume right. The nurse, I assume."

"I serve my master in whatever capacity he needs."

"Clearly."

"Let's go."

I followed her to the front, where several cars were parked. She seemed oblivious to the pony she'd shoved so hard, bringing up the rear. I caught a hint of Agna whispering to it, but even I couldn't make out what she was saying.

The pony darted forward, pushing me to one side, and bit the nurse on her right arm. Her screech brought the waitress and another man—probably the landlord—running out the front door. The sound of galloping hoofs receding into the forest drew everyone's eyes for a few seconds, but there was nothing to see, however much they strained.

Good old Agna.

"That filthy creature bit me!" the nurse screamed.

"What creature?" the waitress asked.

"Well, he's gone now, but look at my sleeve. There's blood."

"Well, now," I said, trying to sound soothing. "He's gone now. You're a nurse, so I'm sure you can take care of it. No real harm done."

The nurse shot me a venomous look and pulled me to her car. She opened the back door wide. I felt the faint breeze of Agna entering before me. "Don't try anything funny. Remember what I said."

"How could I forget? You talked about murdering my daughter."

She smiled—thereby sealing her fate—before getting in, starting the car, and backing out. All with her left hand. So, her right arm was really bothering her. "Damn that beast," she muttered.

"Where are we going?"

"You'll see soon enough."

I noted our position to the sun and all the turns we made. After about fifteen minutes, we pulled up outside a cottage that stood alone at the end of a narrow lane. No neighbors to worry about.

I said, "I see you've been planning this for some time. Renting a place in an isolated spot, and so on."

"Not so long. You haven't been away for more than a few weeks, after all. I'm efficient. Plus, my parents came from these parts."

"I'm sure they'd be proud."

That earned me another nasty look in the rear mirror. As I got out, she almost sprang out of her seat to plant herself in front of me.

"Don't worry, I'm not going anywhere. I wouldn't forsake my daughter."

She took me roughly by the arm with her left hand and walked me to the door. Her right arm clutched her waist. The door wasn't locked, and she went in, bolting it behind her.

So, Margareta was locked up. These cottages wouldn't have basements, although there could be a root cellar.

We turned left into a small sitting room where a shriveled Loki sat in his wheelchair in front of a lively fire. The room was stifling.

He turned his head, staring at me with glittering yellow eyes.

"So, the little princess has walked into my parlor."

"The spider has an innocent little girl caught in his web."

"She's comfortable. Sleepy. We will dump her at the pub when this is over."

I knew what he meant by "over."

"I want to see her."

"Of course, I will allow you to spend one last night together. Just one thing. You will allow Lilian to chloroform you so you can't do any damage. Before you see your daughter."

"Why do you think I can't just take my daughter now? I'm stronger than both of you."

"Huh, don't you think I've thought of that? Her room is booby-trapped. Any funny business and it will blow up."

I took a deep breath, hoping Agna had heard that. "Very well."

Lilian placed the cloth over my mouth. I felt my mind swirl even though I held my breath. I guess a little entered through my nose. That is one of our few godly weaknesses. Even a little anesthesia saps our strength, and Loki knew that. I wasn't out but pretended to be, draping my arm over Lilian's shoulder before sagging. She dragged me through a door in the kitchen and down some stairs to the cellar. It smelled of rotten apples and mold.

"Mama!" Margareta rushed to me, and we fell in a heap onto the dirt floor.

"Your mother has been chloroformed, so she'll be out for a while," Lilian said. "Make the most of your last night together."

"What do you mean?" my daughter cried. "What are you going to do to us?"

"You'll find out soon enough." She laughed, turned on her heel, and left, bolting the door behind her. She could expect no mercy.

My poor girl clung to me and wept. I was not entirely out of it, but still compromised, my strength sapped. I held her as tightly as I could and patted her back.

"Don't worry, little one, I'm not completely finished. And there is help in the house now, someone they know nothing about." I pushed myself into a sitting position against a rough stone wall. "Let me rest a little to get back to rights."

After about a half hour, I started to feel normal. What was Agna up to? And just how would they get rid of me, an immortal? Did Loki know something I didn't?

"Lin, are you all right?" Agna stood in front of us, fully visible. Margareta gasped, and we both shushed her. "The nurse is busy packing in the bedroom, and Loki is listening to music in the living room, so I slipped the bolt."

"Do you know how they plan to get rid of me? There don't seem to be any explosives down here. Did you see any around?"

"No, I checked when I heard Loki mention a booby trap. I heard them talking about fire. There is torn-up newspaper all over the house, especially in front of the door to this cellar. The nurse has scattered all kinds of other scraps around, too. And there's a big can of petrol in the kitchen."

Fire. It couldn't kill me, but it could make me want to die. Immortals can will themselves to die. Well, that could work both ways. They'd never planned to let Margareta go. I had always realized that was a possibility, but it still shocked and infuriated me. I shivered, not entirely due to the damp cold that emanated from the walls and floor.

"We need to get hold of that chloroform," I said.

"Already done," said Agna, patting her pocket.

"After we've put them out, we can start the fire and leave. We don't really need to chloroform Loki. It's not as if he can move."

Margareta clutched my arm. "Mama, you can't let anyone suffer fire. It's too cruel." She had a tender heart.

"You're right, princess. We'll chloroform him, too."

I suppose I should have been shocked that she was okay with killing them at all, with or without the chloroform, but that didn't occur to me until later. I had moved into avenging-god-mode.

Agna said, "I'll go and chloroform the nurse first with a good dose. She'll take at least five minutes to put under. I'd better hit her over the head first to make it easier. Then Loki with whatever's left. You two wait at the top of the stairs. Lin, you must find her car keys."

We all crept up the stairs, my girl and I waiting until Agna had completed her mission. I was concerned because she'd started to limp. New spell be damned. She'd stayed invisible too long.

"All down," she cried out, and we emerged. "Her car keys were on the hall table. Margareta, take these and wait in the car."

I was glad the girl wouldn't have to watch us do the deed. We splashed accelerant around before I went to have a last look at Loki. He was even more unattractive in a coma than he was in life, all twisted and dried out. Lillian didn't look much better, with her open mouth drooling and her pink, woolly knickers showing.

"Okay," I said. "I'm ready. Strike the match." Silence. "You didn't find any matches, Agna?"

"Er, no. There must be some. They planned to set fire to the place, after all."

"Oh, good grief, start looking."

We searched for a few minutes and came up short.

"Now what?" said Agna as we stood in the middle of the kitchen floor, ankle-deep in crumpled newspaper. Then it struck me. Loki was sitting in front of a fireplace. That chloroform must have really sapped my smarts.

"The fireplace, Agna. We'll throw more petrol around, make a torch out of a wad of cloth, and make sure the paper catches in several places. And we leave the gas on so everything blows up after we're safely away."

Agna looked at me funny. "You've got a better idea?" I asked.

"No. My legs." She sank to the ground. Just what I needed. I picked her up and carried her to the car, her noodle legs slapping against mine with each step. After setting her in the front passenger seat, I walked around to the driver's side and started the engine.

"Have you finished, Mom?" asked Margareta. "There're scary shadows out here."

"Not quite, sweetheart. I have to go back and finish up. Only a few minutes."

Back inside, I rearranged the scrunched-up newspaper, taking it all out of the kitchen and leaving a good heap in front of Lilian's room and the living room where Loki sat. I doused it all with petrol and took the precaution of letting some soak into the living room carpet. Then outside to sprinkle the rest around the front of the house. I left the can sitting by the front door. They'd know it was arson, anyway, so there was no point in concealing it.

Now to make the torch. I jumped over the paper barrier into the living room and picked up the poker before going back to the kitchen, where I'd left some cloth scraps. I found a newspaper on the table and wrapped it around the poker, covering it with a cloth before ripping off a curtain cord to tie it all up. It needed only to be lit.

Back down the hall, I leapt back into the living room and thrust my torch into the embers. It had just started to catch nicely when a cold, clammy hand slapped my left ankle and yanked me down. I tried to pull away, but a cold slap and curl around my left wrist stopped me. These were tentacles, fleshy, huge, and full of suckers.

I thrust the torch into the tentacle wound around my ankle, and it dropped away, but not before I, too, felt the burn. The tentacle around my wrist pulled me towards Loki's wheelchair, where tentacles whipped in a frenzy around his withered body, waiting to ensnare me again.

I kicked his chair over, nearly taking myself with it. I gritted my teeth and stabbed the thing that still clung to my wrist with the torch. Nothing. It must have gone out. I tried to pull away, but it threatened to pull my hand off. I had only one other weapon at my disposal. I leaned down and bit hard, heaving as my mouth filled with putrid slush and the horrid thing retracted.

I spat a couple of times before igniting the torch again, dodging the parry and thrust of the tentacles, which seemed to be growing longer. Nearly there. I have quick reactions unimaginable to most humans, but I couldn't evade the snaky tentacle that wound around my neck and started to tighten. I roared in surprise, regretting it instantly because I knew Margareta would have heard it and been scared witless.

Loki's raspy cackle rang in my ears. I might lose consciousness, but he couldn't kill me. Although there was fire.

I struggled and pulled at the thing around my neck. It was more like a snake than a tentacle because I could feel muscles contracting under my fingers. But it was even stronger than me. I was losing.

"Mama! What's happening?"

I could only grunt and hope she would run. After a minute or so, the thing around my neck seemed to spasm before it dropped away. I staggered to my feet to see a scowling Margareta holding a large kitchen knife dripping with sludge. A fat tentacle curled at her feet. I couldn't believe that this fierce little warrior had saved me. Loki spat out vile curses in our old language while she stared at him in horror.

The tentacle started to wriggle.

"Watch out! Go back to the car. I'm coming soon. Now!"

She started to cry and fled.

I ran back to the kitchen, where I turned on only one gas ring—I didn't want the house to blow up until we were well away—before running back down the hall.

I'd set fire to Lilian's pile first but had an unsettling surprise when I got there. She'd crawled to the door, opened it, and was now pulling herself up on the frame.

"What'sh goin' on?" Still groggy.

Too bad she woke up, but she'd planned the same fate for us, after all. I torched the paper, and it burst into flame immediately. Lilian stumbled back, not noticing that her skirt was on fire, and tried to crawl to the window. I left her to it and turned to the living room opposite. I hoped Margareta wouldn't hear her screams.

A shadow blocked the fireplace, growing and coalescing into some kind of vile creature. I looked over at Loki, seemingly surrounded by ghostly images and a cacophony of voices, some of those I'd known and loved. So much babbling, so much misery, as if Loki were channeling all those souls he'd wronged into his core, perhaps to feed on their strength. A few of them tried to reach out to me but were pulled back by some sort of force they couldn't resist. Others flailed and wailed.

Odin looked down from just behind Loki's chair. His one-eyed face was thunderous. I felt as if I'd been stabbed in the heart when I saw my lady Frigg hovering close enough to touch, gazing at me with eyes full of sadness. I tried to clasp her hand but found only cold air when I desperately tried to pull her to me. But I heard her voice, as lilting and loving as ever.

"Act," was all she said before retreating behind Odin.

The shadow in front of the fireplace continued to grow until I realized it had become a monstrous serpent with scales of changing hues that sometimes looked deep ocean blue, sometimes pond scum green, and sometimes a melody of dancing starlight. It slithered forward, raising its hooded head to the ceiling and fixing me with eyes that burned like a tropical sun devoid of warmth. It opened its jaws, swaying toward me, ready to strike with fangs like scimitars. I thrust my torch into the paper bonfire, and it caught, soon igniting the carpet. The serpent fell back.

That gas had been on for a while. I ran like the wind, slamming the door behind me, jumped into the car, and peeled away, slowing as we came out of the lane onto the road. No need to attract attention.

"It's done," I said.

"What took you so long?" Agna asked.

"Complications. I'll tell you later. But it's done."

"Where did Margareta go? I couldn't get any sense out of her."

"She saved my life."

Agna gaped.

"Later," I said again.

"Now what?" Agna said. "We'll have to dump this car."

I looked at Margareta through the rearview mirror. She was still sobbing.

"Don't touch anything, understand? We mustn't leave fingerprints."

She cried harder.

I guess I was a little insensitive. She'd never seen gods in otherworldly situations before. As far as she knew, she'd never seen a god before.

"Don't cry, honey; it's for the best. They were planning to kill both of us. And you are a true heroine. Thank you."

"You're welcome. But it was awful," she blurted out between sobs. "I've never seen anything so horrible."

"I know, honey, but it's all over now. Try to sleep."

"But it's just, you know. Bad. I heard the lady screaming. She must have woken up."

Agna turned around. "Margareta, look at me." She started to sing and chant, holding Margareta's eyes with her own. Soon, the girl yawned and curled up on the back seat.

I said, "I'm surprised you had the strength to do that."

"It took every last bit I had."

"How are your legs?"

"Useless."

"Agna, do you have your cell phone?"

"I think I dropped it."

"Shit, you mean it's still in there? I hope they won't be able to trace it. And we should call Hunter."

"I took the nurse's purse, plus the suitcases, and put them in the trunk after I chloroformed them. Let's pull off and see what we can find."

We soon came to one of those lay-bys for buses to pull into. Margareta still slept.

Agna couldn't get out, so I took the purse to her and watched through the window as she rifled through it. Lilian's phone was in there.

"We can't use it. If there's an inquiry, they'll trace the call." I smashed it under my heel and threw it into the weeds.

"Well, even if we'd found my phone, we couldn't risk it being pinged in the area, either," Agna pointed out. Farfetched but not impossible.

An almighty explosion made us both jump. We were too far away to see the flames, but they no doubt roared well above the treetops.

I glanced through the back window at Margareta. She stirred a little and muttered something unintelligible before falling back to sleep. I went back to the cases.

One was full of money. There must have been thousands. I snapped the locks shut. The other contained only clothing and toiletries. I searched carefully to make sure there were no identifying items.

I found a stack of letters tied up with a green ribbon. I'd read them later. We had to get farther away. I started the car again and told Agna what I'd found.

"We must only use the money bit by bit, not all at once," I told her. "Who knows if it can be traced? I just don't know enough about these things."

"We'll put it in the attic," she said. "No one will find it there. I've got a spare sarcophagus."

Why wouldn't she?

"Tell you what, we'll dump the car near the pub where I met that horrid little pimp, Eddie. Someone will steal it within the hour. First, we'll leave the case with the clothes just inside the entrance to the flats where he lived. It'll disappear in no time. Then I'll run home with Margareta, and you can fly."

"No, I can't. I'm spent. And we need to get Margareta to bed before she wakes up. That way, she'll forget."

"Best to take you both home first, then. We've got to get away from here."

I did all of that. I carried them both upstairs and into bed. I drove back to the building estate and dropped the case before dumping the car behind the pub, leaving its keys in the driver's seat. I ran home and found Agna downstairs.

"How did you manage to get back down?"

"My legs got strong enough. They're still not back to normal, but I can manage. I bumped down the stairs on my bottom."

She limped out to the kitchen, grimacing slightly. It must have been painful. I couldn't help thinking of the Little Mermaid. She came back with chilled champagne as usual before sinking onto the sofa. I have no idea where it came from because I never saw any in the fridge.

When she handed me a glass, she said, "Lin, I'm sorry I'm such a nuisance with my legs."

"Agna, you saved our lives. You are never a nuisance." *Even though your timing sucks.*

I called Hunter from her landline.

"We've got her, Hunter."

"Oh, my darling princess. Let me talk to her."

"She's asleep in bed. Exhausted by her ordeal, you know."

"What happened?"

"It's complicated. I'll tell you when I see you."

"When will that be?"

"Why don't you come over with Sven? I'd love to show you around London."

He hemmed and hawed a bit but agreed to fly over the coming Friday night. The kids would just have to miss the first week of school.

"What shall I tell Lettie?"

"Tell her we want to know how they got her out of Washington and into the U.K. Neither of you should question Margareta or mention this situation. Agna made her forget, at least for now." Such a comfort to hear his voice again. "Goodbye, my love. I missed you."

Agna and I spent the rest of the evening giggling over Lilian's packet of love letters from Loki. Ever the con man, it was all quite nauseating.

The four of us had a wonderful touristy time in London for a week, and my burned ankle healed quickly. Both children were clingy, especially Sven, but I loved the extra hugs.

I couldn't resist following the news each evening.

"Reports have come in about an explosion at a cottage in the New Forest. There are no details available yet, although the fire service suspects arson."

"The police have interviewed the landlord of The King's Forest Tavern about an incident in which a guest was badly bitten by a New Forest pony. She was reported to be with a young woman with short brunette hair. The older woman is thought to be the individual who rented the cottage that exploded yesterday. They urge anyone who may have been in the vicinity and witnessed anyone or anything unusual to come forward."

"And now, back to that explosion in the New Forest last Tuesday. The body of a woman has been found in the wreckage of the cottage. She was burned beyond recognition and has not been formally identified, but police believe her to be the person who rented the cottage. The young woman who was seen with her is asked to come forward."

Only one body? It must have been in bits, but the BBC is always tactful. What would happen to Loki in that kind of situation? Perhaps Eir would know. I didn't want to risk discussing it on the phone. Our phone was unlikely to be tapped but still. I hoped Agna's cell phone had also been blown to smithereens.

The day before we flew back to Dulles, the kids wanted to visit the Tower of London. Not my favorite memory, but I could deal with it.

The beefeater who showed our group around kept a stack of peanuts in his pocket to feed a squirrel who would jump on his shoulder to get his treat. He was the biggest hit, as was one of the ravens, who flew behind our group and perched on a railing to offer his ten cents to the discourse. That beefeater seemed to have an understanding with these creatures—he even told stories about their resident fox. As far as the children were concerned, the history couldn't compete.

As we exited the hall that held the crown jewels, I spotted an untidy, bleached, curly blonde ponytail in the crowd waiting to enter—the pub waitress. I turned my head and almost pushed my family out of there. Hunter started to protest, but I shushed him as we hurried away. I whispered, "I'll tell you later." My hair was different, but she would likely recall my memorable face.

We met Agna for dinner at a fancy Indian restaurant near her house. The children had never tasted Indian food, although they'd eaten spicy chili. I chose for them carefully, and they loved it. Samosas, huge prawns, fragrant rice. It was a feast for all the senses. I had to rein them in on the chapatis, though. They went through two orders in no time. I guess they're the Indian version of potato chips.

The next morning, it was time to leave. It was so hard to say goodbye to Agna. I had tears in my eyes, as did she.

Hunter thanked Agna and pecked her on each cheek before striding to the cab with our cases.

"You are my sister," I said as we embraced.

"Yes, you are my sister," she replied. "Come back soon."

"You must come to us. I think your boy's going on tour over there soon."

She straightened suddenly, joy suffusing her face. "That's right! I'll be there."

The children looked bemused. They weren't used to their mother being emotional.

"What boy?" Sven asked.

"Never mind!" we chorused.

He pouted.

"Well, I can see why that was a very upsetting time, but it turned out well," I said.

"Yes, it did. But it reminded me painfully of our children's mortality. We could have easily lost her to that evil creature."

"Yes, I do see that. When humans lose their children, it's apparently the worst grief possible. Parents are supposed to die first."

Lin's eyes welled, and she fled upstairs.

Why can't I just keep my mouth shut?

12

I was feeling very tired that morning. I went upstairs at about 7 a.m. and helped myself to some cereal and orange juice. No one was about. I went back down and got into bed, only awakening when Lin shook me.

"Mary, are you all right?"

"Yes, sorry, I was so tired. What time is it?"

"It's ten-thirty."

Shocked, I sat up and swung my legs out of bed.

"No, no, Mary. No work for today. I brought you some tea. Just rest as much as you like."

I repositioned myself and sat back gratefully. "I don't know why I'm so tired. Thank you for the tea. It's delicious."

"It's a special one Dora makes whenever the children are under the weather. If you are feeling better tomorrow, we can get back to the stories."

I read and watched TV all day and ate fairly well. Hunter came down for a cuddle. He asked a lot of questions about how exactly I was feeling, clearly concerned. Selfishly, I luxuriated in his concern.

The next morning I announced at breakfast that I was feeling much better so Lin would know to come down. She came bearing coffee for her and that delicious tea for me.

I sat down, took a sip, and switched on the tape.

Tape 9, Volume 2

After returning from London, I had to scramble to make sure the children caught up with their missed week of school. Sven was the easiest because his tutor could cover the material his teachers sent home over a couple of evenings and a weekend. Margareta refused a tutor. I asked Hunter to speak to her, but she charmed him, as always, by showing him she could figure out the math problems on her own. In fact, she did make it all up quickly by reading at night and having a couple of meetings with the science and math teachers.

One morning, after Sven had left to catch his bus, we had a heated discussion about tutoring. She said, "Leave me alone. Let me fix things myself. I remember everything, by the way."

An icy shock rendered me speechless for a few moments. "Remember what, exactly?"

"First, the journey."

"I've been wondering how they pulled that off."

"Chloroform soon wears off, you know. I just pretended to be out longer. She got me into her SUV, then there was a private plane. When we landed, I was given a shot and strapped in a wheelchair. I really was out that time. They must have told immigration I was a sick child. Then a long car trip, for which I was awake for about the last hour, then that cellar."

I was horrified. "You poor darling, you must have been terrified."

"Interested, mainly. I wanted to see what they were up to. I didn't think they would kill me. When I heard them talking, I realized they wanted to kill you and didn't mind killing me. But I knew that wouldn't be so easy."

"Why did you think so?"

"I've always known you and Papa were different. Especially you. I'm a bit different, too."

I felt rooted to my chair. How much did Margareta really understand?

"I remember Aunt Agna, how she could appear and disappear before her legs turned funny. And how fast you move sometimes and how strong you are. Papa is stronger than anyone else's father, too. And you haven't changed at all since I can first remember your face. Not a wrinkle, nothing."

"I see. Have you discussed this with Sven?"

"Oh, no. He's clueless. Boys don't notice much. They're too focused on whatever they're into at the moment."

"We'll talk tonight with Papa. You get along to school now."

"I don't want to ask my friends home anymore. One or two of them have made comments about how young you both look and how fast you move sometimes. It's embarrassing."

"I'll try to do better. And move slower."

I hugged her tightly before walking her to the door.

"You see what I mean, Mom? That would have crushed anyone else."

I collapsed into a kitchen chair, sipping cold coffee. Good thing Dora was upstairs cleaning the bathrooms and making the beds. She couldn't have resisted chipping in. We would have to tell Margareta everything, including the fact that we are immortal and she and Sven are not.

I finally went up to Hunter's study.

"We have to talk," I said.

He registered my mood and hit a couple of keys on his computer before swinging his chair around to face me.

"What has happened?"

"Margareta knows about us. Some of it, anyway."

He went rigid. "How?"

"She is unusually observant. She also remembered much more of her abduction than I thought she would. Agna's spell didn't last."

"What shall we do? She'll be devastated."

"Not really. Every human knows they will die, although we should point out why we must eventually leave them. Haven't you noticed how dispassionate she can be?"

"That's not true. She can be very passionate about things."

I sighed and swallowed my irritation. "You misunderstand. Dispassionate means detached, unemotional … cool about most situations. Anyway, I told her we would talk to her tonight. We must tell her everything."

"And Sven?"

"That can wait. He's very young. We can trust Margareta to keep the secret."

While Sven was working with his tutor, we spoke to Margareta in Hunter's study. I sat in Hunter's desk chair and did most of the talking. Hunter shared the loveseat with his daughter, adding little bits and pieces of largely irrelevant information, alternatively patting her shoulder and rubbing her back. She only interrupted a few times for clarification but, as predicted, remained calm and expressionless.

"I'm glad you told me," she said. "I'm just sorry for you that you outlive your children. It must be very distressing."

Hunter's tears ran over, and he blew his nose so violently that Margareta and I couldn't help laughing. He got up and beckoned me to him. He hugged us both, swaying and rocking.

"Papa!" Margareta finally exclaimed. "I might be stronger than most girls, but I can hardly breathe."

"Sorry, sorry. I just love you so much. I cannot bear the thought…"

"We'll leave you with your thoughts, my love," I said. "Dinner's in an hour."

Margareta was quiet for a few days, obviously thinking things through. At breakfast next Sunday morning, she said, "I would like to go to boarding school."

Hunter's spoon hung midair while he took this in. "I do not like that."

"I think it's best," she said, her chin jutting upward in a familiar gesture of obstinacy.

"Have you a school in mind?" I asked.

"I have. It's in Connecticut. I have a couple of friends who went there."

Sven piped up. "If she goes, I want to go, too."

Margareta said, "It won't be the same school, you know. Mine is only for girls. You have to go to one for boys."

Sven thought this over as he chewed. "That's okay. I'd like mine to be in Connecticut, too, though. That way, if you are in danger, I can come quickly to save you."

I flashed a warning look at Margareta, but I needn't have worried.

"That's very sweet of you, Sven. You are a good brother."

The boy puffed up as he went back to scooping and chewing.

Hunter was dead against it, but I explained that, yes, we'd miss them, but it would help keep our situation under wraps. I hadn't told him about the comments some of Margareta's friends had made, but when I did, it shocked him into agreement.

They applied and were admitted to good boarding schools, and both would depart the following September. I was at once sad and relieved.

We'd always promised to take them to Disney World but had never gotten around to it. I assured them that this time it would happen, assuming they got good end-of-year grades. Margareta declared herself too mature for that kind of thing, but she had a good time and loved SeaWorld nearby. I enjoyed several rides, especially a pirate cruise I did twice, but refused to go on the roller coaster. When the three of them got off, Margareta and Hunter were laughing and joking, but Sven was quiet, and his complexion had acquired a greenish tinge. I sat on a bench with him while the other two lined up for another turn.

I felt nostalgic throughout that trip and couldn't help thinking of it as a "last fling" event. Silly, I told myself. They'd be away for a few months and home for the holidays and summers. We had our whole lives ahead of us, I told myself, a cheerful thought. If only I had left it there, but I also reminded myself that while Hunter and I had umpteen lives ahead of us, our children had only whatever was left of their human span. Not such a cheerful thought. I'd managed to depress myself again.

After we returned, they settled into going to the club and enjoying the pool. Margareta took tennis lessons from the coach. Sven and Hunter went on a fishing trip in the Chesapeake Bay. That was the start of an obsession that never let up. He fished in his school pond, only to throw back the poor specimens he caught. He fished the Potomac and caught a catfish that, even when cooked, I could only describe as slimy. God knows what it had eaten over its too-short life.

His new school was not far from the sea, so sailing and other marine activities would be frequent occurrences. Hunter fitted him out with a collapsible rod and all the junk that goes with it, including a bag. Now Sven couldn't wait to go.

One lunchtime, before she left for her new school, Margareta came rushing into the house after a tennis lesson, her nose bleeding and her racquet broken.

"I was attacked," she panted. "He punched me and tried to brain me with a rock."

"Oh, no." I held her, forgetting to restrain myself until she broke away. "Who? What happened?"

"I don't know. He was walking past, and I hardly saw him move. Mom! Why me?"

"Did anyone call the police?"

"There was no one around. I stayed behind for a while to practice my serve."

"Sit down and tell me exactly what happened."

She took a deep breath. "This man was walking toward me. We would have passed on the corner by the Carruthers' house. As soon he was close enough, he punched me in the face. Then he picked up a rock and tried to hit my head with it. He had these mad eyes. Yellow flashing eyes. I hit him with my racquet, over and over, until he dropped the rock and fell down. He looked up at me. He looked terrified. His eyes looked normal, though. Brown."

"Was he still there when you left?" She nodded. I tore out of the house, reaching the corner in seconds. I looked to the left and spotted a man staggering down the road.

I jumped in front of him and planted my feet wide, arms akimbo. He looked to be at the end of his tether.

"Did you hurt my daughter?" I asked, my fury clearly terrifying him.

"No, a girl hurt me. I was just passing her when I had this strange, dizzy spell. It felt like a current passing through my head. I've never had anything like it before. When it wore off, this girl was assaulting me with her tennis racquet. I'll tell my wife to call the police when I get home."

"Were you unaware that while you were having your dizzy spell, you punched her in the face and tried to hit her head with a rock?"

His eyes widened. "You're completely mad. I would never do such a thing. Not ever."

"I suggest that before you call the police, you call the doctor. I have a witness. You could go to prison for a long time."

"No," he cried, reeling to the point of collapse. "What's happening? I don't understand."

"Where do you live?"

He lived on the street we stood on, so I picked him up and ran him home, leaving him at the bottom of his driveway, even more demoralized.

I walked home slowly, thinking it through. That man was a sad character and had obviously been possessed somehow. But by what? I hadn't come across this kind of thing before. Loki might have been able to do such a thing, but he was dead. Wasn't he?

"Did you get him?" Margareta asked when I got home. She sat in the kitchen with a bag of ice on her eye. "That slimeball has ruined my face."

"It will fade, dear, don't worry. I found him. You did quite a bit of damage, so well done you. But I don't think he meant to." I told her how weak and upset he was and what he told me. "I think he was possessed. I told him there was a witness, so I don't think he'll make a fuss."

"Seriously? Possessed? Like in bad movies?"

"Not quite. Let's be on the alert. I'll tell Papa. I'm afraid one of us will have to be with you both at all times outside the house until this is cleared up."

Margareta slumped further down in her chair. "Oh, great."

The next week I was watching her tennis lesson, reflecting on how my little girl, nearly thirteen, was growing up. She was all smiles-and-charm with her coach and tried mightily to impress him. She succeeded, too. She moved fast. She placed the ball accurately most of the time and developed a killer serve. I heard him tell her how she'd performed miracles after a few short weeks and could perhaps go professional.

"It's entirely due to your coaching," she said, looking into his eyes.

He blushed. She blushed. No shit.

"Why don't we go inside and get some water?" she said.

I trailed after them, watching for her next move in the empty clubhouse. Thank heavens her father wasn't around. From time immemorial, he's always gone ballistic when his girls show any interest in boys.

Margareta bent down to drink at the water fountain. The coach went rigid, and his eyes flashed yellow. He raised his fist and aimed for her neck. He howled as I twisted his arm behind him, probably wrecking his shoulder.

"I'll get one of them sooner or later." The voice was unmistakable. I squeezed the man's jugular vein hard enough to snuff the life out of him. His yellow eyes glared back at me, gradually fading to blue before they closed.

Had I dispatched him quickly enough to destroy Loki? I watched for any sign, maybe an emanation of some kind.

I glanced at Margareta, who stood teary-eyed on the other side of him.

"Sorry," I said. "I had to get him before whatever it was left the body. I hope it worked."

I jumped when she screeched. "Look, Mom, what's that?"

I jumped over the body in time to see what looked like a large cockroach scuttling behind the water cooler.

"It came out of his ear. Ugh, gross!"

I thought about pulling the cooler away from the wall, but I knew those creatures could hide in the smallest cracks, and he'd be well away by now. Besides, there'd be even more of a mess to clean up for nothing.

Now to deal with the body.

"Mom. Look." She sounded weary, close to breaking.

A hand fluttered. He groaned. Had Loki's exit allowed him to pull back?

"Margareta, help me get him to a chair."

We dragged him to an armchair close to the bar area. Thankfully, it was still early, and the lunch crowd hadn't arrived. I examined him. His right arm flopped badly. His neck showed a bruise or two. But he was breathing. Now to spin the story.

"Okay, darling, we have to explain this."

"Yes. I guess a dead body would have been simpler." My girl was full of surprises.

"Don't you believe it," I answered.

Margareta began. "He had a bad fall."

"That wouldn't wrench his shoulder like that. And what about his neck?"

"Guess not," she said.

"After your lesson, he came in to get some water. We heard him yell and ran inside. A man was roughing him up. When he saw us, he ran away."

"That might work, Mom. We'll have to call the cops."

"Yes, an ambulance, too."

The cops and EMTs came after about five minutes, which gave us time to square our description of the miscreant.

After that, my first thought was that I couldn't wait for the children to go to boarding school. But a second thought soon followed. What form had Loki transmogrified into? Would he always be a cockroach, or was he really another sort of being? Were my children safe anywhere?

We told Hunter the story we told the police, agreeing that he'd lock them in the house for months if we told him the truth. As it happened, things went smoothly for the rest of the summer. We had a big barbecue for the kids' friends a week before they went off to their respective schools.

We both felt glum for a while but soon fell into our new routine. Which wasn't much of a routine anymore. Their letters and phone calls were enthusiastic, and I felt we'd done the right thing.

But Loki, where was he? What was he?

"Why was Loki going after Margareta so much?"

"Because he knew hurting my child was the best way to hurt me. When you have your child, you will understand."

I would try to visualize my baby sometimes, but it was just some amorphous blob. Maybe I wasn't cut out for motherhood. Depression hung over me for the rest of the day.

13

I was getting so big now that Lin only came down a couple of times a week. I didn't like sitting at the table for so long. The chair was hard, and no matter how much I wriggled, I couldn't get comfortable. I did miss hearing all her fabulous stories, though.

The next one wasn't quite as awful as the huge serpent, but not far off.

Tape 10, Volume 2

Loki wasn't finished with me yet. I thought he might have been fatally weakened after that tennis coach incident where he seemed to have been promoted from a cinder to a cockroach, but he still had the power to take over people's minds.

One spring, I spent a long weekend with a friend who lives in Maryland on the Chesapeake Bay. I fell in love with the area. Not too developed, beautiful views, and peaceful. While out walking one day, I spotted a for sale sign at a house with a wonderful water view and a small beach. I knew right away it was for me. It took under two hours to drive there from Salton, which was a huge plus. I went to work on Hunter, who, predictably, dragged his feet. Too much money, people would want to know how we could afford it, and so on. But it was really cheap compared to Northern Virginia, so I finally persuaded him to take a look.

Being by the water affects him deeply, as it does me. It's our culture, I suppose. We may have spent most of our early lives living in a blue heaven, but we often came down to Midgard, most of which was by the sea at that time. Njord, a god of the Vanirs, was sent to live amongst the Aesir as a hostage after the war between the two races of gods ended. He soon became a trusted friend of our gods, especially of Hunter—Hoenir, then—and was allowed to move freely. They often dived to one of the palaces scattered on the ocean floor to cavort with mermaids. I've asked him several times how that worked, given their tails and all. He just clams up.

For me, the sound of waves rolling and crashing or caressing the wet sand is the most lyrical music I can imagine. Around the house I loved, tall trees ensure breezes ruffling through leaves and birdsong adds to the symphony. I had to have it.

We called the agent and arranged a showing. The place needed work, but it was in acceptable condition. One bedroom downstairs and three up, so it could accommodate our family and Dora. An aging kitchen with avocado green appliances would soon be modernized. There was no central air conditioning or heating, but we could live with that, and maybe a retrofit was possible. We signed the contract and, because we paid cash, took possession in a few weeks.

I went to a chain store over the bridge in St. Mary's County and arranged for a kitchen designer to visit. In a month, we had a white kitchen and a new washer and dryer in the utility room. I ordered furniture, not worrying about aesthetics too much but opting for comfort and durability. It was great fun. Different from furnishing the everyday house. This was a retreat.

When the children came home after their first year in boarding school, they fell in love with the place, too. Sven invited a friend—I'd put bunk beds in his room in anticipation—and they swam, fished, and rode bikes all over the development. He wanted to spend most of the summer down there, and I did, too. Hunter would often join us. It was glorious.

I went down to the Bay for a few days in October. The children were back at school. Hunter was grumpy about the stock market, and I felt restless. No interesting new men had come my way lately, either. I reckoned that reading a novel on the beach would calm me down.

A chilly wind swept in from the Bay, but I don't feel the cold much. We only had two neighbors, and they were also weekenders, so no one would be around to wonder about my strange behavior.

Footsteps up on the front lawn caught my attention. Very soft, far from where I sat, but not too soft or far for my godly ears to pick up. A burglar was my first thought. I got up and ran up to the house. The sliding doors were wide open, and a man in an industrial mask and a tank on his back stood by them. He startled when he saw me "materialize"—in other words, slow down.

"What are you doing?" I asked.

"Pest control," he said.

"I haven't contracted with any pest control company yet. We haven't owned the place long."

"Oh, I guess it's still under the previous owner's contract. Would you like to sign up with us?"

"I don't know anything about your company."

"May I come in?"

"You need to take off your gear first."

"Okay."

I went into the house, and he followed just as he was.

"I said—"

He sprayed me in the face for what felt like several minutes as I spiraled into semi-consciousness, but not before registering the yellow eyes flashing through the mask before they faded. The man staggered away, dragging off his helmet and shaking his head.

Loki. Still powerful.

You remember what even a little anesthesia does to me, and this stuff was especially potent. I was robbed of my strength, my wits, my godliness. Hardly able to keep upright, I staggered to Dora's bed, unable to defend myself or care much. My foggy mind drifted, vaguely registering hammering and heavy footsteps. Bang, bang, stomp, stomp. But I didn't have the strength to lift an arm, let alone defend my house. At last, it stopped. Heavenly peace.

I must have slept for hours, sometimes half waking before drifting off again. I remember a pitter-pattering against the windows. Rain, I thought. When I awoke, dim light filtering around the edge of the blinds showed morning, although it seemed cloudy. A strange rustling—maybe wind through the trees. It was October, after all.

Why did I feel so strange, so befuddled? What was wrong with me? I groped through my memory until images of the attack started coming back—the man, the spray, the yellow eyes. Loki.

A few punches and leg lifts in bed confirmed my weakness had not lifted in any meaningful way, so I got up to see what had happened. The first time I fell, my head cracked against the corner of my nightstand. I had to get to the bathroom mirror. Surely I wasn't showing my age. Panicking, I fell several times because the floor felt like a waterbed.

Holding the rim of the sink and staring down into the white porcelain, I finally found the courage to raise my eyes. My face was unlined. But I was pale in an unhealthy way, not a Nordic way. Shadows underlined my eyes. Not old but not quite beautiful. Not to my standards. The anesthesia would work its way out of my system eventually. It always did. While I told myself that, the hard knot in my belly stayed put. I went through to the living room.

I fell again after the shock of seeing why the weather had seemed cloudy. Thick spiderwebs festooned the windows, layers of them. The little creatures—not that little, when I looked closely—still swarmed, busily creating some sort of barrier. A prison. I pulled myself up against a chair and turned toward the door that led upstairs, but it was barricaded by heavy bars hammered into the jambs. I walked carefully around the lower level and found every possible exit barred—the front door, sliding glass doors, the windows over the kitchen sink, my bedroom windows, and even the fireplace. All the windows were reinforced outside by webs, which grew thicker by the minute.

I sat on the recliner that faced the bay to think, trying to quell my panic, trying to expel the raw fear. I have always been a fighter because I am strong. But my strength had been drained. I was nothing.

Why the webs? If there were enough layers, they would be strong and hard for me to get out of in my weakened condition. Loki could have just set fire to the house while I was asleep. He knew I would have suffered agony and possibly willed myself to die. So, what was the plan? Loki wanted me to suffer, obviously. But how?

Instead of sitting around, I should call Hunter. After a frantic search—slow motion—I realized someone had taken my cell phone. There was no landline. He would have had it cut, anyway.

I started to feel hot. Maybe I should drink some cold water. But the fridge was warm inside and didn't smell too good. I tried turning on the kitchen light. No power. I went back to the recliner to gaze at the thickening blanket of webs. A huge cockroach crawled up the window under the webs and looked straight at me, waving its antenna as if mocking my plight. It turned sideways, and a flashing yellow eye winked before it scuttled off.

Horrified, it came to me what Loki intended. He meant me to suffocate. But that couldn't kill me. Could it? Maybe if I spent long enough without air, I could die. We always considered ourselves immortal, but most gods died at Ragnarok. Granted, there were extraordinary weapons—swords dipped in a magic potion, a monstrous serpent's poisonous breath, and so on. And look how our powers had weakened over the millennia. Partly because, after the fall of our heaven, no one believed in us anymore. That did more damage than the passing of time.

Lack of belief has always weakened gods. Even the Greek and Roman gods couldn't overcome it. Men have always constructed gods to explain the otherwise inexplicable. And as more and more believe more and more strongly, we come to be, giving life to their hopes and fears. They need us, but an evolving form of us as their knowledge and expectations change. One race of gods fades away, and another rises. In the last few hundred years, monotheism has become fashionable in its many forms—still the comfort, still the strife, and still the rationale for good or evil. Nothing really changes.

I continued to sit there with my eyes closed.

Her voice in my head. *Act*.

How strong would those webs be? I was probably strong enough to break a window. The sliding glass doors would be tempered, but the one in front of me should break easily enough. What to do if I couldn't get through the web? Fire? Was my car still okay? Loki probably assumed I wouldn't be able to get out and use it.

How long should I wait? Perhaps until I felt stronger.

The sound of a car jolted me upright. The situation was so fantastical—how could I explain this to outsiders? I guess I'd have to play dumb.

Running feet. A huge shape appeared at the window. Hunter!

"Lin, are you all right?" he bellowed.

"Yes. Loki did it! Everything's boarded up. He sprayed stuff at me, so I'm weak."

Poor Hunter—his enormous strength pulled away the cobwebs, but not before entangling him, so he was cursing, punching, kicking, and yanking strands that looked like silk but reacted like steel, at the same time sticking to his skin and clothing. He looked like a gorilla that disturbed a hornet's nest. He got to the window and kicked it in. He squeezed through with great difficulty and accompanying obscenities before wrapping me in his arms.

It felt so good, so safe, and so warm, the air full of salt and seaweed … for a while. I pulled away. The webs had reattached, huge spiders now weaving the broken ends together again.

"Why did you come?" I asked.

"I dreamed of you last night. I missed you. Good thing, huh?"

Yes, indeed.

"Let's get out of here. Can you break down the front door? It's nailed shut."

My hero looked around for something he could use as a battering ram. Nothing. He kicked and shoved and cracked the door open. Same blanket of webbing, only thicker.

"Hunter, did you see any webs upstairs? They boarded up the door to the stairway, so perhaps they didn't bother."

This door was flimsier. We ran upstairs, me quickly out of breath, which I found most alarming, given my usual hyper fitness. They were only just beginning up here. Most likely, their commander-in-chief had realized we would try that route. There was a kitchenette up there, so I grabbed some matches and pocketed them. Those webs had to go.

We got out of the door and down the outside stairs. I ran around to the front of the house. Hunter called me back, but it had to be done.

There was my wonderful outlook to the bay, covered in a disgusting mesh of spiderwebs where thousands of the creatures still labored. And there was that big cockroach on the sill behind the webs staring at me.

I struck the match and started the fire. It raced through the entire network, hopping from window to window, trapping everything in its path. A flame licked at Loki before he scurried through the gaps to safety. I was too slow to catch him as he shot through the grass to the creek. A snake reared up as it ran over its tail and struck. I hoped Loki would enjoy his tour of its digestive system. With any luck…

"Lin!"

I turned to find Hunter holding the hose up to the house. All the webs had melted away, and the flames began consuming the walls. Spiders swarmed, some over Hunter and me as they tried to escape. I slapped and stomped as many as I could, crying and cursing Loki.

It was no good. The fire was in charge now, consuming my lovely house.

"Hunter, put away the hose. We have to leave before anyone comes."

He coiled it up on its stand. "Are you strong enough to drive?"

"Yes, I think so. I'm feeling a bit better." I wasn't feeling that much stronger, but it's all relative. I was probably up to the level of most humans.

He kissed me again before we climbed into our cars to drive home. I cried all the way back. My dream house. My refuge. Gone.

We got the phone call a half hour after we got in. Vandals, the fire chief thought. The fire started outside. That was clear. They couldn't save the house. He was sorry.

One of these days, the homeowners' association will demand that we clear the lot. Then what? Did the snake kill Loki? Knowing him, he simply took possession. The perfect container for such a one.

How could I feel safe there again? What kind of haven is that?

Poor Lin. I dared to have different dreams now, but I'd had to accept that I was never going to become a successful novelist, a bitter pill to swallow. A house on the Chesapeake Bay? How special that must have been.

"One day, you will vanquish Loki," I said.

"I don't know, Mary. I can only hope Eir comes up with something."

I watched her climb the stairs slowly, her shoulders drooping a smidgeon. Not her usual bright self.

14

I got out of the shower one morning to find Lin sitting on my bed. I felt shy because I wasn't used to parading around naked. She, of course, was oblivious to my hang-ups, having none of her own.

"Mary, I got a letter from an old friend yesterday. She's invited me to visit her for a few days. I'm leaving tomorrow morning around 10."

I whipped a pair of mammoth panties out of my chest of drawers, pulling them up and over my belly. "Oh, that's nice. Where does she live?"

"In Charlottesville. She's a professor at UVA."

"How do you know her?"

"She used to be a member of our neighborhood watch—you remember me talking about that lot. She was one of the sensible ones, although she's quite fun and knows hundreds of good jokes. Her husband does some hush-hush work for a defense contractor. It'll be a nice change. It's less than a two-hour drive from here."

"Sounds good. Maybe I'll visit Auntie." I struggled with my bra until Lin obligingly came over to hook it up.

"Yes, you should, and give her my love. Keep Hunter company, too."

"Of course." *Delighted to.*

It still felt weird being so open about Hunter and me. Less weird than it used to be, though. I could do with a rest and was quite big now, only two months away from D-Day. We were having unseasonably hot weather, so I stayed indoors more than I liked, which made me restless.

Dora called us to dinner, and we went upstairs, a feat that rendered me short of breath by the time I got to the kitchen.

Chapter 14

We enjoyed a scrumptious spanakopita to start, followed by a creamy, lemony chicken dish. Lin had bought several containers of gelato from a local café. I chose one scoop of hazelnut and one of rose. Rose flavoring was one of my favorite new tastes.

Dora was scrupulously polite now that Lin had apparently put the fear of god (which one?) into her after her jealousy had gotten out of hand, but she couldn't hide the hate in her eyes. Not only had Hunter fallen for me, but I was bearing his child, whom she knew he'd adore. She'd never forgive me. I hoped she wouldn't stoop to betraying Lin and Hunter in some way. She depended on them, so it would be foolish. This demoted woodland nymph had been turned into an unacceptably obese nymph when she rejected Pan's advances, and she'd unwisely irritated Zeus when she butted into one of his feasts to complain. That nasty old god had banished her to earth, condemned to a life of servitude. Lin and Hunter had seen the whole sad episode but had no idea where she went until they ran into her being shamefully overworked in a Texas mansion. They'd brought her to live with them. Although still a servant, she was well treated and allowed to indulge in some of her nymph habits, such as prancing naked through the woods.

As I watched Dora circling the table to serve, occasionally sneaking a sideways glance at me, I had a disturbing thought. I'd realized months ago that she'd look for a way to discredit me sooner or later, but would the baby be safe around her? I'd have to be careful how I put my concerns to Lin and Hunter. It wasn't as if they could have just anybody working in their house. They needed her.

The next morning, Lin left soon after breakfast, and Hunter disappeared to his study as usual. I decided to go back to bed with a novel. I'd brushed my teeth and combed my hair but only threw on a robe before coming upstairs since there wouldn't be any work. I hadn't slept well because the baby was kicking a lot.

Needless to say, I fell asleep about three pages into my book. When I awoke, I became aware of heavy breathing beside me. I turned, more clumsily than intended, and found Hunter fast asleep beside me with what looked like some company's annual report balanced on his chest. I snuggled up next to him and luxuriated in the warmth and intimacy, dozing on and off for an hour or so.

A vacuum cleaner rumbling around the basement and knocking into baseboards had Hunter up like a shot, roaring at Dora to stop that infernal racket. She stomped upstairs, not bothering to take the appliance with her, as I later discovered when I tripped on the cord. I saved myself by grabbing the back of an armchair, but it shook me. Hunter was halfway up the stairs when it happened but raced back down when he heard me cry out.

"It's okay, Hunter. You do realize how much she hates me, don't you? I can't help worrying if we can trust her around the baby."

"I know she is probably a little bit jealous. I think she had some hopes … you know."

Knowing him, he'd given her ample cause to hope. "I've had a lot of trouble with her. Lin had to give her a talking-to. She behaves well now, but the hate radiates from her eyes. It worries me."

"Don't worry, I will keep an eye on everything. If she causes trouble, she will be sorry."

That comforted me only a little—he couldn't watch her all the time. She was a sneaky one.

We settled down again, Hunter slipping his hand under my nightie and rubbing my bump. The baby kicked, and he became very excited, insisting on lifting my nightie to see it with his own eyes next time. The baby obliged, and he laughed with delight, as did I.

I told him, "You know, we always talk about a baby kicking, but it could be throwing a punch at you!"

"You called the baby it. Do you not know the sex yet?"

"I asked, but the doctor didn't say anything. I don't like him that much."

"We have an old friend who is a baby doctor in Alexandria. Dr. Ayre. I am surprised Lin did not refer you. Come to think of it, we have not seen her for ages. She is always so busy, as she has built up quite a practice. I will ask Lin about it."

I didn't know what to think about that, but I suspected who he was talking about. She was, no doubt, very competent. "I like the idea of a woman obstetrician. Thank you."

I hadn't thought about Eir's story since wrapping up the first volume of Lin's memoir. She had been the physician to the gods before Ragnarok and had travelled down the millennia with Loki. When Lin told their story, they had run a sex slave trafficking ring out of the Middle East. She had repudiated that way of life and Loki, winding up her practice in Manhattan to start again in Washington, D.C. I knew she must have moved down here from New York by now, but Lin hadn't mentioned her again. And she hadn't visited since I'd been in residence. Was there a problem? Well, Lin would let me know what was going on. My next appointment wasn't for a few weeks.

Chapter 14

I'd picked a local OB/GYN Auntie Peggy said a friend's daughter had used, assuming that if he had a thriving practice in Salton, he must be okay. Auntie didn't know I was pregnant then and assumed I was going for a gynecological exam. I wasn't sure but made the appointment as soon as I suspected without telling Lin. I told the doctor's office that my husband and I were separated, but they probably hadn't swallowed it.

I didn't want to talk about it anymore until I'd spoken to Lin. Time to change the subject.

"Hunter, why don't you like dogs? It's unusual for someone like you."

"What do you mean, someone like me?"

"Well, you know, people often keep a dog. Man's best friend and all that."

Hunter closed his eyes and took a deep breath. "I was bitten badly years ago. I do not wish to talk about it."

"Okay." Well, that was that. I gave him a big hug.

He sat up and stretched. "I had better do some work before lunch. I will see you upstairs."

It was high time I showered and got dressed. I'd call Auntie, too. I could go after lunch, have tea with her and take Sam for a walk. It wasn't so hot today, only in the high 70s.

Sam jumped all over me, pushing at me with his paws. I sat down quickly so as not to lose my balance. The dog fetched his leash and put it on my lap. Auntie was happy to see me, too, and exclaimed over my size. She also had a cake in the oven, which smelled divine.

"You look well. Is everything all right?"

"Yes, I'm fine, Auntie. I'm not that keen on my doctor, though. He is very abrupt and doesn't really listen."

"To tell the truth, Alice told me her daughter has found a new doctor. Said much the same thing. I'm really sorry."

"It's not your fault. I should have done an online search on him. I think Lin knows a good doctor, though. She's away for a couple of days."

"How's your novel going?"

"Quite well. I'm making progress, although too slowly for my liking." How long could I keep this up before admitting that after all this time, I had absolutely nothing? She couldn't know about the memoirs, my real project. I felt like a failure. I had plenty of time to work on the novel as well as the memoir. I was stuck, horribly stuck. No inspiration, no ideas, and, lately, no interest. That was the real problem.

We had a pleasant afternoon and a wonderful tea after a good walk with Sam, even though I confined myself mostly to sidewalks. I lucked out with his poop, as he did it in a wooded area behind an elementary school with no one around. Bending down to pick up after him was getting beyond me. This was a big baby. No surprise there.

Lin got back the next evening. We all had dinner and went into the living room to watch a movie. Lin and Hunter performed their usual tug-of-war, finally agreeing on a thriller which turned out to be rather gripping, especially in the last scene when the protagonist found himself hanging from a puny branch over a gorge. I don't know why I was so tense about it because we all knew very well that the hero would survive. That's how it works.

The next morning at breakfast, Lin said, "Hunter tells me you're not too happy with your doctor, Mary. Would you like to meet our friend, Dr. Ayre? She has a very good reputation."

I swallowed. *Oh, why not?* "That would be great. I don't really like the man I'm seeing now."

"Yes, Hunter told me. I'll call her after breakfast."

"Which hospital does she use?"

"I'm not sure. I think she has privileges at several. Maybe even Fairfax."

"Fairfax would be ideal."

"I'll ask."

"Isn't that the lady who trafficked those girls with Loki?"

"Yes, but don't worry. She's fine now. She's got other family."

"What family?"

"Us, of course!"

"But you never see her."

"But we are here. For us, a few months is a mere blip."

Lin came downstairs as I was putting the finishing touches on my transcriptions of our latest tapes.

"Dr. Ayre would be happy to take you on, and she does have privileges at Fairfax. We have an appointment tomorrow morning at eleven."

"Wow, thanks! And I have something to tell you."

We sat on the loveseat next to the sliding glass doors. I wedged a pillow behind my back. She turned to me, seeming concerned.

"I found out why Hunter won't have a dog around." I told her about the conversation.

Fleeting emotions crossed her face, from shock to pity to sadness.

"How could I not realize? I should have known. Poor Hoenir." Tears rolled down her cheeks.

"Oh, Lin, I'm so sorry. What is it?"

"I'm going to get the recorder. This is worth getting down."

Tape 11, Volume 2

I'd forgotten that horrible dog. Garm was his name. Do you remember I told you how I found Hunter badly injured and carried him down to Hel so he could be safe while healing?

Garm was a massive hound that guarded the entrance to Hel, chained to a rock. As it was prophesied, he would participate in the destruction of our world at Ragnarok. He was always covered in blood—it was rumored, the blood of those who were not evil enough nor noble enough to enter.

Gods occasionally needed to enter for one reason or another. Odin frequently visited. I'm not sure why. Remember, Hel was the disgraced goddess who ruled Hel, but I can't think she was the attraction—one side of her face was utterly repulsive.

Anyway, Garm was there, but his chain was broken. I'd seen him running alongside Fenrir as that son of Loki devoured the earth and the sun. Garm tried to swallow the moon, but Fenrir snatched it from him. I suppose he ran back to the only home he knew after that. He was covered in even more blood than usual.

There he sat, a piece of his broken chain still jangling from his collar, staring at us as we approached. He began to howl and lick his lips.

"Stand down," I shouted. "The god, Hoenir, requires safe haven."

"You are all finished," he growled. "Die now."

I set Hoenir on the ground as gently as I could and prepared to do battle. I had no weapon, only my agility and strength. And one other thing: the battle cry of the gods.

Garm picked up a human bone and gnawed at it. "You are my next meal," he told Hoenir, whose eyes fluttered open. "Will you be juicy or dry? Tender or tough? No matter, my jaws can chew anything." He bore down harder on his bone after craning his neck toward Hoenir, sniffing voraciously.

Hoenir moaned in agony, his face contorted with fear.

Garm bounded forward and tore a lump of flesh from Hoenir's leg. My poor god howled in pain; probably the first time he ever felt that sensation. I knew then how weak he was—perhaps he'd caught a whiff of that monstrous serpent's poisonous breath that killed so many others.

I was no longer tired and dispirited but enlivened and furious. With blood-curdling fervor, I let out the battle cry I'd heard so often that day.

Garm shrank back, his haunches blocking the entrance to Hel.

"Who dares cry for battle in my realm?" A woman, her face veiled in black linen, pushed Garm aside and stood in the entrance to Hel, feet wide and arms crossed. A sword hung in its iron scabbard by her side. "Who goes there?"

"Do I have the honor of addressing my lady Hel?"

"You do. You are a god? I do not know you."

"I am Lin, handmaiden to the lady Frigg, who has perished this sad day. On the ground beside me is the god Hoenir, brother of Odin, grievously wounded in battle and now wounded again by your hound Garm. We seek refuge, my lady. Garm helped Fenrir destroy our world. Now he threatens to kill and devour us." I clasped my hands and cast my gaze down in what I hoped was a servile posture.

"You may enter. Garm, sit before me." She drew her sword and decapitated the hound, drenching all of us in its blood.

"He has served his purpose," she said. "There is nothing to guard against anymore."

I lifted Hoenir and followed her down a hundred steps onto a ferry steered by a faceless demon and into her damp halls. Hel directed one of her handmaidens to show us to our quarters. I washed the blood off us both with sulfurous water from a spring in the middle of the floor. We lived there for a millennium. You know the rest.

"My god, no wonder he doesn't want a dog. What a ghastly ordeal."

"Indeed, it was. For all of us." Lin got up. "I'm going to rest on my bed with a book."

What awful trials they'd suffered, what terrible sights they'd seen. And yet, they could still be so kind and generous. Their sense of justice had been forged from a different metal than ours.

15

Dr. Ayre's front office looked as nondescript as any other American doctor's office. Lin and I walked up to a windowed reception niche containing a desk-bound secretary guarding his credit card gadgets and computer equipment. I gave the young man my ID and insurance card and filled in a form that demanded I check boxes concerning all kinds of medical information, most of which hadn't happened to me yet. Next to the window was the closed door that must lead to the exam rooms.

I sat next to Lin on an upholstered loveseat that was the color of rusty sludge.

"This place is so ordinary," I whispered to her.

"What did you expect, gossamer and sequins?"

Fair enough.

"Will you come in with me?" I was in two minds about this. I didn't know what to expect from this doctor who, after all, was not human. On the other hand, I didn't like the idea of the exam not being private. Those stirrups are the ultimate indignity.

"I'll come back to make the introductions, then I'll leave you to it." As if she'd read my mind.

The door to the inner sanctum swung open.

"Ms. Lambert!"

We both rose at the strident summons of a hefty middle-aged woman who turned on her heel and strode back out without checking whether we had followed. She stopped outside a small examination room, opened the door, and went in, her eyes scanning the counter and trays before handing me the robe folded on the couch.

"Everything off, opening in front," she rapped. She left, closing the door so firmly that it was almost a slam.

"What a battle-axe," I said, not bothering to whisper.

"Eir's told me about her. 'Very efficient and a heart of gold' was the way she put it."

"Huh."

I started to undress. Lin took my things as I removed them and hung them from the hook on the back of the door. She lifted my pants and shirt to place the undies beneath them—an uncharacteristic display of delicacy. I kept my socks on. Those stirrups...

A knock on the door announced the doctor's arrival.

"Come in," called Lin.

Dr. Ayre was another surprise. Tall and hearty, she was handsome rather than beautiful. Her face looked sculpted because every feature was perfectly balanced. When she smiled, her teeth gleamed like a toothpaste ad. Her blond hair was perfectly arranged in a complex arrangement of braids that would have taxed the talents of any couture stylist.

She and Lin embraced.

"It's wonderful to see you again, Eir. Congratulations on your new office and being so busy so quickly."

"Well, I bought the practice with an existing patient list, and they seem to like me all right. New patients have begun to come in, too, as I make contacts at the Fairfax Hospital, where I have privileges. The place needs sprucing up. It's a bit gloomy and old-fashioned for my taste, but I haven't had time to deal with it yet." She turned to me. "So, you are Mary."

"Yes," I said.

"And you know our ... circumstances."

"I do indeed."

"She is very discreet," Lin broke in. "Well, I'll leave you both to get on with things."

"Get on the table, Mary."

I swung up there and lay on my back.

"Scoot down," she said.

I scooted.

"Farther."

I wriggled my way down some more. She placed my feet in the stirrups. I could feel the chill through my socks.

"I understand you have been seen by a doctor. How far along are you?"

"My due date is August 25th."

She pressed my belly in various places. "Nervous?"

"A little. It's a big step."

She examined my breasts. "Lin and Hoenir will take good care of you and the babe."

"I know."

"And you won't suffer during the birth."

"But I've heard it's very painful."

She straightened and looked down at me. "It certainly can be. But I have my special ointment. I can't use it with my other patients because it would cause talk, especially among the nurses. I can't risk that. When you are nearer your time, I'll give you a jar of it so you can apply it yourself before leaving for the hospital."

"How does it work?"

"You will first apply it to your face and neck, then your abdomen and thighs, and lastly, your genitals. Your mind will compartmentalize. Part of you will look to the outside world as if you feel the pain, but you will only *sense* the pain, not really experience it. The other experience will be of love and peace in your moment of creation."

"Is it safe? Will I be normal afterwards?"

"Quite safe. It will wear off quickly after birth. You will feel well and happy."

"It sounds marvelous."

"It is. Now, keep still. I want to take a quick look around."

I have never liked this part, but she was remarkably gentle. My mind eased.

"Well, everything is as it should be. I'll see you next month. Nice meeting you."

She left, and soon I heard her voice in the room next door, although I couldn't make out what she was saying. I got dressed quickly.

Lin wasn't in the waiting room. I went to the office window to make my next appointment.

"Your friend is waiting outside," the girl said.

I took the elevator down to street level and looked up and down the street. A few seconds later, Lin drove up and opened a window.

"Where shall we go for lunch? What do you fancy?"

I actually fancied bananas, but that was no good answer. "Caribbean?" I said.

"What a great idea!" she said. "I know just the place." Of course, she did. And with any luck, they'd have plantains as a side or some kind of banana dessert.

Chapter 15

It was a colorful little place. Lots of Gauguin-style paintings covered the walls, and the young men and women working there were equally colorful. My appointment had so raised my spirits that this seemed like the perfect celebration.

"Well, what did you think?" asked Lin as we sipped our fresh tropical juices. Mine was banana strawberry.

"I really liked her. She's gentle. And she's going to give me a special ointment so I don't suffer. I have to use it before I go to the hospital because no one can know about it."

"I thought she'd be able to help. I'm so glad it worked out."

Lin could be so kind and warmhearted and yet so callous. I guess it was all according to context and her approach to pragmatic solutions, which was skewed just enough from mine to sometimes send chills up my spine. It was probably like making friends with a tiger. One false move...

My good cheer surged once more when a plate of chicken with rice and sautéed plantains was placed in front of me. I ate the lot. Then a dish of grilled bananas with lime zest and a splash of rum.

Lin had some kind of fish with mixed vegetables.

"Well, you were hungry!" she said, clearly amused.

"To be honest, I've been craving bananas," I said. "I've got a couple of bunches in my room."

"Ah, that explains it," she said, laughing. "Well, you certainly got your fill here! We won't do any more sessions for a few months. You have other things to do."

"You are so kind. But I feel I should do a little work at least."

"Nonsense."

I took a good nap that afternoon.

16

I woke with a start. Was it a pain or a dream? The clock on my bedside table showed 4:00 a.m. At least it was early enough that I could get another good stretch of sleep before breakfast. Lin had stopped the recording sessions three or four weeks before, so I didn't have to get up early if I didn't feel like it. She understood I was uncomfortable sitting in one position while she talked.

She and Hunter had been so kind, making sure I had foods I liked (I'd gone right off bananas), company on walks, and lifts to visit Auntie Peggy whenever I wanted. Lin had outfitted me with maternity clothes, too, often showing up with a pretty new top. It did me good to feel I looked nice. Hunter would often visit me in my quarters and lie with me on the bed, stroking my hair and belly, often singing to the baby. We hadn't made love for a few weeks. I didn't feel sorry for him since he had Lin.

I turned on a lamp and got up to go to the bathroom. Luckily, I'd just sat on the toilet when my water broke. I was still groggy, so I didn't realize it immediately. Another contraction brought me to my senses. What if the baby was born into the toilet? I grabbed a towel and waddled back to bed.

Dr. Ayre said to time the contractions. Okay. I got up at about a minute past four. It was now quarter past. And then it hit me like a tsunami. It was like having a cannonball rolling around in my belly. I wouldn't wake them yet. The ointment was in my bedside drawer. Only when they happen every five minutes, she'd said. Then call me and come.

It took some time to get to the five-minute mark. I looked at the clock yet again. Nearly 7 a.m. I got up and showered before getting out the ointment and applying it as directed, using up the entire jar. The next contraction came. My belly tightened, but I managed to relax and ride with it. I made my way upstairs, holding tightly to the railing to be on the safe side.

I didn't feel like going up another flight of stairs, so I called up. "Lin? Hunter?"

It was almost as if she'd been waiting for me. "Is it time?" she called down.

"Yes, five minutes apart. I used the ointment."

"We'll be down in a minute. I'll call Eir."

They both came down. I'd expected Hunter to be panicky in Hollywood-expectant-father-style, but he was perfectly calm.

"Where is your bag?" he asked.

"Oh, sorry, I left it in my room."

He was back with it in a minute. "Let us go."

"You get in the back," Lin told me. "That way, you can lie down if you feel like it."

The traffic was moving toward rush hour level but not quite there yet. Hunter drove just over the speed limit. I was in no hurry. Birds sang a magnificent chorus to me, so I opened my window to hear them better.

"Isn't the birdsong fabulous?" I asked them. "I feel as if they're singing just for me."

Hunter looked back at me, his eyebrows raised, before settling into a frown.

"What is the matter with her?" he asked Lin.

"Eir gave her a little something special," she replied.

"Ah." Hunter laughed.

"You can laugh," I said, "But they really are singing to me. I just heard my name."

Hunter didn't laugh, but when I glanced at him in the rearview mirror, I could see his mouth working to stifle it.

We were at the hospital entrance in twenty minutes. The beautiful middle-aged lady at the admitting desk already had most of my information. Once they'd copied my insurance card and ID, an exceptionally pretty aide hustled me into a wheelchair and wheeled me to a labor room. I could have walked—run, even. She left me alone, and I sat down, closing my eyes as the contractions came in waves. It felt like bobbing on a choppy sea.

A nurse knocked on the door and entered simultaneously. I gazed at her in wonder because she was just so beautiful. Tall and very, very curvy. Those rolls of fat looked so comfy.

"Use the bathroom," she said. She handed me a pretty gown. "Get undressed in there and put this on. Put your clothes in this bag. I've put a name tag on it."

I managed to pee on command. A pregnant woman can always pee.

When I finally emerged, she helped me into a gown and onto the table, where she doused me with disinfectant as if I had lice. I hoped she hadn't wiped off the ointment.

Lin soon arrived to sit with me. We chatted a little, but I was too busy gazing at the beauty around me to say much. The white walls looked as pure as new snow. Nurses came and went, checking my progress. I watched them from a safe distance, like taking in a movie—present, but not part of it.

My contractions were strong but not distressing. I felt my bed move and rumble. I was vaguely aware of entering another place, a brighter, whiter place filled with gorgeous people, Dr. Ayre the most gorgeous of them all.

I heard a heartbeat. No, two heartbeats. Mine slightly louder and faster than the other. A primal mind at work, waking and waiting with me, trying to kick and punch to escape its tight confinement. Music. Unearthly tones more sweetly beautiful than any I'd ever heard or will ever hear again, calling to me from the earth, the oceans, the wind.

"Push," sang the earth.

"Show us," sang the ocean.

"Make it happen," sang the wind.

"Help me," called the mind.

I became aware of a little cry, then a more lusty one.

My mind began to clear. A nurse was cleaning me up. Dr. Ayre stood next to me.

"You did very well, my dear. You have a lovely baby girl."

"Thank you, doctor. For everything."

"The nurses are taking care of her now. You will be able to hold her in a minute."

I felt exhausted, exhilarated, and restless.

The nurse finished with me. My legs lay blessedly flat, and I was moved to a gurney. A young nurse gently placed a swaddled bundle into the crook of my arm. I gazed down at the little face whose eyes seemed to bore into mine, swollen though they were. I guess the ointment hadn't quite worn off.

"Mother," said the mind. Not the word but the idea.

"Daughter," I thought back, my heart swelling with the sound of it.

We were on the move, but our eyes remained locked until a nurse took her from me so I could be helped into bed.

I couldn't bear it. "Please give her back," I said as soon as they'd settled me.

Soon Lin and Hunter came in.

"She's beautiful," said Lin, pressing a finger on her forehead.

Hunter's eyes filled as he gazed down at her. "Come to Papa."

He took her and rocked from side to side, singing softly to her in his ancient tongue. She gazed up at him quietly before falling asleep. I glanced at Lin. I couldn't fully fathom her expression. I thought I saw yearning and sadness ... but joy, too.

"We never discussed a name," Hunter said.

"I thought of it when I first saw her," I replied. "Rose."

"Little princess, Rose," he crooned.

"Let Mary get some rest," Lin finally said. Hunter reluctantly handed her back, and they went out. He looked back at us both wistfully before closing the door.

When they took me home the next morning, I found a new cradle beside my bed and a changing table next to my chest of drawers, its bottom rack filled with all kinds of necessary items. There was a smaller chest in the little second bedroom next to mine, which we'd turned into a nursery, adding baby clothes from our frequent shopping trips, supplemented with Auntie Peggy's knitted creations.

I had everything. Absolutely everything.

17

Lin hadn't come downstairs for months. I know she said we'd wait for a while, but was she tired of all the telling? Too many bad memories? But she also had related lots of good memories. She liked talking about how she'd come out on top in any situation, although, to be fair, she could laugh at herself, too. Mostly. Maybe she was busy buying presents and preparing for the holidays.

It was silly to fret. My darling baby was the light of my life and, it seemed, of all those around her. I felt a little guilty that I hadn't told my sister, but we only exchanged a terse email every few weeks. I didn't feel like dealing with the interrogation and the jealousy when she realized what a wonderful situation I was in. I didn't know if Auntie Peggy had mentioned Rose. She didn't say.

Rose was sweet-tempered—except when hungry—and smiled early. She seemed to do everything early, and I sometimes wondered if I could see her grow if I stared at her for long enough. She was a beautiful blonde, too. Her hair might change color, but I hoped not.

I loved Hunter to bits, but even that love couldn't compare to the profundity of my love for Rose. Poor Lin and Hunter ... to outlive all their children. What a bitter sacrifice for immortality. I couldn't think about it without tearing up.

Thanksgiving had been fun. Everyone was there—Sven and Margareta, Joe and Helen, Auntie Peggy, Reema, Lettie and her boyfriend, and even Dr. Ayre. I'd been a little nervous because Sven and Margareta hadn't seen the baby. Would they guess who the father was? Would they be jealous? After all, Auntie Peggy had guessed. We hadn't seen Reema for months, as she was doing a residency in Pennsylvania. What would she think about this unmarried mother situation? Hunter had relented somewhat on the subject of dogs, so Sam was there, too.

As it turned out, I needn't have worried. Everyone seemed to take the situation in stride, and Rose was the hit of the party. I worried that being passed from person to person so much might bother her, but she'd just started to smile, and everyone wanted her to smile at them. She smiled away, and I found it quite interesting how they reacted. I wondered if Sam would be jealous, but from the first cautious yip and sniff, he clearly regarded her as under his protection.

Margareta was quite matter-of-fact, taking Rose into a corner while searching her face and having a conversation with her I couldn't quite catch, although Rose listened intently. Then Sven took his turn, walking her around the house, showing her this and that pretty thing, laughing when she rewarded him with her adorable toothless grin. Dr. Ayre held her on her lap for a while, gazing down at her with a look I couldn't quite interpret—nostalgia? Reema bounced her around a little more than I would like but seemed delighted to hold her. She congratulated me on my beautiful baby, seemingly without reservation.

Auntie Peggy, of course, was her usual loving self, both to me and Rose. She'd brought me some perfume because "new mothers need something special just for themselves." She got Rose a new plush rabbit. I had a huge basket full of plush animals next to an almost-full chest of exquisite baby clothes.

Lin and Hunter let everyone have their turn since they saw her every day. Helen held Rose while Joe stood close, looking down at her with a sloppy grin while she clasped his finger. They exchanged a look I had no trouble interpreting. *Shall we?* Sam followed everyone who held Rose, never taking his eyes off her.

When it was time to sit down to eat, Hunter said he'd get the crib from his study. Dora, who had just brought in a magnificent turkey, said, "Oh, no, it's my turn now. I'm going to sit down for a bit, so we'll have a nice cuddle, won't we, my sweet?"

Dora's reaction to the baby had taken me by surprise. I'd been scared that she might want to do Rose harm, but she'd immediately acted like an adoring aunt. I'd been suspicious at first and kept a close eye, but it seemed genuine.

Lin told me she'd been seeing someone. "I suspected she had a beau because her disposition became so sunny. You know how sulky she can be. So I followed her one day. A man picked her up in a truck, and off they went to Great Falls Park. They parked in a spot reserved for rangers before ambling quite deep into the woods, holding hands, chatting, and laughing. He was quite good-looking—about forty, I'd say. Not very tall, but solid. Well, they stopped in a clearing, where she took off her clothes, danced, and sang while he sat with his back to a tree and watched. It was quite obvious where this was all going, so I left."

I wouldn't put it past her to have stayed and watched. "Do you think she wants to get married?" I asked.

"Only if she can still work as a maid. Remember her curse; she can't do otherwise."

"Poor Dora," I said. "Can she bear children, do you think?"

"I hadn't thought of that. Interesting idea."

Lin clearly considered it an unwelcome idea. My additional thought was that perhaps the curse was weakening. They'd be bereft without her, especially during their time of rebirth. Although maybe Margareta would be able to help now that she knew the truth.

I was looking forward to Rose's first Christmas in just three weeks. Everyone would give her a mountain of gifts on the big day. I just hoped she wouldn't get overwhelmed and cry—not that she cried much, as long as she was fed regularly. She was growing so fast. Four months old and wearing clothes intended for babies of nine months. Surely she wasn't going to turn out to be a giant like her father. I thought about that a lot.

Hunter doted on Rose. After breakfast, he had been in the habit of retreating to his study to study the financial markets and didn't like to be disturbed. Now he always took Rose with him. He'd bought a small crib that he kept next to his desk, topped by an infant seat so she could sit and look around. He'd bring her down to me when she got hungry. His mornings with Rose were sacred. Lin liked to rock her to sleep after her midday meal, singing hauntingly beautiful Norse airs while she did. After her last feed was my special time, creating memories more precious than I can say. But I certainly appreciated the built-in babysitters.

The Monday after Thanksgiving, Lin appeared downstairs again after breakfast. I hadn't asked her about her absence, mostly because I was afraid of the answer.

"Ah, nice to be back," she said.

"I was afraid you were tired of it," I said.

"Oh, no, just very busy with the holidays and seeing friends."

I knew what "friends" probably meant.

"Besides, you've had your hands full."

"True enough."

Chapter 17

"Agna is coming to stay for Christmas. I can't wait!"

I couldn't wait, either. A real witch. "That's exciting. Really exciting. I never thought I'd meet a witch."

"Did you ever think you'd meet a god?"

"Good point. No, of course not."

Lin settled herself on the couch.

"Wait a second, Lin. I haven't set up the recorder."

"Okay, hurry up."

Soon I was set up, and she started.

Tape 12, Volume 2

When I found out Agna was coming last night, it jogged my memory. It was in London, just after we'd gotten Margareta back, and the night before Hunter and Sven arrived. We had a wonderful dinner at a restaurant in Pudding Lane, supposedly the site of the bakery where the Great Fire of London started. A historical event I'm glad I missed. It's very old, and the food is excellent. Margareta was quite in awe of the atmosphere and history. Agna and I liked it, but we've seen so many much older things that a mere 600 years isn't that impressive.

Anyway, Margareta went up to bed soon after we got back. Agna opened a bottle of bubbly, and we curled up on the sofa and chatted.

I asked her, "How was it living in the Valley of the Kings? It must have been so dull after all you've been used to."

She said, "It was never dull if you focused your mind on its small world." Village life could be a hotbed of intrigue. Women were traditionally subordinate to men, of course, but it was merely traditional hypocrisy upheld by all. The women ran the show. They decided who would lead, who would marry whom, who would be held to account for misdeeds, and so on.

But, she said, there was often what she could only describe as internecine warfare between them. Jealousy was usually at the root of it. Someone's husband built an addition on the house, another bought his wife a piece of cloth finer than that of her neighbor, and so on.

One day, things came to a head when it was time for two young girls to get married. Both mothers were ambitious for their daughters. There were three or four eligible young men, but one was the son of the village chief who would inherit his father's wealth and become rich … relative to their circumstances. One girl was widely acknowledged to be the most beautiful girl in the village. The other wasn't bad looking but couldn't compete with her rival. But the plainer one's father offered a much larger dowry at his wife's strong suggestion. Of course, the dowries comprised chickens, cloth, and other small household items—these people were poor.

After the day's work ended, each mother would stroll around the village with her freshly washed daughter in tow, ending with a slow parade past the chief's house, where the puffed-up man would sit sipping his beer. Sometimes they'd approach at the same time from different directions and almost run to get past first—although I should have thought being last would leave the strongest impression. Both girls were embarrassed by these tactics, knowing full well that the whole village was laughing at them.

Agna was sure that the chief would most likely take the larger dowry and the plainer girl—who, by the way, was in love with another boy. Agna knew both of these girls. She said the beautiful one was very sweet and sometimes walked with her near the tombs—unusual, given the local superstitions. They believed in ghosts that fed on humans.

There are no such things as ghosts, Agna told me—but then she said, "Not really. Close, but not what humans think of as ghosts."

"Well, I had to break in there, Mary," Lin said. "Sort of ghosts? I'd never heard of such a thing … and certainly never met one."

"I've never believed in ghosts, either," I said.

"Well, wait to hear what she told me."

She said, "The dead don't leave us entirely, Lin. Not for years. We think we get a message in a dream sometimes, or we suddenly think of our dead loved one as if they'd just jumped into our minds. But that is their essence. They do sometimes enter our dreams … make us think of them … try to make us take a different course. They even use us sometimes. It only happens with very strong relationships, though."

I asked whether she meant love, as with her and Tut.

She said yes, "Or hate. Like me and Ay." He died only five years after Tut. He had become Pharoah, so they buried him in a spare tomb in the Valley of the Kings. They always had one ready, you know.

Agna tried never to go anywhere near Ay's tomb, but she said that he still finds her sometimes. She keeps her mind set against him, so while he knocks, he cannot enter. She noted that Tut used to come to her often, usually when she was about to fall asleep, but often when she walked by his tomb.

I asked whether she saw Tut.

She said no—he enveloped her in a white mist and sang, always the same song, telling of love and loss. Sad and happy. He stopped coming to her about eighty years ago after he'd been moved away.

But Ay, she said, still tries. His hatred is unrelenting, and her spells do not extend to the afterlife. Hel closed her doors to all but the mortal dead after we left. Now she's been reduced to a state of doom and grief that hovers in perpetuity.

Ay got to Agna in Paris when she visited Tut's first exhibition. She told me that he got into her mind and made her roar like a lion in the middle of the Louvre. Security guards came running, but Agna couldn't become invisible because he'd drained her energy. They took her to a mental hospital, where she was sedated. Of course, you know how that is for us.

When the sedation finally wore off, she was able to disappear and high-tail it back to Egypt. Gathering her strength, she went to Ay's tomb.

He came to her in a dark wind that carried sand and scorpions swirling around her, trying to pick her up and throw her against the rocks. She stood immobile with her eyes closed, her mind pushing against his. He had to fall back. Agna said that was the last time he was able to overcome her, and she gets only feeble emanations now, but she know better than to let her guard down.

"That's unbelievable," I said.

"That's what I said, Mary. But I suddenly wondered if I should visit some of my children's graves."

"Oh, Lin," I said, saddened. "Did you?"

"Not yet. I might. Let me go on."

Anyway, the marriage feud. Agna decided she would have to act. She made sure to run into the plain girl and her mother on their evening stroll. They talked about all sorts of things, although the mother made it clear she would like to be left alone with her daughter. She was curious, too, of course. As you can imagine, Agna was quite an oddity in the village—no husband, a house with nice furniture, and a figure of rectitude, despite what they'd expected after seeing her beauty.

Agna didn't like either of them much. She said they were both sharp-tongued, rather sly, not to mention awash with envy and spite. She left them just before the chief's house.

On her way back, she passed a thicket of thorny shrubs and heard laughter but cries, too. She made herself invisible and stepped over the vegetation to a small clearing in front of a few miserable palm trees. Two boys, one of them the chief's son, were tormenting a dog with sharp sticks. They had the poor little thing tied to a stake in the ground, so he couldn't escape. He bled copiously.

Agna was so full of rage that it almost drained her energy, but she managed to hold herself in check. She got two sharp sticks of her own, one for each hand, and gouged the boys with those sticks from all directions, so they didn't know which way to run. And, of course, they couldn't see her, which made it all the more terrifying. She started to howl and screech before she finally let them go.

"The chief's son became a gibbering idiot. The other boy wasn't much better. They told tales of a ghost who pursued them and beat them. Agna told people here and there about them being cursed. They were both out of the marriage market after that. They never worked a full day again and died unwed.

The two girls went on to marry decent fellows. The beautiful girl and her husband were happy, the other couple not so much—Agna was right; the girl was a sly shrew.

As for that little dog, Agna had enough energy left to heal him right away. She took him home, bathed, and fed him; he was her faithful companion for fifteen years.

"Well, Mary, what do you think of that?" Lin said as she sat up and swung her legs to the ground.

"I'm astonished once more," I said. "I wish I'd had visits from my parents, though. Perhaps they lived too small to have the passion it takes, though."

"I think this is it until the new year," Lin said. "It's going to be a busy time."

I couldn't stop thinking about ghosts. I had troubled dreams that night about my parents. In one, they opened their front door and invited me in. As soon as I stepped over the threshold, they drifted away, faces turned from me, and the house evaporated. That was the only one I could fully remember in the morning. The others were mere flashes here and there that hinted at their presence behind clouds or windows.

The weekend was quiet. I went out on Saturday to buy Christmas gifts but didn't find much. On Sunday, I made a list for everyone except

Lin and Hunter. What do you give people who can have everything and anything they want?

18

Lin came down to breakfast about a week before Christmas, looking ready to cry, the way her eyes and mouth were fixed into rigid containment. She said good morning without looking at any of us. And drank coffee without eating.

I glanced at Hunter, and he shook his head discreetly, so I said nothing and concentrated on finishing my breakfast as fast as possible before kissing Rose and escaping downstairs. Rose, as usual, spent the morning in Hunter's care.

A couple of hours later, Hunter brought the baby down to me. She was fast asleep, so I was surprised to see him. His habit was to keep her until she started to fuss for a feed. He gently set her down in her crib.

"What's up?" I asked.

"It is Agna. She is not coming. Lin is so disappointed. She was really looking forward to having her and showing her around. She regards Agna as her sister, you know."

"I know. Poor Lin. Why couldn't she come?"

"It is rather strange. She said she felt a great upheaval coming. A plague, even."

"That sounds a bit farfetched. Perhaps she didn't want to come."

"She is a witch, remember. She feels and knows things even we cannot. Anyway, I must comfort Lin."

"Why don't you suggest doing some Christmas shopping?"

Hunter thought for a minute. "Maybe mentioning Christmas is not such a great idea."

He had a point. "I know. Tell her I'll get Sam from Auntie Peggy, and you'll both take him for a walk. You know how she loves dogs."

"All right. I suppose."

After Rose woke up and had dined copiously, I took her upstairs to Hunter and went to get the dog. Auntie was a little confused, as I didn't explain very carefully beyond saying we needed to cheer Lin up.

As soon as we returned to the house, Sam raced downstairs to find Rose. When he discovered she wasn't there, he ran back up, then into Hunter's study, when he heard her gurgling. She giggled when she saw him, and he sat in front of the crib, gazing intently at her as if to check her wellbeing.

"I suspect we shall have to take her along, too," Hunter said.

"Definitely!" I said. I would have liked to go, but they needed their time together. "I'll fetch Lin."

"No, you stay here. It is better that I go."

I guess Lin was unapproachable. I heard them come downstairs. I lay Rose down in her stroller, which led to a vigorous protest. She liked being able to look around. She'd quiet once they started walking. I attached Sam's leash and maneuvered the three of us into the lobby. Lin didn't look at me; she just held out her hand for the leash. I fitted the loop around her wrist while Hunter carried the stroller down the front steps.

"These are the poop bags," I said, showing her the cylinder attached to the leash.

"What?"

"Poop bags. You're not supposed to leave it on the street. Just scoop it up and leave it in the trash when you get home."

"Ugh. I didn't know about that. Nasty."

"You get used to it. Didn't you change your babies' diapers?"

"Only when I absolutely had to."

"I will see to it," Hunter called from the path. "Come on, Lin, let's go."

They were away for more than an hour. I went to meet them when I heard the front gate clang shut, wondering if Rose would be fractious by now. Sam pranced proudly by the stroller, and Rose babbled in response to their song. They were both singing to her as they walked. A lively melody, unlike the more haunting ones I'd heard Hunter sing. The same language, I think. I felt the pang of being outside their bubble, although glad to see Lin happy.

When they got inside, I lifted Rose from the stroller and cuddled her, covering her with kisses. *You're mine.* We migrated into the family room. I settled myself in one corner of the sofa, and Sam jumped up to sit on my lap, hardly taking his eyes off Rose. I looked up nervously. Hunter looked a little shocked but kept mum. Lin just looked amused.

"Sam is Rose's guardian angel," she said.

"Yes, he is," I said. "Is it all right, him being up here?"

"Oh yes. Sofas can be cleaned. They need each other," Lin replied.

Hunter kind of grunted.

"Hunter told you Agna can't come for Christmas?" she went on. I nodded. "Well, he suggested I visit her in the New Year, maybe for a few months. That will be such fun."

"I'm so glad you will see her after all. Disappointed that I won't, though," I said.

"Maybe I'll bring her back with me."

Yes!

Christmas saw the usual hectic shopping, cooking, and wrapping on the part of Lin, Dora, and, to a lesser extent, me. The usual cast of characters attended, Rose once more being the star of the show. Her pile of gifts was almost embarrassing. I'd need a big basket just to hold the plush toy animals. She got some cute little dresses from Lin that came with their own miniature hangers.

While we were sitting down to dinner, I happened to notice that Helen wore a diamond ring on her left hand. Once we were all seated, I said loudly, "That's a lovely ring, Helen. Is it new?"

She blushed, Joe blushed, and the table erupted into cries of congratulation, with everyone getting up to kiss Helen and, if male, shake Joe's hand. Rose, in her infant seat wedged into the stroller next to Auntie, was overcome by too much noise and disruption. I noticed her little chest beginning to heave before she broke out crying. Auntie cooed at her, and Hunter came over to pick her up, but Dora pipped them at the post, swooping out of the kitchen and whisking her away.

Auntie looked bewildered by her sudden loss.

"Happens to me all the time," I told her. "There's a lot of competition around here."

Sometimes it annoyed me, too, although I felt fortunate to have time for myself.

I went to stay with Auntie Peggy for New Year's Eve, as the Thorens never celebrated. Auntie Peggy wouldn't be able to stay up that late, nor would I, as Rose woke early. But being together made her feel good. Just having someone to wish Happy New Year on the first of the year. She was getting frailer, her arthritis bothering her more. I always waited until she was sitting down before letting her hold Rose. I wondered how long she could keep up with the house.

Seeing me eye her with concern as she struggled out of her chair, she anticipated my thoughts. "This house is getting too much for me," she said. "I've started to look at retirement communities around here. They'll have to accept dogs, and I don't want to be too far from you and Rose."

"I was a little worried. I'm quite close, but you need someone closer for emergencies."

"I know," she said. "And I don't want to be a burden."

"Never a burden, Auntie. Never."

"Well, you've got a little one now. She must come first."

"We could move in with you," I said. "I could go to the Thorens' every morning."

"Oh, I don't think Hunter would like that very much, do you?"

Dumbstruck, I stared at her. She was almost laughing. Someone of her age should have been scandalized. Just about anyone would be.

"He's a lovely man," she said. "And they're different. Anyone can see that."

"I don't know what to say," I said.

"Best to let matters rest at that," she said.

That was Auntie all over—let sleeping dogs lie.

Did Helen and Joe realize? And Reema?

A couple of days later, Hunter took Lin to the airport. Lin promised to be back for Easter, which she always made special. A whole three months of Hunter. I loved Lin, but I longed for more of Hunter.

In March, COVID forced a shutdown. Not only would Lin miss Easter, but everyone would.

19

It was an anxious time. I was terrified for Rose. Dora did all the shopping as she wouldn't catch any human disease. The first time she went out after the announcement, she came home in a panic. The freezer shelves were completely empty. No bread. Not much of anything. She'd bought plenty of flour and other staples and soon went to work baking bread. She'd found steaks and a chicken. Produce was available.

I worried about Auntie. I took some bread and chicken over, and she was so relieved. She'd been to the supermarket but with a scarf tied over her mouth. She couldn't find masks. I'd managed to find some online, but they'd take a couple of weeks to arrive.

It got worse. Hospitals were overrun, shortages of everything, and every person was a possible threat. Thank god, I had Hunter.

"I think you should bring your Auntie here," Hunter said one day in May. "Gas is getting short, too. She will be safer with us."

I called Auntie at once. She reluctantly agreed that I would bring her and Sam over next Sunday.

"What time is best?" I asked, forgetting church wasn't an issue any longer.

We all kept going as normally as possible. I felt the undercurrent of fear, the insecurity of the food supply. The tension always buzzed just underneath my skin. I'm sure it was the same with everyone, especially for parents.

Hunter called the children back, too. I wanted them to be safe, but had my qualms.

Margareta arrived first. I answered the door wearing my mask. She wore one, too.

"Hello, Mary," she said. "Super to see you. I'm going to stay in my room for a week. Dora can bring up my meals. Can't risk Rose getting it."

"Oh, Margareta, I'm so glad you understand. I didn't quite know what to say."

"Well, we have to be sensible. Don't worry, I'll make Sven see sense."

And she did. We remained in a bubble, glad of each other's company. Margareta and Sven were able to take their classes online, so they spent a lot of time in their rooms anyway. They grew very fond of Auntie Peggy. She was a rare species for them, a kind of grandmother figure they'd never experienced. Their parents didn't have any older friends—in a manner of speaking.

It wasn't unusual to see one of them in deep conversation with Auntie, probably venting their angst about something or other. She never said. She seemed to revel in the company, too. I wondered how she'd adapt to being alone again. Sven always took her arm to help her upstairs to bed. Margareta always took her a cup of tea in the morning and remembered just how she liked it—the British way, with milk and a teaspoon of sugar.

Rose was loving life, too. She lived in a house full of adoring relatives. Her life was all about love and play.

Hunter avoided coming down to me until everyone had gone up to bed—luckily, fairly early as a rule. The kids liked watching their shows on TV, and each had one in their room. Sometimes, they watched something together, but not often.

Air travel was an issue. Weeks turned into months. Lin and Agna weren't susceptible to COVID, so why not fly once the airlines were moving, albeit infrequently?

Lin and Hunter FaceTimed every week, and we soon got our answer.

"I keep testing positive," Lin said.

"I don't understand," I said. "I thought you couldn't catch diseases."

"Well, I don't get ill, but apparently, I can carry this one. Until I can show a negative test, I can't travel."

"Maybe Agna can think of something," Hunter said.

"She's working on it. Anyway, I can't risk carrying the virus home."

"Have you asked Dr. Ayre?" I said. "Maybe she has some advice."

"Good idea," Lin said, her voice flat and unenthusiastic.

Hunter's lips tightened. He'd noticed, too.

"I am so glad you are having a good time," he said.

The conversation turned frosty-polite and ended soon after.

"She does not want to come home," he whispered after the children had left.

"She's feeling a new kind of freedom. She'll soon tire of it. Remember, a few months is just a blip in time for you two."

"Yes, that is true." He looked more cheerful.

We'd enjoyed most nights together, always in my bed, even though it wasn't king-size. Hunter somehow curled himself around me. I loved being held and loved. He did, too. But he was getting restless.

"I am going to rebuild our house on the Bay," he announced one September morning. "It's about time."

"Is it safe?" I asked. "Are you sure Loki has gone?"

"Well, he has not made his way here. And how long do common black snakes live?"

"I don't know. Do you?"

"Can you look it up? You know, internet stuff."

I went downstairs to my laptop and discovered they lived between three and four years.

"Well, it has been that long," Hunter said, rubbing his hands together gleefully.

"Loki seems to be very resourceful," I said. "Anyway, isn't there a shortage of building supplies?"

"If you can pay, you can find anything," he said. "I am going to my study to start the design. Do not tell Lin. I want it to be a big surprise."

I just hoped she'd appreciate it. From what I'd heard, Loki was not to be underestimated.

Hunter barely emerged from his study for the next few days. I missed him but wasn't about to play the needy nuisance.

One Friday in October, he sat down at the dinner table and announced, in the manner of one who had been awarded a Nobel prize, "I have engaged an architect. Tomorrow we will drive down to the Bay, and he will see if he can fulfill my design. Would you like to come, Mary?"

"Of course," I said. "Rose can play on the beach a little." She was fourteen months by then, big for her age, and had been able to walk without toppling over for a couple of months. "Auntie, would you like to come?"

"No, thank you, dear. Sitting on the sand is not for me anymore. Why don't you leave Rose here with Dora and me?"

"Yes, maybe that would be best. Thank you."

Auntie and Dora had made friends fast, bonding in the kitchen while they exchanged ideas for meals. Auntie was teaching Dora to knit, too.

"Hunter, can I see your design?"

I followed him to his study and marveled as he showed me around his huge layout. The living area began on the second floor as, at ground level, he'd planned a garage and storage space. The first level had the utility room, kitchen, two small attached bedrooms with a bathroom for me and Rose, and a powder room. Four small bedrooms with two bathrooms around a sitting area occupied the next level, and at the top were a master bedroom suite and a study. It looked palatial.

Carole Weiss, the architect, turned out to be a middle-aged woman with that formidable "Don't mess with me" air about her. We all chatted amiably enough on the way down to Southern Maryland.

"One thing," she said. "We have to make sure your land will permit for all those bedrooms. Why don't we call the bottom two a den and storage area? Then it's four bedrooms."

"Yes, of course." Nothing could daunt Hunter's good spirits.

When we arrived, I was dismayed by the dismal look of the place. The charred framework, the half-burned furniture, the skeleton of a house. I soon took myself off to the beach. I regretted not bringing Sam. He would have found all kinds of new smells on what looked like great walks around the coast. The view was great. I could see across to a long spit of land where military aircraft soared and landed behind a thick barrier of trees. Hunter told me later it was the Patuxent River Naval Air Station.

I went back to the small road between the property and the beach and took a walk, keeping to roads close to the water. I soon came to a lake with houses dotted around the edge. Standing by the lake and looking out to the Bay was an exercise in serenity, despite the chill in the breeze playing off the water. COVID felt far away, a bad dream.

I returned to the house, such as it was, to find Hunter and Carole waiting for me.

"Sorry," I said. "I discovered a pretty lake not far away. It's strange to see a lake so close to the sea. It's beautiful here."

"Man-made lake, no doubt," said Carole. She seemed impatient to get going.

Hunter said, "It is all going to be fine. Carole will draw up the plans, and we will choose a construction company. She even knows a good one down here and does not foresee any problems. It should not take long." He was like a little boy anticipating his birthday party.

"Let's not forget the permit," Carole said. "It can take a while."

The permit didn't take that long, as it happened. The building went on all early spring through July. Hunter drove down at least once a week, and I accompanied him in July. I didn't expect the house to be so far along. It would be ready by the end of the month.

"I'll leave the furnishings and so on to Lin," said Hunter.

"Why don't we do the bedrooms for Rose and me and Dora?" I suggested. "That way, we can use the place right away. And why not let the kids choose their own furniture?"

"Okay. I suppose we do not know when Lin will be back."

He looked downcast, and I was almost sorry I'd mentioned it. Not very sorry because I just wanted to be there as soon and as often as I could. The sea beckoned me, somehow.

"Let's have a little party on the beach for Rose's second birthday. She won't know what's going on, but it'll be fun."

It was quite a procession that drove down there in August. Sven had bought some beach umbrellas and chairs online.

"Did you design a shed?" he asked.

"Of course I did. That reminds me, I had better take a padlock."

We had coolers with sandwiches, drinks, and a cake. It was a merry time. Sam stayed in the house a lot because of the heat. Rose didn't seem to feel at all uncomfortable. She loved sitting in the water at the edge and giggled delightedly whenever a wavelet splashed her. Hunter gazed at her dotingly and made a few little humps in the sand, which she immediately smashed with her fist. Hunter and I took her and Sam for a walk to the lake, which he hadn't yet seen. Quite a few people were out walking, and they all greeted us warmly and admired Rose, albeit from a safe distance. It was another world.

Rose and Auntie Peggy slept all the way home. Luckily Margareta and Hunter drove, as I was pretty sleepy, too.

We picked out the furniture, as I'd mentioned, adding a guest bedroom set so Auntie Peggy could join us. Margareta said she wanted to be able to go down there at once, so she would pick furniture for her and Sven. Sven was keen to go fishing, so he was fine with that. Hunter decided to pick out his study furniture, too.

That left the living room and the master suite for Lin—except that we ended up getting a few chairs and sofas for the living room because we needed somewhere to sit down. We needed a table to eat at, too. I hoped Lin wouldn't be mad. Margareta and I, double-masked, made a few trips to a furniture store to decide on most things, and Hunter joined us to pick out his study desk, chairs, and shelving.

We had a glorious few days there in September and October and decided to have Thanksgiving there, too. I loved that—a walk on the beach after lunch. What could be better?

20

We continued to communicate with Lin every week. Christmas came and went. We ordered gifts and food from Amazon, and there were enough of us to enjoy a jolly time. We all missed Lin, though. We all kept everything in order—I had wisely let Margareta call the shots on the home front so as not to step on any toes. She was a remarkably intelligent and capable young woman. Hunter and I enjoyed our time together. Auntie Peggy was now part of the family. Dora seemed happier for having Rose in her life. But Lin was a presence strong enough to make us acutely aware of her absence.

We were all having breakfast in March when Hunter got the call.

"That is a number I do not recognize," he said. He declined the call. It rang again. "What?" he almost yelled down the line. His face became suffused with joy. He said something in his language and hung up. "She and Agna are coming this afternoon!"

The children whooped and rushed off to their rooms with talk of a welcome back sign. Auntie looked a little concerned.

"Did she test negative?" I asked.

"I forgot to ask. Maybe she did talk to Dr. Ayre. They came over to New York on some kind of boat and have rented a car. It will take them at least five hours."

That made me nervous. Could Rose catch COVID from them? Auntie and I had received our vaccinations, but there weren't yet any for children. I had such conflicting feelings. Jealous that he was so happy, but happy she'd be back. I loved her, too. Excited to meet a witch. Concerned about what Auntie Peggy would make of it all. And dinner!

"We have to tell Dora right away."

I went to the kitchen to find Dora sitting at the table, wiping her eyes. "Did you hear?" I asked.

"Yes. I'm so happy. I need her. And she needs me. They all do. I'll start thinking about dinner." She took a deep breath and went to clear the dining table.

I decided it was time to talk with Auntie Peggy, whom I found in the living room, looking sad. Everyone else had dispersed to carry out their own preparations. Sam was probably glued to Rose's side, as usual.

"Hello, dear. That is such good news. I think it is time for me to leave. I will pack my things if you wouldn't mind driving me home."

"Oh, that isn't necessary," I said. "Lin is the most generous of people. She wouldn't want you to be on your own. I wanted to explain a few things to you."

"I know they are different, dear—is that what you mean?"

"Well, they are very different. You will find this hard to believe, but they are from another age. Lin and Hunter are gods."

"Gods? My goodness. What kind of gods?" I couldn't quite make out her demeanor—shock seemed to have been overtaken by excitement.

"Norse gods who escaped the final battle. Their powers are much weakened, but they are very ancient and go through many rebirths and lifetimes."

"Are you sure, dear? I knew they were odd, but I never imagined such a thing."

"Auntie, Hunter is paranoid about anyone finding out. Margareta knows, but I don't think Sven does. It's a very long story. But they mustn't know I told you. I just wanted you to know why some things might seem a little strange. And this friend Lin is bringing with her from London. She's another one."

"Good gracious. I'd better sit here awhile while I take it all in."

I don't know if she believed me, but if she saw something odd, she'd remember what I said instead of being frightened. I wrestled with the idea of telling Hunter what I'd done but didn't want to spoil his mood.

No, let's face it, it was cowardice.

21

Lin called from Dr. Ayre's office to say they'd be late. They'd stopped to make sure they were not carrying the virus. Dr. Ayre apparently had them disrobe before spraying them with her own anti-viral concoction and making them swallow something disgusting. She declared them clear. A huge relief.

When Lin and Agna entered the house at around 6, I could hardly believe my eyes, even though Lin had told me about the likeness. They were almost identical, except for Lin's shiny golden hair as opposed to Agna's fall of white blonde.

Lin kissed both children after thanking them for the lovely welcome home sign. The children greeted Agna politely, temporarily dumbstruck as they stared at her and Lin as if seeing a mirage.

After a big hug, Lin introduced me.

"Mary," Agna said in a soft, musical voice, clasping my hands in her shockingly cold ones. "Lin has told me so much about you. I am very pleased to meet you."

"The pleasure is all mine," I said. "I so enjoyed hearing your story." I caught my breath and glanced at Hunter. Fortunately, he was busy enjoying the reunion of the children and their mother. While he knew I was aware of their true nature, he knew nothing of the memoirs.

"Don't worry," Agna whispered. "He didn't hear a thing."

We exchanged a grin like two naughty children.

Lin, Hunter, and their children were soon chatting away, interrupting each other excitedly while Agna stood to one side.

"Come and sit down," I said, leading her to the sitting room. "May I introduce my aunt, Peggy Cartwright?"

"I am so pleased to meet you," Auntie said, clearly taken aback by seeing a woman who could have been Lin's twin. "You must be tired after your long journey."

I whispered to Agna, "I've told my aunt about you, Lin, and Hunter. But they don't know I told her. Please don't tell them." Agna nodded and squeezed Auntie's hand.

"It was a very tedious journey," Agna told her. "Cargo ships are not exactly luxurious. When you are obliged to remain invisible but have to find a safe hiding place to take a nap when it wears off before repeating the spell, it's really annoying. The ship stank, too. Fuel, unwashed bodies, and so on. When we stood on deck to get some fresh air, it seemed to hasten the lapses, so we couldn't do it as often as we would have liked." Agna sank into an armchair and looked out of the window. "The trouble is, we have become more human. We used not to need sleep and food. And indeed, we still don't. But we are accustomed to it and want it, so we think we need it."

Auntie opened and closed her mouth a couple of times before responding. "Er, goodness me, how exhausting it all sounds. Yes, indeed."

"I think that applies to many of us," I replied. "I am used to a much finer life than I ever had before. I also think I need things I could only dream of in my former circumstances."

Agna suddenly turned to the door, smiling, with her eyes wide. A few seconds later, it opened as Dora led Rose in slowly—the little one wasn't becoming very steady on her feet. "Oh, is that your little girl?" she exclaimed. "How lovely she is, just like her mother."

I glowed.

"She woke up when she heard all the noise, didn't you, my love? Doesn't want to be left out," Dora said fondly. She still didn't like me that much but doted on my child.

Rose launched herself at me, and I picked her up for a cuddle before settling her on my lap.

"Does she like stories?" asked Agna.

"Oh, she loves them," I said. "My aunt has bought her lots of books, and Hunter tells her stories about the old world."

"Well, I have plenty of stories for her," Agna said.

"But are they suitable for a little one?" I found the idea alarming.

"Oh, yes, I have some charming ones about beautiful Egyptian princesses."

"That sounds wonderful. You'd be surprised what she understands at such a young age."

"I clever," Rose suddenly announced, making Agna break into laughter that sounded like a cascade of fairy bells.

"Yes, I think you are, Rose," Agna said, stroking the child's back.

"Actually, I'd love to hear more of your stories," I said.

"Lin told me about your morning sessions. Tomorrow morning I'll come down and tell you one. I'm sure Lin will be busy with her children. Or she can come and listen ... if she wants."

We all enjoyed champagne before dinner, for which Dora had outdone herself. A huge leg of lamb that, in truth must have been mutton, was cooked in yogurt with all kinds of spices. She'd prepared a medley of vegetable dishes, along with potatoes and rice, followed by a wonderful array of pastries and custards for dessert. Rose sat in her highchair and nibbled a few things before falling asleep. Hunter picked her up and carried her to bed.

The next morning, I left Rose with Hunter after breakfast and went downstairs in case Agna wanted to join me. She arrived about an hour later and sat on the sofa.

"Do you mind if I record you?" I asked.

"No, certainly not. I'd like to be in Lin's book. She told me it won't be out for years, so that's fine."

"I just wanted to ask one thing that's been puzzling me. How come the story of those men being turned into pigs never got out? From what Lin said, there were lots of witnesses."

"Oh, I erased their memories," Agna said. "Of course, I couldn't quite control how much of their memories I erased, but it wouldn't have been that much. For most of them."

"I guess I should have thought of that," I said, laughing.

Just then, Rose came down the stairs, bumping from step to step on her bottom, the way I taught her. Sam followed carefully. She came running over to Agna and climbed onto the sofa next to her. Agna put her arm around the child, and Rose nestled against her chest. Rose was a friendly child to a point, but I had never seen her behave like that with a stranger. Sam didn't seem concerned and lay under Rose's feet.

"Well," said Agna, "I think I'd better choose a different story this morning. Let me tell you about Ramses and the lion."

Tape 13,
Volume 2

One day, the great Ramses decided to go hunting in Nubia. He was loved and revered in those parts, so his party was welcomed by any settlement or town in which they wished to set up their tents. He always kept his favorite falcon, Trey, close, even taking the bird into temples to pray and offer libations to the gods. When he performed his ablutions before entering, he would wipe a wet cloth over Trey's feathers and talons to show respect. He believed that such a noble creature should be welcome. The priests weren't comfortable with this but dared not complain.

On one excursion into particularly wild terrain, he walked ahead of his entourage. Trey started to mutter and fidget, flexing his talons on the leather strap that protected his master's forearm.

As Ramses rounded a bend, he came face to face with a big lion. He stopped and looked into the animal's eyes.

"I am Ramses, Pharoah of Egypt," he said. "I wish you no harm."

"I am Leb, king of the animal kingdom as far as the distant horizon. I wish you no harm, but I am hungry."

Ramses turned to Trey. "We will find you food," he said, extending his arm to the sky.

Trey soared until they could scarcely see him. By now, Ramses's men had caught up and drawn their weapons.

"Be still," he told them. "This noble lion wishes us no harm. Trey has gone to find him sustenance."

With a great flapping of wings, Trey hovered overhead and dropped a rabbit at Leb's feet before flying high once more. Leb sat and ate the rabbit quickly. He licked his lips.

"Trey will be back soon with more," said Ramses. He turned to look at his men. "This king deserves our respect. You will do him no harm."

Over the course of an hour, Trey fed the lion until he was sated. The falcon settled back on Ramses' gauntlet, and his master replaced the hood.

"You have shown me kindness and mercy," said the lion. He rose to his feet. "I pledge to serve you to the end of your days. Then I will return here to rule my kingdom." He looked up into an old acacia tree. "Hawk, take a message to my wife, Lebua. I will be gone for some years, and she must assume my duties."

Ramses had not noticed the hawk perched near the top of the tree. With a hearty squawk, the bird took off.

"Spare the hawk," commanded Ramses, lest the bird become another casualty.

Leb took his place at Ramses's side, where he remained until the great Pharoah's time had come to pass into the underworld. It is said that Leb and his wife still rule the animal kingdom with wisdom and love.

"Well, what do you think about that, my sweet?" Agna asked, looking down at Rose, who had been staring at her entranced throughout the story.

"Rose luv Leb."

"She understood. Well, I'd better go and find Lin. Where's your aunt?"

"Maybe in her room. Between you and me, I explained a few things, but not everything. She'd be bound to notice odd events and behaviors. I know Lin and Hunter will be mad at me, but I felt I had no choice. I haven't told them. Auntie's had a shock."

"I'm not surprised. I'll talk to her, too. You seem to be coping well."

"It took me a while. But they are so kind. And Hunter..."

"Yes, I know, Lin told me. She's happy for you."

"I love them both, just Hunter in a different way."

"Nothing wrong with that. And your child is exceptional. As is to be expected." She patted my arm and kissed Rose.

"Thank you. I haven't had much to do with small children, so I don't have any to compare her to."

"Never compare. It can only lead to either discontent or conceit."

She went back upstairs.

"Rose want walk. And Sam want walk."

Sam pricked up his ears at that magic sound "walk" and pranced in circles while I got Rose's shoes and coat on before making my way upstairs.

I peeped into the living room, where Agna sat in deep conversation with Auntie Peggy. They had their backs to me, but all seemed calm.

"Just taking Rose and Sam for a walk," I called. They turned around, both smiling. Not a hint of tension.

"Have a lovely walk," said Auntie.

"Look after Sam," said Agna.

"Rose do," replied the babe.

We took the stroller because, at eighteen months, Rose couldn't walk that far. There was a park about a twenty-minute walk away with swings for toddlers, which Rose loved.

"Where go?"

"The park. You like that."

"'Wings."

"Yes, you can have a go on the swings. I know you love that."

"Agna like 'wings."

"I'm sure she does. But they're not for big people."

"Agna can get 'mall."

That sent shivers through me as she had trouble saying so many words but could manage Agna? What was going on? I didn't know whether to be proud of Rose or scared for her.

I heard heavy footsteps coming up fast behind me.

"Mary. I wanted to be with you both."

"Hunter!" My heart fluttered. "I thought you'd be busy with the family."

"You are my family, too. And I want to watch the little one as she enjoys the swings."

Just then, Sam edged over the median and pooped. Hunter took a bag off the leash and did the honors. There was a trash bin at the park we could deposit it, thank goodness. I don't think it was intended for that, but needs must.

When we got to the swings, Rose began to squeal and clap her hands. Hunter lifted her into one and pushed her gently.

"More!" she cried.

Hunter pushed a little harder, and she giggled and babbled. I watched like a hawk as Hunter sometimes forgot his strength. Sam sat at full alert, not entirely comfortable with the situation. The trouble would start when it was time to leave.

"It's nearly lunchtime, Rose," I called out.

"No!"

"Lin and Dora won't like us to be late."

"No!"

I had a better idea. "Maybe Agna knows another story."

"Okay."

Well, that was easy. Except that Agna might not have another story.

We got back just as Dora was putting the food on the sideboard—a platter of fish and other dishes of vegetables. I took Rose to wash her hands and wondered what Hunter would have to say.

When we got back, though, he was already seated with a bloody T-bone in front of him while everyone else helped themselves. Hunter settled Rose in her highchair while I fixed her a plate.

Agna asked, "How was your walk?"

"Very nice. But she always makes such a fuss getting off the swing, and today was no exception. I tried all kinds of things, but when I said that maybe you had another story for her, she came off immediately. I'm afraid she expects a story when she goes down for her nap."

Agna laughed—how I loved that laugh—and assured me that would be no problem. I was rather looking forward to it myself.

We had a lively time and ate too much. Rose and I went downstairs, and I got her ready for her nap. Agna came down soon after.

"Do you mind if I record this?" I asked.

"Of course not." Agna sat in the rocking chair where I used to nurse Rose.

I set the recorder on Rose's chest of drawers and turned it on before sliding down the wall to sit on the floor.

Tape 14, Volume 2

Once upon a time, there was a little girl called Rose who lived far, far away in a country called Egypt. Her father was the mayor of their village. She was a happy little girl who loved playing with her dog—who looked very much like Sam—and her family. The family ate well, and she enjoyed her favorite sweet baklava at least once a month. She had all she wanted. The sun shined every day, even in winter when the air felt cold.

When Rose had just turned seven, two strangers rode into her village. One was a tall man who looked very strong and carried a hooded falcon on his arm. The other was not quite as tall but looked strong, too. Their horses looked tired and thirsty.

Rose's father and her two older brothers approached them.

"Good morning, my friends," said her father. "Welcome to our village. May I offer you refreshment?"

"Thank you, my good man," said the tall man, clearly the leader. "I would welcome that. We have traveled for the hunt farther than I intended. While we would welcome refreshment, our horses need some food and water, too. I will be glad to pay."

"Friends, you are our guests, and I cannot accept your gold. My sons will see to your horses. Please enter my house. I see that you are fine gentlemen used to finery, so please accept my apologies for our humble dwelling." The mayor extended his arm to show them in.

They drank cool beer and ate figs with honey and yogurt and special little cakes. They chatted for a long time about things Rose didn't really understand. She did hear a few words she knew, like "Pharoah" and "loyal." Eventually, the men came back out into the sun and reclaimed their horses. They rode away with calls of friendship and thanks. They came back when Rose was eight, nine, and ten. She would soon have her eleventh birthday and supposed they would be back in a week or so.

When she got older, Rose liked to take walks. Her mother and father told her never to go so far that she couldn't look back and see her house. That wasn't very far, and Rose really, really wanted to see more of the world. There wasn't all that much to see, just a lot of huge stones and one pyramid quite far away, quite a small one as pyramids go, with its stones arranged so that each side looked like a wide staircase.

One day, Rose decided she absolutely had to see that pyramid up close. She was almost eleven, after all, and big enough to take care of herself. She had never disobeyed her parents before, but it was an urge she couldn't resist.

She started walking farther and farther. She got to the first big stone, one that was much taller and wider than her, and looked back. She could just see the top of her house. So that was all right.

A big hiss made her freeze. That was what she'd been taught to do if she heard such a dreadful thing. Without moving the rest of her body, she moved her eyes to the side and down. A huge viper was almost at her feet, all reared up and ready to bite. Then she heard an even scarier sound, the roar of a lion. The snake didn't like that sound, either, and lowered itself before slithering away as fast as it could.

Rose stood still and listened hard. No more roars, no other sounds, except her pounding heart. The lion was probably very far away. She should go home. But she had come this far, and it would be such a waste not to see the pyramid.

She went past the big stone and passed several more, stumbling on the rocky ground. The pyramid didn't look a whole lot closer. A huffing and snuffling behind what must have once been a wall halted her again. A foxy face peered through a gap in the wall.

Jackals. They'd eat anything, especially little girls. Rose now understood why her parents had told her never to go beyond sight of their house. One by one, they came around the wall and circled her. She spun this way and that, knowing that if she screamed, that would set them off. They looked thin and hungry and mean. They stared at her, so there was nothing else to do but stare back.

A lion roared. The jackals lifted their snouts to sniff the wind before slinking away, finally breaking into a flat-out run across the desert. Rose felt a lot better until she remembered the lion.

Being a very stubborn little girl, Rose decided to keep on walking. She was getting hot and thirsty. She should have brought water. She decided to sit for a few minutes, so she squatted with her back against a stubby, knobby tree trunk, the only one around. This was not a place to sustain trees and flowers. Too much sand and rock and not enough water. Rose bent her head and closed her eyes. She must have fallen asleep for a few minutes because a thud jolted her awake.

A massive lion sat in front of her. This was the end, then. She should not have obeyed her parents.

"Yes, you should not have disobeyed your parents," said the lion. "It is dangerous out here. Your parents understand that, and I think you do now."

"You talk? Are you going to eat me?" Rose felt tears rolling down her cheeks.

"Yes, I am Leb, king of the animals. I am not going to eat you, although there are plenty that would. You were lucky I was nearby and could tell them all you are under my protection."

"Why? I'm not special."

"Your father has welcomed the Pharoah Ramses generously into his home without knowing who he is and refusing payment. He has also professed loyalty to Ramses. I am also Ramses's liegeman, so Ramses entrusted the family's protection to me."

"How is it you speak like us, King Leb?"

"I was born immortal, with divine skills. I know what you want, too. You want to go to the pyramid."

"Yes. I need to see the world."

"The pyramid is a tomb guarded by spirits. Not all of them are friendly. Some things bring more trouble than their beauty is worth. Such things are better admired from afar. Gold and precious stones are like that, too, because greed makes some people do very bad things."

"I think I understand. I will think a lot about what you have told me. But at least I have had an adventure."

"Yes, you have. I will take you close to your home now as you have come very far. Never go into the desert without water. Get onto my back now and hold tight to my mane."

Leb lay down so that Rose could climb aboard. He ran faster than the wind, and Rose had to hold on very tight. When he stopped behind a large stone, Rose got off. When she walked around it, she could see her house. When she turned around to thank Leb, he had disappeared.

"I love you, Leb. Thank you for saving me," she called out anyway.

A distant roar answered.

She walked home, looking forward to a long, cold drink and a rest before lunch on the cool veranda. Her mother met her in the doorway.

"Where have you been, child? I've been worried."

"I took a walk, and when I sat down to take a rest, I fell asleep. I'm sorry." And she was. She resolved never to disobey her parents again.

"Silly girl. Don't you ever do that again. Have you never heard of scorpions and snakes? You come and help me with the lunch right now."

At least her mother gave her a cold drink.

"Leb good," murmured Rose before her eyes closed.

I switched off the tape. How much had she understood? Although it was a child's morality tale, I had enjoyed it.

"Agna, was that a true story?"

She laughed. "Heavens, no. But it's quite a good one. I'm going to find Lin."

"I'm ready to take a nap myself. I ate too much."

Before I dozed off, it occurred to me that I hadn't heard a word about the new Bay house. Was Hunter hiding it from Lin for some reason?

22

We all lived together like sardines. I didn't mind, and no one else seemed to. Auntie Peggy flabbergasted me the way she took things in her stride. I suppose she hadn't ever had much excitement in her life. She'd worked "for the government" until she retired but never spoke of it. After a few years living in the Washington area, I realized that people said that when they actually worked for one of the secret services. So maybe she had seen some action.

Rose, of course, thrived. We went for walks, rented movies, and played board games and cards. I'm pretty sure Lin cheated from time to time. I sometimes caught a little draft when I suspected her hand snaked out to pick up or drop off a card or token. Human eyes couldn't see it, but I caught Agna grinning at her whenever it happened. So, she wasn't a good loser. There were worse faults.

But when would we go down to the Bay again? I needed the sea breeze, the sound of the waves lapping the shore. Finally, I had enough privacy with Hunter to ask.

"I'm waiting for a few days when I can take her down and surprise her. I'll say I've had a letter from the association, and we have to do something about the site." He looked excited about the prospect.

"Soon, please, Hunter. I'm dying to go again."

So it happened one Saturday that Hunter announced at breakfast that he and Lin must go down to the Bay and arrange for the property to be cleared. Lin looked irritated and sulky. Bad memories.

It was a wrench saying goodbye. I wanted to go so badly. But Agna suggested we take Rose for a walk in Great Falls Park. Rose loved it, of course. A river, a waterfall, and Sam to trot alongside her. We even saw a line of horses trotting up a trail into the woods, their riders' calm demeanor impressive to one who had never sat on a horse. They looked scarily high off the ground.

Agna said, "I know you've felt left out since I've been here. I'm sorry about that. We are so delighted to have found another of our own kind; we can't get enough of each other."

"Oh, don't worry about it," I said. "I understand how lonely it can be to have to hide your true self from everyone. Lin and Hunter are very good to me, and I feel as though I have a loving family. They have been so kind taking Auntie in, too. I'd been worried about her living alone, even without the worry of COVID."

"Your aunt is a remarkable woman," said Agna. "She's like an ideal grandmother."

"Yes, she kept me straight after my mother died. I didn't know quite what to do or where to go. She took me in, and it didn't take long to feel much better about life. And then Lin came along."

It was getting close to dinnertime, and Rose was looking fretful, so we turned around and walked back to the car park.

"Rose hung'y, Mommy."

"Yes, darling, we'll soon be home. Dora's sure to have some lovely dinner for you."

Just as we were about to sit down for dinner, Lin and Hunter arrived back from their jaunt. I was relieved to see that Lin's eyes shone, and she looked happy.

"You liked it?" I asked, eager to hear her reaction.

"I love it!" she said. "And thanks for all the work you put into the furniture. I like what you did."

"Well, Margareta helped, too. We did it together."

Phew. Now perhaps we could get down there.

Rose wouldn't give us much privacy for recording anymore, so it was April before the three of us sat together in my basement living room, chatting and sipping coffee. Or rather, Agna and Lin chatted while I listened, my head turning from one to the other as if they were playing ping-pong. It was a nice break while Hunter took Rose out in her stroller.

Agna said, "And what about that poor sailor with the webbed feet?" And that was enough to send them into helpless laughter. It sounded like a harpist practicing arpeggios.

"Er, webbed feet?" I asked. "No, wait, I have a feeling I need the recorder for this."

Lin was the first to recover herself and tell the tale.

Tape 15, Volume 2

We were hiding in one of the lifeboats when a terrific storm blew up. Agna poked her head out of the cover to see how bad it was, and this sailor who was on his way up to the top deck saw her. He rushed down to grab her, so she turned him into a frog. We couldn't stop laughing.

They still couldn't stop laughing. Agna took up the story.

Only the wind was so high, it looked as if he'd be swept overboard because he was all tangled up in his ripped clothing and trapped in one of his shoes. Being a very nice sort of witch, I took pity on him and turned him back to his real self. Except he was naked now, and the spell didn't work on his feet. They were the right size and everything ... but webbed.

I wish I'd seen how he explained it all away. You should have seen him starting to run and tripping over what used to be his toes.

Agna broke in again.

And what about those two sailors seeking a little privacy? We changed our location from time to time, but the lifeboats were the best place to sleep when I needed to recharge. Both these men, no spring chickens, chose the lifeboat we were in for the same reason—they were furthest away from prying eyes. They slurred their words and fumbled the tarpaulins. Each time a hand or finger got under the tarpaulin, I stuck my nail into it, and the guy yelped, causing the other one to shush him with the subtlety of an angry asp.

Meanwhile, Lin had fished some pins out of her bag. She hissed loudly and stuck two of them into his hand, drawing blood. We watched him zigzag the length of the deck, gabbling about poisonous snakes, while his paramour stumbled after him as best he could. We decamped to a boat on the starboard side.

"All that laughing has made me peckish," said Lin.

"There's a cheesecake in the fridge upstairs," I said. "Agna, if I get it, will you tell us a good story?"

"Ah, I've got a real corker," she said. "I haven't even told you this one, Lin."

A corker? That was a new one, although the meaning was obvious. I found the cheesecake and put it on a plate. My first instinct was to cut three slices and take them down, but I thought better of it. I, for one, might want more. I put a big plate and knife, plus dessert plates and forks in a bag and carried it all downstairs together with the cake box. While setting it out, I suggested making more coffee, as I had supplies in my kitchenette.

All that accomplished, I set up the recorder with a new tape before we all tucked in.

"Let me ask you ladies something," I said. "You each arrived with two suitcases. Where did you hide them?"

"Oh, that was easy," Lin said. "The ship was carrying all kinds of electronic equipment. We simply pushed a few boxes forward and concealed them at the back."

"Of course," Agna added, "We caused a few people nasty surprises when we bumped them into their legs going down the gangway. I said, 'Sorry,' once, and that made a couple of people uneasy. The Brits are always saying sorry. I supposed I picked up the habit. Now it feels churlish not to do likewise."

They started laughing again.

Finally, we all had two slices of cheesecake and poured a third cup of coffee. The two of them sat back, sighing with contentment. I was happy Lin had found a true sister but a little jealous, too.

I moved to my seat at the small table where I kept the recorder and turned it on.

"Storytime?" I asked.

Agna closed her eyes and leaned back against the cushions. Lin sat almost rigid, her eyes fixed on her friend without blinking. A tableau of goddesses.

Agna said, "I'm ready to tell the story now." I hit record.

One day, while Tut—I'm going to use his nickname for simplicity—was taking a nap, I decided to explore the palace. The complex was huge and had obviously been extended several times—easy to do then, as buildings comprised a series of rectangles attached to one other, sometimes with the addition of a tower or two.

I walked a long way along stone paths skirting the outside walls. The vegetation seemed to have dried up by the time I reached a corner edifice, more of a cube than a rectangle, with a high wall around what must have been a small garden, judging by the palm tree canopies lining the space. I stopped when I thought I heard muffled sobbing through the slits in the tower. As I looked up, a tough old woman came storming out of a doorway cunningly disguised by alternating walls that didn't completely touch the wall.

"Get away, in the name of the Pharaoh!" she screeched. "I'll call the guards on you! What business have you here?"

"None, old mother," I said. "I was just taking a walk, exploring the palace. I am also in the Pharaoh's employ."

"Well, get out. Mind your own business."

She followed as I rounded the corner and watched as I walked quite a distance before losing myself in an orange grove.

Needless to say, I couldn't let it go. I rendered myself invisible and flew back. I didn't bother with doors and stairs, but willed myself inside the tower. There, I found a young girl sobbing on a low bed with feet carved in the likeness of crocodile heads. Before I could make myself known, the old woman burst into the room and slapped the poor girl's face.

"Be quiet, you stupid girl. There was someone snooping around outside, and I think she heard you. You know how angry Ay would be if I told him."

"I can't help it. I'm so lonely. And you shouldn't talk to me like that. I am Pharaoh!"

"Don't put on those airs and graces with me, miss! You are just an ordinary girl now and always will be. Be quiet, or I'll tell Ay."

The old woman stormed out of the room and slammed the door. The girl fell sideways and buried her head in a fat, red cushion, which muffled her cries.

Pharaoh? I vaguely remembered hearing about a seven-year-old girl whose father, Akhenaten, had declared her the next pharaoh to ensure the continuation of his dynasty. That was before Tut's time. After her father's death, she had disappeared before the official consecration.

Some said she died, but there was no public funeral. Others muttered about more sinister possibilities, but no one thought of her anymore after the two old pharaohs and now Tutankhamun. This girl, pasty and flabby on her commoner's bed, looked anything but regal.

I made myself visible. "Can I help you, my dear?" I asked.

She shot up and peered up at me with swollen, bloodshot eyes. "Who are you? How did you get past Gar?"

"I am advisor to Pharaoh Tutankhamun," I said. "I was exploring the palace and heard your cries. I have special powers, you see."

"We must whisper. I had a half-brother, Tutenkhaten. I am Nefereferuaten."

"He is now Tutankhamun, the Pharaoh. Why are you held here? What happened?"

"I was just a little girl when my father, Akhenaten, declared me his successor. I think he knew he was close to death, and he didn't trust Tut's mother. He had a horrid old cousin who protested that he should be the next pharaoh, but my father persisted. Dear Father."

She paused and turned away for a minute, taking a deep breath. She dug under a cushion and drew out a grubby white cloth that she used to dry her eyes and blow her nose.

"I'm sorry. It's just that I think I'll go mad sometimes; shut in here talking to no one except Gar. I don't know her real name, but Gar sounds ugly enough. Anyway, the month before my consecration, the old cousin said he would take me and my best friend to a secret place where he had a special plaything for us, a magic horse. He brought us here and locked us in. We cried for a long time, first because we were so afraid, and then when we got hungry and thirsty. Finally, Gar came in with a box of horrid food. We pleaded with her to let us out, but she just laughed." She unclenched her fists and started unravelling an edge of the cloth.

"You poor things," I said. "Where is your friend?"

"We tried to keep track of the days for a while but got discouraged and didn't see the point anymore. I think it was after about three years that she got sick one day, getting paler and hotter until she couldn't sit up or talk anymore. That's when I met the man, Ay. He came in with Gar and looked at her. I asked for a doctor. He laughed and said I was never to ask for anything, not ever. He picked up my friend and carried her away. I never saw her again. I suppose she died. I've been alone ever since."

I was really angry by this time. "How do you pass the time?" I asked.

"I sleep a lot. Sometimes Gar lets me into the garden. I like that. There's a pond with big golden fish and some flowers and trees where birds nest sometimes." Her face almost allowed a smile. "So much nicer than up here. I am forbidden to make any noise outside, which used to be hard when there were two of us. Now it's easy. But she's spiteful. I don't get out there every day. And more and more often, only at night. That scares me. I've seen snakes there in the twilight, and scorpions, too."

My heart bled for this girl. And the situation was perplexing. Why hadn't she been killed? It would have been easily covered up, and it's not as though that was the first time Ay had disposed of someone he deemed inconvenient.

"I suppose you have never had a tutor," I said.

"Oh, yes, Father had me and my brothers tutored. We could all read and write and add numbers by the time we turned six. I was given papyrus and writing tools, which is what stopped me from going completely mad. I have to show Gar what I have written. She takes my poems about the trees, the birds, and the flowers and burns them. But I secretly write a daily journal, which she has never found. Someday, people will know of my tragedy."

"I will try to help you get out of here," I said.

This time, a real smile lit up her face, making her look quite pretty.

"But you will never be Pharaoh," I said. "If I find you a home, it will be modest. And you must promise never to breathe a word of your true identity."

"I promise." The joy on her face was heartbreaking. Could I trust her to be discreet? I couldn't risk my boy's reign. And if Ay learned of her whereabouts, she would die.

"You understand that if Ay were to find you, he would have you killed?"

She shivered. "Yes, he's wicked. I don't know how he knew the old cousin, but he carried on his work."

"Your father's cousin probably paid him. And if it's any comfort, he's been dead awhile, and I suspect Ay had a hand in it."

"My father did have a witch cast a spell on me to protect me from harm. But look at me; it didn't work."

"I think it did. You are still alive, after all. The spell probably only concerned physical harm."

"Oh. I hadn't thought of that."

"I have to go now. I'll think of something."

She sat motionless while telling her story, all the stuffing knocked out of her. Suddenly, she stood and took my hand. "Thank you, thank you."

I patted her shoulder, became invisible once more, and flew back to the royal quarters. I had a lot of thinking to do. That girl could not be allowed to disrupt my boy's reign. And what could I do with her that assured both her safety and her silence? If I placed her as a servant, she would soon disdain her circumstances as beneath her. She was not fit to be highly placed. Marriage? Maybe that would be the best route.

Tut was awake and grumpy when I got back. "Where were you? I needed help with this document." He gestured at what looked like a substantial scroll on his writing table.

"What is it?" I asked. Ay usually took care of all written communications.

"I don't know. It's too big. I don't feel like reading it."

"You are the Pharaoh. You must learn to take care of Egypt's affairs."

"Yes, yes," he sighed dramatically.

I opened the scroll and started reading, a laborious process, as my skills in hieroglyphics were not that strong. It was a proclamation of regency and succession. Ay was to remain regent until Tut turned twenty-five. And he would become Pharaoh if Tut died without issue. Even if the boy had issue, I doubted their chances of survival. Tut's marriage was set for a few months from now, which was why Ay had presented his claim.

"Don't sign it," I said, explaining the contents. "Ay is an impatient man."

That led to quite a row once Ay came to collect the scroll, expecting it to be the end of the matter.

"Is this her doing?" he shouted, pointing at me.

"I am Pharaoh. I make my own decisions," Tut declared, nose in the air.

"She has her hand in everything you've ever done, which is not that much when I think about it. Everything achieved in your reign has been thanks to me. Me! You hear?"

That caused Tut to fly into an almost laughable ball of fury, given his high voice and incoherence and Ay's deep bass and cutting comments, which cut even deeper for their truth. But Ay left without the signature he craved. I feared for my boy.

We ate dinner in near silence that evening.

"I should have a taster," Tut said suddenly.

"Good idea."

I had to find Nef—I simply cannot say her full name all the time—a husband. A kind husband who would treat her well because she deserved a good life. She must have been about eighteen then, really late to marry in those days, so an older man. A widow with children, perhaps. A good family.

I started to mingle with the courtiers more than before. They didn't bother to attend Tut because he was too young, so I suppose it was really Ay's court. Ay never socialized with them either, though. I found the social pretensions as annoying as they are today in certain circles, but I was on a mission. I'd been back to see Nef several times and had explained my solution, to which she agreed at once. But not before asking what it meant to be married. I explained. She only said that she'd seen her father doing that to one of the servants once and that he was making funny faces, but she seemed to like it. After imparting a few more details to tie up loose ends, I left.

One day, a couple of courtiers were talking about a young man who was arranging to visit his father for a while. His mother had died the previous year, and there were still young children at home. He wanted to help his father find a wife. I sidled up to them and asked about the young man's whereabouts. I soon ran him down in his quarters.

Asim was a nice chap, polite and well-spoken.

"I'm sorry to hear you will be leaving us," I said. "You will be missed."

He blushed. "I must help my father. There are still three young ones at home. He has someone to clean and cook, but he has a very responsible job. He needs a wife."

"Oh, what is his position?" I asked.

"He is scribe to the governor of Thebes."

"I think I have just the lady for you. She is of noble birth but was orphaned and imprisoned by a greedy uncle who used her inheritance. I recently assisted her escape. She needs good food and exercise, and, most of all, company. She is very agreeable to marriage to a kind man."

"This sounds very interesting," he said, intrigued. "Is she pretty?"

"She will be. She has been shut in a tower for ten years and needs the sun, although not too much. She is a delightful lady who deserves a good life and will be grateful for it. How long will the journey take you?"

"At least a month, depending on the availability of river pilots."

"Enough time for her to regain her strength. I will reward you well." I named a sum that would pay for his journey and more.

"I leave tomorrow morning at dawn. Can you have her here before then?"

"Not here. Where will the barge be moored?"

We struck an agreement. I would meet Asim at the dock with Nef and a bag of coins.

I went straight back to my rooms. Mercifully, Tut was sound asleep. I had a long hooded cloak Nef could wear to hide her identity. Several hours later, I flew to Nef with the cloak and a good portion of my savings in a silk bag.

"Wake up," I whispered, holding my hand across her mouth. "We're leaving."

She was scared at first but soon rallied and donned the cloak.

"I must take my journal," she said.

"No, if anyone finds it and betrays you, it will mean your doom. Where is it? I'll hide it somewhere safe. That part of your life is over, gone, finished. You will start afresh today."

She dragged a few thin rolls of papyrus from a loose stone under the window opening and handed them to me.

"Please, a safe place. I want someone to know, even if I'm long gone."

"I promise. Now, we must go. The man's daughter will take you to your new husband. The journey will take at least a month. You must get healthy and strong. Walk when you can. Eat well. At least you have pale skin, the mark of an aristocrat. He will like that, so protect your complexion. Now, be brave. We are going to fly."

I hoisted her up, and off we went. To her credit, she only squealed once. It took mere minutes to get to the dock, where oarsmen were already helping load the barge. Where was Asim? He arrived after a half-hour or so, during which time I could hardly conceal my anxiety. I handed off Nef and the money and watched them board. Nef kept her eyes downcast and didn't say a word. "Asim" means protector, which I took as a good omen. I didn't wait for the departure, as I had to conceal Nef's journal.

First, I went back to the palace to find a protective covering for the papyrus. I found some tight-woven cloth in which I'd kept sweetmeats for some time. I stuffed the last one in my mouth before wrapping up the treasure. Then off again to some caves not far to the south. I selected one that looked like it went deep into the rocky cliff, hoping I wouldn't come across any territorial wildlife. I was too tired for a fight and only had just enough juice left to get home.

Loud snoring and a pungent scent sent me back to the surface. No, couldn't take that on. I had better luck in the next one, inhabited only by a couple of mating asps that were too befuddled and tangled to react quickly to an invisible threat. There were plenty of loose stones in the back of the cave, and I was able to pluck plenty from their resting place and rearrange them to form a little hole for the journal. The place was dry as dry could be, so it should still be there. I have often wondered who will find it.

A few months later, Asim returned. The first time I saw him at a gathering, I managed to take him aside. He reported that Nef (she'd changed her name to Ama) had become healthy and happy during the journey—a journey which most young women would have complained bitterly about—and his father had been pleased. His young siblings had taken to her after a brief spate of resentment because she was to replace their mother. She had told them all about her incarceration and that she would need help taking care of a household, as she had never learned how. The oldest daughter, not much younger than her, had liked that, and they quickly became close. His father was happy, so Asim was happy. And she sent her love and undying thanks to me, her savior.

So that's my story of the female pharaoh who became the wife of a provincial scribe.

"Wow! And no one but us knows the real truth," I said, awed by this privilege. "Did you hear about any repercussions?"

"I did go back to the tower the next morning. I heard the old woman wailing and Ay roaring. Then, sudden silence. Of course, she had to be silenced. But I couldn't feel sorry for her after the way she'd treated poor Nef. She must have realized what would happen if Nef died, for example. Ay was certainly in a fouler mood than usual in the days that followed. He drowned his sorrows in strong drink and flogged a myriad of slave girls and boys, often savagely."

"Why didn't you kill him?" I asked.

"Lin asked me the same thing. And I almost did after Tut died. I didn't because he had surrounded himself with men like him, so things probably wouldn't have been any better. And Tut was not yet ready to rule. The fact is that Ay reformed Egypt after a long period of stagnation and established many good bureaucratic structures and important alliances that survived him for centuries. But he was never happy. Did Lin tell you about the spell I cast on him?"

"Yes, she did. Rashes and boils."

"He scratched for the rest of his life," Agna said with obvious satisfaction. "And he couldn't have sex anymore, either."

How odd it felt to be the keeper of such a secret. "Maybe we should go and find that journal one day," I said.

"And how would you explain knowing where it was?" asked Agna. "Tell people a witch told you?"

"Yes, I see your point," I said, crestfallen.

Lin sprang up and cleared up the plates. "Come on, it's nearly lunchtime."

I trailed behind them, feeling a little stiff. I'd been sitting almost motionless for an hour, as had we all. I don't know if I'd use the word "spellbound" in my writing because it's rather trite, but it certainly describes my state during Agna's revelations.

23

Agna stayed with us for months, which kept Lin too occupied to resume our sessions. The house was so full that Hunter and I didn't have much time for ourselves, but he managed to visit occasionally. Lin and Agna went out a lot; I'm not sure where. They laughed and sang and often played with Rose.

We all went to the Bay often, where Rose delighted in the sand and water. Hunter liked nothing better than to watch her. He taught her to swim, too, and Sven helped her along when he wasn't studying. She was a strong little girl whose speech progressed by leaps and bounds. I had to warn people to be careful about what they said in front of her—she was like a sponge, soaking up anything that was said with emphasis—which was usually embarrassing.

The weeks passed by, becoming monotonous. I couldn't help feeling left out of things. Lin used to take me when she went shopping. I missed our morning sessions.

Margareta and Sven both received good grades in their final exams. Margareta had received early acceptance to Duke, and Sven was finishing his freshman year at MIT online. No prom for Margareta, which probably didn't bother her much as she was a couple of years older than the other kids. And no real settling into college life for Sven. It was a rough go for so many people for so many reasons.

I wondered when Rose could make friends. She was around adults all the time, which was great for the love and attention she received, her vocabulary development, and her good nature. But she should develop social skills with her own age group, too.

Chapter 23

One morning, I remembered some questions I'd written at the back of my notebook to ask Lin. Maybe it was time to bring them up.

I waited for a moment when I had her alone, or at least with only Agna present. It was a Sunday morning after breakfast. Even though the stock market was closed, Hunter was in his study because he liked to read Rose stories on his sofa, where she'd nestle under his arm to see the pictures. Auntie was in the kitchen helping Dora make a couple of peach pies.

"Lin, we haven't had any sessions for months. I feel as if I'm not earning my keep."

"Oh, never mind that," Lin said. "You're family now. We'll get to it."

"Well, I pulled out my notebook the other day and remembered I had written down some questions to ask you." I'd been sitting on said notebook and retrieved it.

"Fire away."

"Near the end of the recording about Margareta's abduction, you remarked about an unhappy memory to do with the Tower of London."

"Yes, that's a sad one."

"Then there was that stabbing you said you witnessed here in Salton. How did that end up?"

"Nothing much there, as I didn't look into any details. Joe would know all about it as he was involved, but he can't know about these tapes."

"Okay. I was wondering if you did anything exciting during the two world wars."

"I was in London during the Great War, and Hunter was still young. We were in Texas during the Second World War. There was an incident there, but to my annoyance, I missed it. It might have been exciting."

"Texas? What on earth could happen in Texas?"

"In the early forties, the government started to build a lot of munitions factories in Texas, and warships at Galveston, too. Lots of spies came to the U.S. to look for information, but they tended to be undertrained and usually managed to bungle their assignments. This one was a real loser. I noticed him one day, walking around town, taking photos of just about everything, including the signposts. Talk about subtle."

Agna jumped in. "I did a lot during World War II in Egypt. Would you like to hear about it?"

"Of course, I would," I said, happy to have the extra input.

"Anything else?" Lin asked.

"If Agna is willing, I'd love to hear how she escaped Ragnarok and where she went for all those years. And how she ended up in Egypt. Speaking of Ragnarok, you mentioned that Baldur's death led to the final battle, but you didn't go into how he died. I gather Loki was involved, but I was curious to know how it all happened."

"Well, that's all going to end up the size of an encyclopedia." Agna thought for a moment. "But I can break it down into small segments. You've heard a lot of the Egypt stories, so I won't go into any particular exploits, just what happened during Ragnarok and the places I've been. I'll let Lin tell you about the death of Baldur, as he was the son of her lady Frigg."

"That sounds wonderful," I said, excited to hear more stories. "I think that will give me enough for a second volume. Let's start with the Tower of London."

We arranged to meet the next day during Rose's nap. Even if I asked someone to keep her occupied for a while, she always ended up coming downstairs to see what was going on. Naptime was easier, as she slept deeply for two hours after lunch every day.

Tape 16, Volume 2

Hunter and I were taking a break from each other after a terrible fight. He was getting very boring in his paranoia about not drawing attention to ourselves. First of all, he's too big and handsome to go unremarked, and as for me, well, need I say more? I turn heads wherever I go.

Anyway, Henry VIII was on the throne at the time. He'd been such a handsome young man, but a life of excess had him well on his way to being a fat pig with bad indigestion, leg ulcers, and a terrible temper. Everyone complained of his bad breath, too. He was by no means stupid, but belief in his semi-divine persona led him to indulge in sudden whims rather than consider the advice of his cabinet and take measured action.

I had attended court several times in the company of a peer of the realm who turned out to be a lot less vigorous than I would have liked. And I didn't like the way His Majesty eyed me whenever he caught sight of me. I always stayed at the back of the throng, behind a pillar if possible, because I knew the King's reputation and didn't want any part of it. The very thought of being with him nauseated me.

I was attending a soiree at the earl's mansion one evening, endeavoring to keep at least one room between me and his wife, when I spotted this very attractive man standing alone in a corner. His face looked as if he'd just come from a funeral. He clasped a goblet of wine in one fist and rested the other on the hilt of his sword. I caught an air of contempt in the way he surveyed the room. Definitely not a courtier. I decided it was my duty to cheer him up.

"Good evening," I said. "I am the Lady Lin Thoren."

"Madame," he replied with a curt bow. "I am Peter Longtree, Keeper of the Ravens at the Tower of London."

"My, how fascinating," I cooed. "What does that involve?"

He went into a lengthy description of his duties that I won't bore you with—not that I remember much of it after all these years. His eyes lit up, and his whole body relaxed when he spoke of the ravens. A man with a passion.

"And where is your good lady?" I asked, hoping there wasn't one.

"I have never married. First, I served many years in the King's army, and now I am a Yeoman of the Guard at the Tower. There are often important prisoners kept in the Tower, so we need to be ready for anything."

"What brings you here? You don't seem to enjoy the company."

"The earl wants to keep ravens himself. He hopes to persuade me to join his household. I do not plan to do so. It would only take one word to the King to put me in danger of losing my head. He's always concerned about his ravens. You know the legend, I suppose?"

"No, actually, I don't. I've traveled widely for many years and am not yet *au courant*."

"It is said that if the ravens leave the Tower of London, the kingdom will fall."

"I can see why His Majesty wants his birds safe and well."

I went home with Peter that night. I left first after bidding the countess *adieu*. Her icy tone belied her stated wish that I visit again very soon. I did not see Peter slip out, but he joined me in my carriage after about ten minutes. I'd asked the liveryman to wait by the horse for a tall man in a long green jacket.

We could hardly go to my rooms provided by the earl, as he would be sure to come looking for me later. Fortunately, Peter had an apartment to himself near the birdcages, so we had privacy. The other Yeomen were obliged to share rooms. We had to be discreet, though, as visitors to the private quarters were prohibited.

I mostly came and went at night to avoid prying eyes. If I wanted to go out during the day, I either ran very fast so as not to be seen or carried a basket of dirty washing as if I were a laundrymaid. I found that demeaning.

This went on for months, and I got tired of being restricted. I heard the earl had put the word about that he should be notified the moment I was seen. His wife came from a powerful family, so he couldn't be too loud about it, but his pride had been injured. He hadn't minded parading me at court—to proclaim his manly virtues, I think. He always lectured me on the subject of court etiquette before each appearance and inspected what I planned to wear. Sometimes he ordered dresses without even consulting me.

Thankfully, he didn't know I had left with Peter, who had been able to let him down gently about being his personal raven keeper by declaring loyalty to the Crown; he was sure the earl would not want to anger His Majesty. The earl, although disappointed, agreed that it was never wise to cross the King. People had lost their heads for less.

Peter was a stern man by nature, although gentle with me and his birds. A good man, he was quite well-read for the times—remember, books were costly then. He had plenty to talk about and entertained me with all sorts of legends about the Tower. I don't remember them anymore. It's been several hundred years, after all.

One summer evening, he was due to take part in one of their military exercises. I decided to go and watch. There was a rampart from which I could see everything and remain hidden from view. The men were milling around, chatting while waiting for their officer to arrive, when I heard a piercing scream. Two rough-looking fellows emerged from a side door carrying a scrawny woman, whom they dropped in the dirt so one of them could lock up. She convulsed and screamed again. I stared at her, unable to believe what I saw. Her clothing was thin and mostly torn away from her body. What repulsed me was that I could see the ball ends of her arm and leg bones protruding from her shoulders and hips. As she sprawled on the dirt, her limbs lay completely awry, her joints no longer functional. Her shins lay at odd angles, with ankles backwards. The lay of her arms and hands was all wrong, too. Her grey face stared up at the setting sun as she moaned, a low, guttural purr from deep in her chest.

The rack. I'd heard about it, and here was the broken horror it produced.

'Be quiet, you," growled one of the men. "It's off to Smithfield for you and an end to your misery."

They hoisted her up, one holding her under the armpits, the other by her ankles. The agony roused the woman to another howl, at which the man holding her ankles twisted them until she fainted. I don't know how she lived through that pain. They threw her into the cart as if she were no more than a sack of cabbages.

Although some of the yeomen spared her a pitying glance, most ignored the woman's plight entirely and carried on with their banter. One of those was Peter.

I waited until the cart taking that poor creature was out of sight. I thought of following, but there was no point unless I wanted to subject myself to the horror of watching her being dragged out to the stake and burned alive.

I collected my possessions and left well before Peter returned. No more men, I vowed. Well, I'd said that before and would no doubt say it again.

"That's gruesome," I said. "I've heard of the rack, of course. Who hasn't? But I've never thought about the outcome too much. How can people do that to another human being?"

Lin said, "Life was pretty brutal in those days, and there wasn't much empathy spared for the pain of others. But even today, there are always those who are not averse to inflicting torture, and there are certainly those who enjoy it."

"Yes, of course, you are right."

Lin lay back again. It seemed she wasn't through.

I had to get out of England once more. The earl had his spies everywhere, and Peter probably wasn't best pleased with me, either. But where could I go? And where was Hunter? I was beginning to miss him. It wasn't that far off the time of our rebirth, either. Neither of us could manage it on our own. Only about ten years to go. So, where? I thought of France, as it was nearest. But Henry frequently sent troops over there to conquer land for England. And Toulouse had been in a state of unrest for years. Avignon was a temptation, but the memories of my dead children, Jean and Marie, would make me too melancholy. I didn't want to go north. I was no longer accustomed to cold weather for so much of the year, and those Nordic kings were constantly fighting with each other. I was so sick of war. Spain was dangerous with its relentless execution of heretics, too. I could overcome any attempt to execute me, but I was tired of all that. When humans and gods lost their moral compass, our world and most of the gods were destroyed. I wondered how much longer this lot would survive.

Maybe a little farther north, but not much. I'd heard about Bruges, a nice old city where things were relatively quiet. Maybe I'd give that a try.

I got passage to France on a merchant ship. I still had plenty of money, thanks to Hunter's financial acumen and my making sure I absconded with a good portion of it after our row. Would he ever try to seek me out? What if it was over? I admonished myself to stop thinking that way. He was probably as lonely as I was, however many people he surrounded himself with.

Needless to say, the few men on board all tried it on, but I only had to throw one overboard. The captain had no idea what had happened to him. Who would suspect a delicate little thing like me? Anyway, we docked at Calais. I started to walk. I still spoke French fairly well, so I got the occasional ride on a donkey cart and one good long ride in a gentleman's carriage. He, of course, expected payment in kind. I left him clutching himself and almost weeping while the coachman tried vainly to stifle his laughter. I ran so they couldn't see me any longer. They no doubt thought I'd run into the woods that bordered the road, as I couldn't possibly have run out of sight that quickly.

I ran through the next town as I knew the carriage would stop there and inquire after me. I soon came to a poor village, where I found several peasant women washing their linen by the riverside. I wished them a good day and asked where I could find a bed for the night. They regarded me with the usual suspicion of peasants. I told them I was following my husband, who had departed for Bruges some weeks earlier. I hired a carriage, and the driver put me out and made off with all my worldly goods. I still had a few coins and some things in the small bag I held, enough to pay for dinner and a bed.

"You'd better come with me, then," said the oldest. "My name is Celine." She looked grim and humorless, but a bed would be welcome. Autumn was drawing in, and I was no longer accustomed to the cold. I could deal with it, of course, but I didn't want to.

I followed Celine to her stone dwelling, just one large room. The wide glowing fireplace with its hanging cauldron served as her kitchen. Two wooden platforms with fur covers stood against one wall, and a rough table with two chairs graced the center of the room. It felt colder in there than outside and damp, too. But those fur covers would help. She lit the candle on the table, as the house had no windows.

"My husband died last month in that one," Celine said, waving her arm in the direction of one of the platforms. "You can sleep there."

"Thank you, you are most kind," I said with forced courtesy. I rummaged in my bodice and produced a few sous. "I hope this will suffice."

She looked at them, bit them, and transferred them to her own bodice, which was already under considerable strain given her girth. "Unh."

Celine took two bowls off a shelf next to the fireplace and set them on the hearth before ladling a portion of stew into each. She broke two portions of bread off a loaf in a covered basket and added them to the bowls. She put them on the table and went back to the shelf for two spoons. The shelf was now bare. The stew was surprisingly tasty due more to the herbs she'd added than the other mystery ingredients. I found a couple of small pieces of meat amongst the greens, possibly rabbit.

I thanked Celine and complimented her on her cooking skills. She almost smiled. I could tell that night had fallen outside because the room's dark corners had disappeared into the gloom.

"We rise early, so we sleep early," the old woman said. "Besides, candles are costly."

I went to the platform she had indicated and got under the cover, fully clothed. I closed my eyes, but not all the way, as I wanted to watch her. She removed her outer garments and quietly turned one of the kitchen chairs to face me. She drew her bed cover around her shoulders and sat wrapped in fur, watching me intently. Did she fear I meant her harm? She had nothing worth stealing. She wanted to rob me.

I waited a while before starting to snore gently. She laid the fur on her bed and tiptoed over to stand over me. I felt her hand reach into my bodice. When I grabbed her wrist, she squealed.

"No, no, sorry. I was just making sure you were all right. Let me go."

"Celine, Celine. This is not nice. I have paid you. If it wasn't enough, you had only to ask."

"Everything is so expensive. We are poor. You say you lost everything, but you still have coin. I need it more."

"You are a Christian, are you not, Celine?"

"Yes." She crossed herself.

"What would Jesus say?"

I let go of her wrist, and she ran weeping to her bed. I wriggled around to try to get comfortable on the old straw-filled pallet before I slept and dreamed. In the morning, I heard Celine moving around but didn't feel like emerging from the warm bed. After a while, I felt her by my side.

"Eat."

I joined her at the table, where the same bowls, wiped out after dinner the night before, contained a thin gruel. After we'd finished, I thanked her, picked up my bag, and went to the door. Before opening it, I retrieved another coin—a gold one this time.

"Here, Celine. This is for giving shelter to a woman alone in the world."

She gasped in disbelief. She wept again. I left, feeling quite the moralizer.

I ran until I was out of the village and well down the road. I came to a signpost for the next town. There, I discovered that Bruges was only a two-hour journey by carriage—and managed to get a ride with a courier. He didn't ask for much, and I was relieved that he looked too old and run down to give me much trouble.

Soon, there I was in Bruges. I didn't look so good by this time but managed to find a hotel that offered a private room. The poor maid carried upstairs many pails of hot water for my bath.

I slipped her some coins. "Our secret," I said.

She gasped and bobbed a curtsey.

I lay in the bath and cleaned myself thoroughly with a cake of rose-scented soap from my bag. I put on a fresh gown.

When the maid returned, I gave her the dirty ones to be laundered. She washed them in my bathwater before pouring it out of the window, pailful by pailful, incurring some powerful cursing from below.

"I'll rinse them out in the river," she assured me cheerfully. I thought I knew how she'd deal with the chamber pot.

Now I had to decide what to do next. A job? A rich lover? First, I would explore the city. It was a beautiful place with well-built, pretty houses and a magnificent cathedral. After a few hours, I wanted to get something to eat. I found a café on one of the side streets, but it was full of men. Perhaps it wasn't common for women to eat alone. Judging by the looks on their faces when I entered, it wasn't. But the proprietor grudgingly brought me a plate of meat and greens, which he slammed down on the table so hard it splashed my dress. I shot him a glare, which he met without flinching before stomping off. They probably thought I was a whore.

Afterwards, I resumed my tour. People on the streets looked mostly cheerful, and there were plenty of groups chatting and laughing. It started to rain. I ducked into the nearest church before getting soaked through, with the intent of sitting quietly in a pew. To my surprise, the church was full of nuns and poor wretches on makeshift beds who seemed to be on their last legs.

"Can I help you?" asked a young nun with a face more angelic than those of the cherubs that adorned the ceiling.

"I just came in out of the rain. What is this place?"

"It is The Church of Our Lady Bruges," she said. "Here we care for the dying who have no one to care for them and no roof over their heads. But you are most welcome to rest." She pointed me to a pew in a quiet corner.

I sat and watched the nuns at work, soothing the fretful, cleaning wounds, and wrapping those who had passed over. They seemed to have a couple of men on call who removed the corpses after prayers were said by a priest who emerged from a side chapel when called. The same men brought in new patients—at least five during the few hours I spent there. I noticed that many patients were oriented to face a vast painting of Jesus on the cross. They seemed to pray in that direction but with their eyes open. I supposed they drew comfort from knowing that Jesus also suffered pain.

Others faced the altar, where a moving statue of Mary and her infant stood, only a little smaller than life-size. I found out later it was the only Michelangelo work outside Italy at the time, originally intended for Siena's cathedral. After a dispute, two wealthy Bruges merchants bought it for this church.

I marveled at the selfless toil of the nuns, their patience and love for this mass of destitute beings whom society had tossed aside.

I had to do something. Would I work with the nuns? No, didn't fancy that. But they must need money for food, medicine, and bandages.

I went over to the young nun who had welcomed me and gave her a couple of gold coins.

"Go with God," she said, her delight a stark contrast to the plight of the poor creature who gasped for air beside her. "In a while, I will give this to the Mother Superior. But first, I must help Pierre pass to his rest."

No more than a minute later, Pierre passed after a sort of gasp and rattling in his lungs before his chest lay still.

I left and ran back to the hotel. I must start a business, I thought. But what?

"That's enough for today," Lin said. "Next time, I'll tell you how I helped those nuns and found Hunter."

"After that, why don't we do Baldur, and then we can go on to Agna's escape and life until Egypt? Next, her war stories," I said.

"Let's just do it once a week," Lin said. "Monday afternoons. Is that all right with you, Agna?"

"Of course," said the witch. "I'm delighted to be in your book."

I was pleased, too. I'd been bored lately, a little left out.

Lin came down by herself the next week. She seemed a little edgy, fiddling with her sleeve, putting down her coffee cup, and picking it up again.

"What's the matter?" I asked.

"I'm not sure how you're going to take this next part," she said. "I was involved in something you people would shame me for."

You people? "If I've learned anything these past couple of years, it's not to be judgmental, to know that different cultures have different approaches to things. Don't ever worry about me."

She flashed her brilliant smile my way and settled herself on the sofa.

Tape 17,
Volume 2

Depressed by my encounter with the destitute dying, I trudged upstairs to my room. Michelle was there, sweeping the floor. She must have been waiting for me because she put down the broom at once, eyes sparkling and an eager smile breaking through.

"You cannot imagine what has happened."

"No, indeed I cannot." I found her excitement amusing.

"There is a brothel in town, right behind The Church of Our Lady of Bruges. The madame there is—was—said to be cruel to her girls, not feeding them enough and whipping them if they displeased her. Well, she was found dead by her maid this morning with a knife in her back. There are no clues anywhere to suggest who did it, even though they have searched the place. I expect it was one of the girls. I hope they don't torture them to find out."

An angry bellow from downstairs summoned Michelle back to her work. She winked at me and scurried out, carrying her broom like a pikestaff.

I lay on my bed, thinking about this news. Who owned that brothel? The madame? Who would run it now? The more I thought about it, the more I wondered if this might be the opportunity I needed. I didn't have too many scruples about the girls. They would likely be from poor families and would have been half-starved if left to their familial home or married off to some brutish fellow. Plaything or broodmare were their only options.

I got up and found my clean clothes folded on the table under the window. I should look respectable if I were to change my circumstances.

I ran back to the church and circled around it. I found a big stone house at the back with a crowd of girls hustled in a cluster outside, clutching their belongings tied up in cloth. A skinny man with a large nose and pot belly stood on the front steps, yelling at them.

"Got away, you miserable whores! Go!"

I approached him. "What is happening?" I asked.

"I own this house. The woman who rented it is dead. She owes me money. I will keep everything she left behind. It is my right. What is it to you, woman?"

"Do you still want to rent it? I am looking for a house. I only recently arrived in Bruges."

He looked me up and down. "I doubt you can afford it."

"You must excuse my appearance. I have been travelling for days. My driver pushed me out of the carriage some distance away and drove off with my chests. Fortunately, I had my coin safe around my person. How much?"

He gave me two prices—one for an empty house and one with the contents.

I asked to see inside. The reception rooms and small "entertainment" rooms were gaudy with their red velvet curtains and chairs, as were the madame's set of rooms, but the rest of the house was pretty squalid.

"The condition of the house is terrible. The furniture is not to my taste, but I need somewhere to eat and sleep for the time being until I can get things straight." I offered him one rate for three months, at which time he was welcome to take back all the furniture, and a lower rate for two years, effective immediately. He wavered, thought about his problem being solved without delay, and nodded. He stuck out his hand.

I shook it, knowing full well what he meant.

"Where is your coin?" he asked in an unpleasant tone.

"You will get it as soon as I have the agreement in writing."

His face took on an ugly look. "I will not waste my money on notaries."

"I will pay for the notary. Let us go there at once."

Only somewhat mollified, he locked the door and led me a few streets away to a dark basement office where an ancient, who looked more gnome than man, scribbled on parchment with a quill.

"Greetings, Monsieur Fernon," the gnome said, half rising from his stool.

"This woman wants to rent my house."

"I suppose you mean the brothel? I heard of the sad demise of Madame Pontine."

"She gave shelter to poor orphan girls. I would never allow a brothel on my property," Monsieur Fernon said in feeble protest.

"*Pardon*, of course not."

I broke in and described the terms before my prospective landlord could try to change them. The document was soon written twice and signed by all of us. I turned away and retrieved several gold coins from my cleavage. "This is for the first six months. I will pay monthly thereafter."

My landlord looked more cheerful once he clutched his rent.

"The keys, please."

He handed over two large iron keys, which I tucked into my bag with the rolled parchment lease agreement. I excused myself and left, hoping to find at least some of the girls still there.

They were all still there. I stood and stared at them. There were seven of them, all pretty except one, all too thin and too pale.

One approached me nervously, her greasy, almost black hair draped around her face like curtains. She dropped a curtsey.

"What is your name?" I asked.

"Katia, madame. We have nowhere to go. Our families sold us to Madame Pontine. They won't want us back. Can you help?"

"Everyone get back inside," I called and ran up the steps to open the door. The girls followed with happy squeals. I turned into the main salon.

"Sit down." I waited until they had settled down. "I own the business now. We are going to close for one week. Is there a maid?"

"Me," said the plain girl, her pudgy face finally showing animation. "I have to do everything."

"Well, that has to change. This is a big house. I will find a cook and a washerwoman. Will you girls help clean the whole house? The parts not used by the clients are dirty. I want this to be a nice place to live for all of us. With good food, too."

"Yes, oh yes," they chorused.

"I am new to Bruges. Do you know where I can buy furniture?"

There was apparently a workshop not far away with a large supply. I would visit that very day.

"I will stay in what were Madame's rooms. I don't like the furniture there or in the client areas, but it will have to do for now. Is there food in the house?"

"Yes, Madame," said the maid. "I am Aimée. There is one cupboard for Madame and one for the rest of us."

"Show me."

The two of us went downstairs to the kitchen, which was none too clean. I peered out the window to the yard beyond, bare but for a well and a chicken coop where a few birds lolled around, listless and probably unproductive.

Madame's cupboard yielded a good supply of beef, vegetables, and sweetmeats, the other little more than bread and moldy cheese. I gave Aimée instructions to prepare a meal for us all, using the contents of Madame's cupboard before making my way upstairs again. I told the girls that dinner would be ready in an hour or so and suggested they start cleaning while I went to the furniture maker. I rooted around in Madame Pontine's desk to find a good sheet of paper, upon which I wrote a notice saying that the house would be closed until the following Saturday. I told one of the girls to nail it to the front door. I needed to retrieve my meager belongings from the hotel and give my notice there, too.

The week passed in a frenzy of activity for all of us. The girls alternated shopping and helping Aimée with the housework and cooking. I had a quick word with Michelle at the hotel, telling her I needed a cook, a maid for the rough work, and a washerwoman, which she sent me surprisingly quickly. The washerwoman would collect our dirties every Monday and bring them back a few days later, dry and ironed. The cook was willing but mediocre. Aimée was actually the better qualified of the two. I suggested to the cook that they share the duties to lighten the load. She agreed readily. The maid scrubbed floors and everything else with satisfying vigor.

I ordered furniture for the private quarters—beds with fresh pallets, some chests, chairs, and tables. Michelle told me about a small house where a widow had recently died, and the contents were for sale—solid country furnishings and good linens. I bought it all, mostly for my rooms. Soon we would have a comfortable home, and the girls were well fed and happy. It was time to reopen.

That Saturday, I removed the notice at noon. The girls had warned me that some gentlemen enjoyed "love in the afternoon," as they put it.

I bought myself some new gowns. Formal, but ladylike. The salon would have a new ambiance. I'd gone over the books carefully, so I knew what to charge and the peccadillos of some of the regular clientele. We needed to bring in money. My supply of gold coins was running dangerously low.

When the bell by the front door jangled, Aimée ran to open it in her new dress, cap, and apron. She showed a couple of gentlemen into the salon, withdrawing to stand in a corner near the door.

"And you are?" asked one of them, a rather bloated gentleman with a goatee. I extended my hand to him, then his swarthy companion, who remained silent.

"I am the new proprietor, Madame Lin Thierry. Welcome. Would you care for champagne?"

We sat and chatted over our sparkling cut-glass flutes. I ascertained that one preferred Katia and the other Ann-Marie.

"Aimée, please ask Katia and Ann-Marie to come down."

"Yes, Madame."

"Would you like to conclude our business before the girls arrive?"

Money changed hands, and I dropped it into an oriental box on the table next to my chair. Clink, clink—a cheering sound.

Soon the girls appeared, wearing new silk negligees and looking pleased to see their clients. There were expressions of delight from all, even the quiet, swarthy man. The men were soon led to the small rooms with their freshly washed linens sprinkled with lavender water.

I retrieved the money and locked it in a strong box in the study—which I'd found empty, no doubt raided by my landlord. The key had been secreted on top of an ornate cabinet. I tucked it in my bodice.

After an hour, the four appeared in the salon again, and the girls kissed the men goodbye before seeing them to the door.

"Go and wash yourselves," I said. "You will find hot water in your rooms and some food and drink, too. Then rest."

"Oh, Madame, you are so good to us!" said Ann-Marie. They both scampered upstairs.

We had good custom that evening. It must have been exhausting for the girls to pretend lust and affection all evening. But I had ascertained that Sunday was not a working day, so they'd have time to recuperate.

On weekdays, the action was surprisingly steady. I tried to have one girl off duty each day, but sometimes a client would ask for her, and I had to relent. The box was filling nicely. One Sunday afternoon, four men came and emptied the salon of its furniture. I had notified Monsieur Fernon, and he came to give the order to send it to an outdoor market. After it was all gone, different men brought the new furniture.

New heavy silk drapes that matched the upholstery were hung, a lush carpet rolled out on the floor, and the room finally looked tasteful, setting the new tone I hoped to bring to my establishment. Aimée had been cleaning the chandelier and sconces since noon. I had gradually replaced everything in the small entertainment rooms. My landlord's own men took the old stuff, no doubt for some of his more squalid properties, the same with the girls' old bedroom furniture. It was all gone within three months. We had a nice home, a cheerful atmosphere, and everyone was happy.

Except ... I missed Hunter. I didn't know how he'd find me after all this time. Well, he'd found me before. Some sort of sixth sense, which we gods used to have in spades. We still had it, just not as sharp as it used to be. I hadn't even found a man I considered attractive. They didn't have to bother with brothels.

I started to insinuate myself into town life. I introduced myself as a widow. I'd come to Bruges to join my husband, only to find he had died of a fever. I stayed in a little house on the city outskirts. I rented such a house just for appearances when I wanted to entertain some lady friends. It was well appointed, although not overly so. A neighborhood man tended the small garden, and I found I enjoyed spending time there, sipping a *tisane* in fine weather. Aimée attended as my maid when I had company. I furnished one bedroom upstairs, just in case.

The business thrived as our reputation for cleanliness and good taste spread to nearby towns. The only people who could expose me were clients, some of whom were prominent members of the citizenry, and they'd be hard put to it to explain how they knew me. They learned to rely on my discretion as I did theirs. I never used the front entrance and always wore a hooded cloak whenever venturing out.

One Wednesday evening, an enormous character arrived. He was a rough sort, and I felt alarmed for whomever he chose. It was a slow night, so he was the only visitor at the time.

"I don't believe we've met," I said, holding out my hand. He ignored it and slumped onto the sofa. He was a little drunk. "May I offer you refreshment?"

"Wine."

I took him some claret and sat in my usual chair.

"Your name?"

"Call me Robert. How much?"

I told him, and he paid.

"I want one with some meat on her bones."

I tried not to show my distaste. "Aimée, fetch Louise." She'd filled out more than the others, which enhanced her fair coloring and large blue eyes.

Louise came down, and I introduced them. The man drained his glass and got up. "Let's go."

I waited a while before running down to the kitchen to find a meat fork. I found two. Back upstairs, I tiptoed along the passage to stand near their door. I heard nothing unexpected for twenty minutes or so, but then the girlish cries of delight were cut short by a choked cry and the rustles and thumps of a silent struggle. I opened the door quietly to find Robert with his hands around Louise's throat, staring into her eyes as he choked her.

I rammed the forks into his backside, one in each buttock. He sprang up with a roar and went for my throat. He roared again as I broke both his arms. I gathered his clothes and pushed the howling man downstairs, through the kitchen, and out of the backyard gate.

"If you ever show yourself here again, I will kill you," I said. I pushed him farther up the lane and into a pile of horse manure, his bare bottom with its eight punctures mooning the world.

I rushed back to comfort Louise. I told her he would never come back. But I wasn't so sure. He could watch for me to leave, or he could set fire to the house. I should hire a watchman. A big one.

Jean-Paul came to work for me and was a great help. He was huge and made sure the clients caught sight of him. If any of them thought they could hurt my girls, he taught them otherwise. He took care of the chickens, too, and drew the water as if the bucket weighed no more than a kerchief. Aimée had made great strides with the chickens once she was able to buy them good feed, but Jean-Paul had the magic touch. He integrated into the household seamlessly. He occasionally played around with one girl or the other, but they didn't mind, so I didn't, either.

Time rolled along, and my cash situation became very comfortable. I made sure to share, giving the girls and maids an allowance as well as buying them pretty clothes and ribbons sometimes, providing Jean-Paul the tobacco he favored, and always feeding them well. The nuns received a weekly donation, too. I bought myself a horse and carriage and cut quite the figure as I was driven to tea parties and soirees. Of course, I had to leave the carriage at my little house, which had a stable with a room where the coachman could stay. I'd go into the house for a few minutes, then run back to the brothel. I couldn't have anyone spotting my carriage at such an establishment. It would have meant social ruin. Life was too good to risk that.

One Saturday night, almost a year after I'd moved to Bruges, I sat sipping champagne in the salon. The last client had left, and the girls were all upstairs—and, probably, Jean-Paul. I lay my head back, enjoying the quiet. Someone pulled the bell strap. Aimée clattered downstairs to open it.

"Please, sir, Madame is resting..."

Heavy footsteps strode towards me. Not that wicked Robert, surely. I stood facing the door, ready for trouble. The door crashed open. Hunter. I shrieked and ran into his arms. Jean-Paul came bursting in, ready to defend me, which rather broke the spell.

Explanations were due. I explained to them both that I had believed my husband's cousin, Monsieur Thierry, to be lost at sea when he did not return from Scotland. Hunter nodded his head vigorously while I told my story. I needed to restrain my enthusiasm as he was not, in their eyes, my husband. Lies do trip one up horribly, sometimes. I sent them both back to bed. I had kept one small bedroom ready and fresh to keep my hope alive. Hunter would sleep there, I said. Hunter looked displeased.

Once the others had left, we had some catching up to do. I explained about the town and the girls.

"Girls? What girls?" he asked. His surprise looked somewhat overdone.

"Well, I took over this brothel when the owner died." Which reminded me that I hadn't asked the girls if any of them were guilty. Actually, I didn't want to know. "It's very profitable. The girls had a miserable life before I came along. Now they have nice clothes and enough to eat. Their families sold them, you know."

"That is a wicked thing," Hunter said, his brow furrowed. "But are they really happy doing this kind of work?"

"They are used to it. And they have no choice now. At least they have a nice home. And you, what have you been doing?"

"Well, years ago, I got involved with the Cathars. Have you heard how the Pope had so many massacred as heretics? I fought with them for years and saved quite a few. In the end, it was a lost cause, so I just escorted a group of them to Portugal, which is a little more tolerant. Then I moved on to Denmark, then Sweden. I bought a big fishing boat and hired a crew. I spent years sailing and selling my catch. I had to move on, of course, because my men started talking about how I was not aging. So I moved over to Norwegian waters. The kings of Norway, Sweden, and Denmark are always arguing about who owns what, but no one bothered me too much. I did not need the money, of course, but loved the life. I started to miss you more and more. I have wandered over half the world to find you." He clasped my hands, gazing into my eyes.

"But how did you know I was here?" I asked.

He stammered and stumbled. "I asked many people and described you."

"You randy bastard, you came here for sex, didn't you? It was just chance."

"No, really, I heard your laugh while passing. I saw all these men going in and out. I waited for hours."

He was lying. I knew it, and he knew I knew it. But I needed him; we needed each other.

We stayed in that house together for nearly ten years. We didn't have too many problems over the next few years. We lost poor Louise. She contracted syphilis, probably from Robert. It's a bad way to go. When her mind began to rage, I could no longer keep her in the house. I went to visit the madhouse but couldn't leave her among that cacophony of demented souls and thuggish warders. I rented a tiny house near the church and hired a woman to take care of her. She had a decent burial; my friends, the nuns, saw to that.

Robert came back just after Hunter joined us. He tried to start a fire all along the back of the house by spreading old rags and kindling. I heard his clumsy efforts and warned both Hunter and Jean-Paul that someone was prowling outside. They both went out of the front door and crept around the back so they could trap him. I heard a brief scuffle, a couple of curses, and then, no more. Somehow, I knew he would never be back.

I'd bought the house at the end of my two-year agreement with the landlord. Hunter hates mixing in society, as you know, so we ended up not telling anyone about our relationship. But it was nearly time for rebirth. We called everyone together one Sunday afternoon.

"My dear friends," I started. "I actually bought this house from Monsieur Fernon a few years ago. It is time for Monsieur Thierry and I to leave." The company gasped, and Aimée began to cry. Even Jean-Paul looked teary. "But today, I visited the notary and changed the deed. The house now belongs to all of you in equal shares. I have designated Katia, the oldest girl, as the new Madame. I hope you will continue as before and enjoy the considerable profits."

They all came crowding around for hugs and kisses, which embarrassed Hunter a good deal. He somehow wriggled himself free and into a safe armchair.

"Just one thing," I said. "You must be aware of those poor souls who come to the Church of Our Lady of Bruges to die and of the selfless work of the nuns who tend them in their last agonies. I have been giving them money every week to help them buy their supplies and pay the men who bring in the sick and carry out the departed. I hope you will be generous after I am gone."

"I certainly will," said Katia. "My mother died there. The nuns eased her suffering as best they could. My father had five other mouths to feed at home, all younger. I had come into the city with him to help carry her to the church. After she died, he brought me straight here and sold me. I don't know how he knew about this place, but I will never forgive him. My life was misery until you came—it was so for all of us. Now we have a real home. And it is ours, thanks to you."

I gave the little house to the Mother House of those sweet nuns and the carriage to the coachman. My household loved me and was sad to see me go, even though I had now made them all prosperous.

We moved to Portugal, rented a little house, stocked it up with supplies, and went through rebirth. Me first, then Hunter a couple of weeks later. So there I was in Portugal, looking for a nanny again. One with the fortitude to deal with the monstrous infant Hunter would become.

I have to admit that I was not shocked until I thought about it later. Lin made it all sound so reasonable. Maybe it was, given the times. Something else to chew on.

She looked at me inquiringly as she sat up.

"Those girls were very fortunate," I said.

Another brilliant smile before she swept upstairs.

25

Lin took me shopping with Agna a couple of days after our last session. Perhaps she realized how I was feeling. We went to a couple of boutiques in Bethesda that had stylish clothes which were finely cut and beautifully finished. She bought me a silky, emerald-green summer dress with cap sleeves and a gently flowing skirt. It made me feel good, especially when the saleslady, Lin, and Agna all said it brought out my beautiful coloring. I didn't know I had coloring. Brown hair, pale skin, greenish eyes. That I knew, but never thought of the whole as being "coloring."

"You need some decent sandals with that," Lin insisted when I tried to tell her she'd been generous enough.

"Let Lin do it," said Agna. "It makes her feel good, too."

We had lunch at a French bistro. They started with escargot. I did not. Then back to Tysons Corner in Virginia to a store that sold a marvelous assortment of shoes. I got a pair of sandals that were comfortable yet chic. I hadn't known that comfortable and chic could coexist.

The following Monday, I settled Rose down and went back into the living room to set up the recorder. Lin and Agna were already there with cake and a carafe of coffee. There would not be a graceful pose on Lin's part today, apparently, but the three of us sitting around the coffee table with the recorder nearby. Suited me just fine.

Tape 18,
Volume 2

Baldur, the God of truth and light and the most handsome of the gods, was the son of Frigg and Odin. Baldur was also knowledgeable about healing herbs and runes, which made him a favorite among the people of Midgard. Baldur lived in the Palace of Truth with his wife, Nanna.

Baldur had been having frightening nightmares, although he didn't complain because he didn't want to upset his mother. Everyone noticed that he didn't look like his usual cheerful self. Finally, his mother, my lady Frigg, pressed him to tell her what the matter was. He confessed that he'd had nightmares about being killed by someone or something in the most unexpected way. He never saw who or what or how ... only felt pain and falling into a dark void.

No lie or bad thought could pass through the walls of the home of the God of Truth, so when Baldur spoke of having frightening nightmares about his own demise, the other Aesir gods took them seriously. Even a Norse god could be killed by some extraordinary event.

I was standing behind Frigg's throne when he told his sad tale, his voice faltering, his face drawn and exhausted. I will never forget his demeanor, his look of misery.

Frigg was horrified and went to her husband, Odin, the king of the Norse gods. All three of us handmaidens accompanied her. Odin sat upon the throne of the Aesir gods with his companions, the two ravens, Hugin—Thought—and Munin—Memory—whispering in his ears. From this position, he could look over all of the nine worlds.

After she told him the story, he said he would consult the Goddess of Death to see what could be done. He had his eight-legged steed saddled, rode to the gates of Hel, and summoned the Goddess. He alone knew how to call her from her lair.

"We have grand rooms ready for Baldur," intoned Hel. "He will soon be amongst us."

Sorrow flooded Odin. "What can we do? He is the most beloved of all the Aesir. We must keep him with us, no matter the cost."

"You must have the promise of every living thing and every other thing not to harm Baldur. That is the only way to save him."

Odin went to Frigg's palace and told her what the old woman said. He was worried, not only for his beloved son's life but for the universe, as he knew Baldur's death would be the beginning of the end, as prophesied so long before.

"I will call every living creature to my palace and make them swear not to harm our son. I will then seek out everything and everyone who has not answered the call and demand their agreement not to hurt Baldur."

Odin gave her his blessing.

First, the gods came to Frigg by Odin's command, all eager to show their love for Baldur. Next, the call went out far and wide, and Frigg's palace was surrounded by a mob of humans, gnomes, elves, and spirits, eagerly waiting their turn to pass by her throne and give their assurances for Baldur's safety. In flew Sickness and Poison, Water and Fire. All knew the terrible price to pay for going against Frigg and Odin. But in any case, Baldur was so universally loved, no one thought of refusing.

Asgard days were very long, but even so, the procession went on for weeks.

It was no good asking the Jotuns and other far-flung enemies to swear an oath, but they got the message that harming Baldur would result in war, one they could not hope to win.

Finally, Frigg went down into Midgard to secure the promise of every creature, be it bird, reptile, insect, mineral, or mammal. Then she pleaded her case with every plant large enough or poisonous enough to pose a threat and any others she came across. One day, she came to a large tree laced with mistletoe. She got the tree to take the oath but didn't bother with the insignificant mistletoe. Her journey had been grueling, and even gods could get tired. She wanted nothing more than to go back to her own spinning wheel.

As she made her way out of the forest toward the sea, she came to a rocky outcrop where she saw a giantess sitting at the back of a huge cave. Relieved to have found this last being, she entered.

"Good day, I am the goddess Frigg. Whom do I have the pleasure of addressing?"

"I have no name. I am just an ugly giantess tossed aside by my kin." Her voice sounded surprisingly high for such a massive individual. She made no polite greeting as expected when addressing a goddess. She didn't even smile but sat on a vast cushion that ballooned around her massive hips.

"I am sorry to hear that," said Frigg, thinking that maybe she should do something nice for this poor exile. She went on to tell her story and asked the giantess to give her word she would not harm Baldur.

"I will do no such thing," was the shocking reply. "Why should I? I'm not one of you, nor do I care for anyone or anything."

"It is not wise to refuse a god," said Frigg.

"I do not care," replied the giantess. "I never leave this cave. You are the first visitor I have ever had. What harm can I do?"

Frigg, drained after her weeks of travel, left the cave and stood outside for a while to compose herself. When she turned back, the giantess who never left her cave was gone. She cursed the wretch and willed herself home, where we handmaidens waited to bathe her, soothe her with fragrant oils, and sing her to sleep.

We all later realized that the giantess was Loki, the master shapeshifter. He had not come to swear the oath with the other gods. He told a few of his cronies that he was half Jotun and not a full god, so he didn't count.

When she had completed her mission, Frigg returned to her palace, where she sat spinning the clouds that floated above Midgard. The palace also served as the afterlife home for married couples who wished to be together. It was a counterpart to the famous home of valiant warriors, Valhalla, where Odin spent much of his time drinking—he had stopped eating when he had been reminded of the inevitable doom of Ragnarok—with his feasting and fighting companions and the Valkyries.

After a good night's rest, Frigg and Odin gave a celebration feast in Gladsheim, the gods' meeting hall. After a few rounds of drinks and toasts, the gods decided to test Baldur's invulnerability. A small rock thrown at Baldur bounced off without hurting him, true to its oath. Larger weapons followed, including Thor's motley collection.

A few days later, Baldur was jousting on the sacred fields outside Asgard when one of the lances hit his chest. His partner was horrified until he realized the point had not pierced his flesh but had merely bounced off. The lance had also sworn the oath. After that, all his companions enjoyed themselves, throwing knives and spears at Baldur while he danced around, laughing.

I heard the commotion and came out to watch. Loki leaned against a fence, scowling at everyone having such a merry time. He was never invited to join their games because he was sly and mean. Baldur, on the other hand, was loved by everyone for his ready smile and happy nature, always ready to comfort and encourage. I saw the hate in his scrunched-up face and knew no good could come of it. Hodur, Baldur's twin brother, stood near Loki, turning his head left and right, eager to catch the sounds of play. Hodur, the god of darkness, was blind.

Shortly after I returned to Frigg's throne room, a very old woman came hobbling in, demanding in a shrill voice to see my lady. She was barefoot, dirty, and clothed in rags.

"I have been traveling far and wide, across the worlds, seeking shelter and food. I came to the sacred fields and saw a crowd throwing weapons at our beloved Baldur. Why are they doing that? They must be stopped."

Initially annoyed by the interruption, she softened at the old woman's concern for Baldur. Frigg explained Baldur's nightmares and told her the story of her arduous journey.

"And did you secure the guarantees you needed, my lady? I pray that you did."

"I did, save for a few insignificant plants."

"Which ones, my lady?"

"Oh, I don't remember. They were so small. There was one, though, that had wrapped itself around an oak, taking the oath. A mistletoe, nothing of consequence."

"I'm so pleased that you met with success, my lady. I will leave your presence now."

Frigg ordered one of my sister handmaidens to take the old lady to the kitchens so that she might be fed a good meal.

We found out later how the catastrophe was brought about. Of course, the old woman was Loki in disguise, as was the giantess. Loki was so consumed with jealousy and hatred of Baldur that he hatched an evil plan. He found the mistletoe, snapped off a strong limb that was not as big as a branch but larger than a twig, and carved one end to a sharp point. The next day, he went to the field of Ida and found Baldur's friends playing the same silly game. He went over to Holdur and told him what was going on.

"Why don't you have a go?" he said.

"But I'm blind. How can I throw something at my brother?"

"I'll help you. I have a good dart here."

And help him, he did. Hodur was so grateful to be able to participate in the fun he allowed Loki to guide him into the throng. Loki put the mistletoe dart into his hand, covered it with his own, and guided a throw right at Baldur's forehead. Baldur died instantly. Loki slipped away as the others all stared at Baldur, horrified and silent. Hodur turned to those around him crying, "What's happened? What's wrong?"

Poor Hodur was inconsolable when he found he'd killed his brother. Odin descended to look at his son's body and let out a howl of grief and fury.

"What have you done, Hodur? How could this happen?"

Hodur, his voice trembling, told his story.

"Loki!" Odin's cry carried to all the nine worlds.

My lady Frigg and all of us came running. Frigg threw herself on her son's body, weeping. She picked up the piece of wood that had killed him. "Mistletoe," she shrieked.

It was a terrible scene, with the whole gathering weeping and crying for Loki's blood. But Odin had made him a blood brother and immortal, so he could not slay him.

Celebration turned to lamentation for the death of the most beloved of the gods. Odin alone was aware of how disastrous this event really was for them all. He knew that with the loss of light and truth, Ragnarok, the end of the world, would come about soon.

The gods lay Baldur's body in his graceful boat and surrounded it with kindling, ready to be pushed out to the celestial sea to the end of the world where Hel waited. His body glowed white as if lit from within. There was loud wailing from some gods and silent mourning from others. Frigg and Odin stood before their son's pyre as if frozen. Baldur's wife, Nanna, collapsed suddenly, her heart shattered by grief. Freya wept her golden tears over Nanna's face before Hoenir set her body in the boat beside her husband. The gods, exhausted by grief, did not have the strength to push the boat from the shore, even after placing great rollers to ease its way.

Odin raised himself from his torpor to call Hyrro, a giantess, to help. She arrived in a chariot drawn by a wolf with vipers for reins. Everyone kept their distance from this strange vehicle, and Odin called on the Beserks to guard the chariot, as he knew its vicious servants might cause trouble. Hyrro gave a mighty heave-ho, sending the boat into the water so violently that the rollers caught fire.

This made Thor very angry, as he felt the giantess had shown disrespect to Baldur. He wanted to slay her with his hammer, but his brothers calmed him down, saying that it was the gods who had summoned her after all. He still muttered resentfully.

Next, Baldur's valiant stallion was sacrificed, his body cut up and thrown into the boat so he might carry Baldur wherever needed in the afterlife.

Odin roused himself to chant the spells of transition, leaning over Baldur at one point to whisper one into his ear. He blew on the kindling to set it alight and pushed the boat toward the horizon and Hel, who would be eagerly waiting for the royal couple.

A gnome, bored with the proceedings, ran in front of Thor to make his way back to the mountain labyrinth that was home. Enraged, Thor tripped him, so the gnome crashed face-first onto the stony shoreline. Thor picked him up and threw him into the boat, now a veritable inferno where he burned to death. He would serve Baldur and Nanna for infinity. Thor felt a little better after that.

A short while later, Odin leapt into the saddle and visited Hel again. She led him down into the underworld, where he found Baldur and Nanna dining in the place of honor at the head of the table. Although their faces were as white as snow, they looked well and were happy to see him.

He asked Hel whether she would release his son. Hel promised that Baldur could return to earth if every living creature shed tears of grief for Baldur. It looked as though it would be simple to arrange, for everyone loved Baldur, and most were still weeping for him, anyway.

Once again, Frigg travelled the world to ask every living creature to weep for Baldur. She made sure to visit the cave where she'd met the giantess but found it empty. On her way to the coast to meet the crabs and the fish, she ran into the old woman who had once professed such concern for Baldur's welfare. She realized it was Loki who had tricked her the last time, so she was prepared.

"Will you weep for my son?"

"Never," said the crone. "I weep for no one."

Frigg slapped the old woman on one side of her face and then the other—a slap terrible in its power and sound. Loki screamed, reverted to his real, weaselly form, and fled, clutching his cheeks but refusing to let a single tear fall from his eyes.

And so it was that Baldur could not return to the land of the living. Baldur and Nanna remained in Hel, where Hoenir and I visited them often.

The all-seeing Odin found Loki where he was hiding, in that cave where Frigg had thought she was talking to a giantess. Thor and Hoenir captured him, and Odin ordered him to be bound to a rock in a cave with snake venom dripping onto his face—I told you about that at our first session in the last volume. His son Fenrir was bound to another rock nearby. You will remember that they finally broke free to take part in bringing our world to an end. Ragnarok.

Both Lin and Agna had tears streaming down their faces. I started crying, too. Somehow the tragedy that had such momentous consequences, all engineered by that loathsome Loki, touched my heart, too. They'd all lost so much. Hoenir lost his whole family. Lin lost her goddess and her sister handmaidens, who were, in truth, her only family. So much pain and loss. People in other parts of the world were in similar straits—not a whole world lost, but their worlds.

After this depressing session, we had more cake. Lin said we needed wine and went upstairs to get some prosecco. We felt much better once the bottle and cake plate were empty. The only problem was I needed a nap, and Rose was about to wake up. I sighed and ruminated on the sacrifices of motherhood.

26

Monday had rolled around again. Life was good. We'd spent three days at the Bay with the whole family, and I felt free and easy as I walked Sam and the stroller around the neighborhood, sometimes with company and sometimes on my own.

Sven often took Rose down to the beach, where he helped her make lopsided sandcastles that looked whimsical with their decorations of seaweed, shells, and pebbles. It was a place where she had freedom of movement that she clearly felt was different from the park. She trotted up and down the shoreline until she wore herself out. It was June now and warm enough to paddle.

Agna and Lin came downstairs with their coffee and settled on the sofa.

"Well," said Agna, "I hardly know where to start."

Tape 19, Volume 2

I knew Ragnarok was almost upon us as soon as Baldur died. I was devastated to realize what would happen to my lady Freya and, indeed, all the Aesir. I told my lady that I would travel seven of the nine worlds in search of a remedy to the prophecy. Odin would parley with the gods of the Vanir and the high heaven. We embraced, and she wept her golden tears into my hair, where they still occasionally appear like precious beads.

I first went far away to Jotunheim, the land of the giants and trolls, but they refused to discuss it. I tried to remind them that they, too, would lose their world.

"You lie," said the most massive Ice Giant. "You Aesir want only to conquer us and rule over our land and people. There is no such prophecy."

"It sounds like a story to me," said the ugliest troll. "I have never heard such a foolish notion. Go away."

Next, I traveled down into Darkalfheim, where the gnomes plied their craft.

"I suppose you want gold," said their chief.

"No, of course not," I said. "We just want to stop this awful prophesy being fulfilled. We don't want our world—or yours—to be destroyed. Help us. You make many wondrous weapons that can protect us and you."

"We are well protected here," the twisted little creature told me. "It has nothing to do with us."

Discouraged, I edged toward Muspelheim, the World of Fire. Even though I'm a witch, I couldn't get too close to that inferno.

"Please come; I need to talk," I called into the center of the white ball of fire.

“What do you want?” whispered a hot breath by my ears.

“Please help prevent the destruction of our worlds. At least do not participate; I implore you. My lord Odin sends his respects and asks that you stay apart from the battle.”

“Fire is our very essence. We are hot and fierce and cruel. We cannot be otherwise.”

This was turning out to be an epic failure. Since I was already far down between Yggdrasil’s roots, I transported myself further down to Niflheim, Hel’s underworld. I wasn’t sure I would be able to call her out—only Odin could do that. Garm, the gruesome hound, barred my way.

“Another tasty morsel,” he said, gnawing a monstrous bone.

“I wish to speak to the goddess Hel,” I said. “I come at the request of Odin.”

“Then he should come himself. You may not enter this gate.”

I rendered myself invisible.

“You won’t get in that way,” Garm said, baring his teeth. “Nifleheim is closed. They are preparing a huge new set of halls and rooms. We are expecting an influx of guests any moment now.”

I tried to cast a spell on the loathsome creature, but he seemed immune to my magic.

“You see? You can’t win.”

At that final sneer, I turned and left. I willed myself to Midgard next, the earth where humans live. There weren’t that many of them at that time, so I would only have to visit a few settlements—mostly in the north and around the equator.

First, I needed rest. I was weary in heart and soul. I found a sweet-smelling stand of trees where bluebells abounded, and birds warbled their love songs. I sat with my back against a tree and wept. I had not accomplished anything. I knew Freya and Frigg had become concerned about the human condition lately, as greed and violence flourished. That was also mentioned in the prophecy. But I had to try.

As I expected, chieftains and kings were not interested in what I had to say. I tried frightening some of them with tricks like felling trees with a slap of my palm, setting fire to a dwelling with a breath, and so on. It made no difference. There was nothing that they couldn’t take care of themselves. And if the gods were so powerful, why couldn’t they take care of the problem themselves?

There was only one world left before I had to return to Asgard to confess my failure. Alfheim, the world of the elves. They were flighty little things, mostly kind and full of laughter and joy. Ghostly in appearance and able to become invisible in a flash, I couldn't see them taking anything seriously. I flew into their kingdom and made a bad first impression. The air was a pale misty purple, and I didn't notice a procession coming up on my right until I crashed into the ghostly elf leading it. The old elf I'd sent flying cursed me in a very un-elflike manner. The cats pulling the silver carriage arched their backs and hissed, unsheathing their claws with scant regard for their passenger, which tilted their charge alarmingly. A very cross elf queen (at least, I supposed she was a queen) tottered out of the carriage and looked daggers at me. Really. Sharp mirrored flashes shot from her eyes to pierce my body like little ice darts. My first instinct was to become invisible, but I remembered that these elves would still be able to see me. It behooved me to grovel.

"Your Majesty," I said, performing a deep curtsy. "My abject apologies for creating such a disturbance. I simply did not see your approach. I was trying to make haste to parley with your leader." I curtsied again. Queens like that.

"Who are you?" she asked. "What do you want with us?"

"I have been sent by the great gods of the Aesir to plead for your help in trying to prevent the fulfillment of a prophecy that will destroy our world."

"What has that to do with us?"

"The first part of the prophecy has come to pass. The bitter end must come soon unless we stop it. Your world will also be doomed."

"Nonsense! I've never heard of such a thing. But now you are here and have made so much trouble, I think we'd better keep an eye on you."

Silk straps stronger than steel suddenly clasped my wrists and ankles. I couldn't shift them, however much I struggled. I tried magic, but it didn't work in Alfheim. The elves were magical beings themselves and knew how to guard against it.

I must have lost consciousness because I woke in a room with no window or door. It was not dark, as a soft light seemed to stream from the ceiling. I called out, but no one came. There was no food or drink, but I'd never needed it anyway, so that was all right. I don't know how long I spent there, but there was something in the air that was soothing and joyful, like lilting music that I could only hear in my head.

Suddenly, one wall disappeared, and a pretty little elf ran in with a knife. Tears poured down her cheeks. Could they kill me, overcome my immortality? Fear gripped my heart. Instead of hurting me, she cut my bindings.

"The end times are here," she cried and ran out again.

The place had darkened now, and waves crashed outside. I had missed the battle. My lady Freya must have thought I'd abandoned them. It was too late to go back. There was only one place to go now.

Underwater. My only hope was to find the mermaids. I must have been kept in the palace because I saw royal regalia floating past as the waters rose. I had to get out, but the pressure of the water held the doors firmly closed. The water moved fast now, carrying pale elfin corpses with their wands and dead cats along with it.

I realized the queen's spell was broken, and my magic would work again. I willed myself outside, where black water boiled as it consumed the worlds. I took on the form of a whale so I would have the strength to navigate the obstacles and currents underwater.

After many days, I think—there was no way to measure time—I arrived at the enclave of mermaid palaces I had sought. The few mermaids who spotted me fled in fear, so I changed myself into a mermaid and followed one into the largest palace, where I found my way to the main hall. There sat Njord, God of the Sea and Wind.

He swiveled to face me. I felt transfixed by his eyes, one the brightest blue and one emerald green.

"What are you doing in my realm?" he said. It took a few moments before the sound reached me, and I could distinguish words distorted by water.

"Forgive my intrusion, my lord. I was imprisoned in Alfheim. When the seas rose, they set me free. I am Agna from Asgard, handmaiden and witch to the Goddess Freya."

"How did you anger the Elf Queen?"

"When I arrived in Alfheim, I accidentally flew into her procession and caused some mayhem. I didn't notice their approach, as I was on an urgent mission."

Njord rolled around in mirth, his belly laugh setting off the whole company of mermaids and mermen. "She was a spiteful little thing, too full of her own importance," he said.

"Well, she has perished now. I have travelled seven of the nine worlds to search for a way to circumvent the prophecy that told of the end of our worlds. I failed. And I ask for safe haven."

"You are welcome here, Agna. Soon you will become accustomed to our ways. Yes, Asgard is vanquished, as are the other worlds. A sad occurrence indeed. I was very fond of Odin and his family. Hoenir and Thor often visited me here. And I can assure you that at least, the Earth will rise again. That is also prophesied."

I wept for all that was lost. I wept for my failure. And I wept for the cruelty of it all. I had no idea then that others of my kind had survived. The loneliness was unbearable. But the merpeople were kind, and I got used to that life. I still love to swim and have not entirely lost the ability to stay underwater for long periods. I have not seen Njord or any of his merpeople for centuries, as I can no longer go that far down.

I grew to love Njord, and only the jealousy of his wife prevented him from taking me as a concubine. Her diamond-white eyes cut into the object of her anger like shooting stars, while her white sheets of hair swirled around her head as if anticipating a duel.

I still miss him. I often wonder if those scientists who plumb the depths will find his palaces. But I know they are well concealed by water and weeds and are probably deeper than man can ever venture.

Agna lay still with her eyes closed, probably still thinking about Njord. After a few minutes, I turned off the recorder. The snap of it seemed to rouse her.

"What a story," I said. "How did you eat down there? What did you do all day?"

"Oh, it's a wonderful life," she said. "We didn't eat, as all the fishes were our friends. We played and danced—sort of water ballets—and sang in a spluttery sort of way. They made love a lot. I had my moments with Njord, too, although we had to avoid his wife's fury. There wasn't much privacy down there. And mermaids have really long hair. It's green, fine as fine can be, and they have to spend a lot of time combing it. I was happy when I could forget my gods and our life on Asgard."

"When did you know to leave?" I asked.

"That's for another day. These memories drain my mental energy."

Rose woke up. Agna rose quickly and went to pick her up. I followed her into the nursery to find her rocking the child as she sang in some unknown language that sounded downright strange and nothing like the language Lin and Hunter sometimes spoke. A language from her water world? At any rate, Rose found it soothing.

27

The week passed quickly as Rose developed a chesty cold. I was terrified at first. The hum of fear was never far away during the peak of COVID infections. Even though the adult mortals in the household had received their vaccinations, none were yet available for toddlers. Many children escaped the scourge, but plenty didn't. And with so many anti-vaxxers out there, I didn't feel I could take her anywhere that might be crowded.

The child was feverish for a couple of days. Hunter heard her crying one evening and spent the entire night on my bed with her sprawled across his chest. But the fever abated, so I relaxed and comforted my grouchy little girl with all the patience and love I could muster. My relief that it was only a cold made it that much easier. By the time Monday morning rolled around, she was almost back to normal.

Agna and Lin came down just as I was shutting Rose's door. I'd already prepared the recorder. I was running low on tapes and resolved to check my Amazon account to see if they were available the easy way. We absolutely could not run out of tapes.

"I'll tell you a bit about my exit from the kingdom of Njord today, my wanderings, and an encounter with a spy in Egypt. I understand that Lin has already told you all about Tut."

"Yes, she has," I said. "And very fascinating it was, too. I found some novels online set in ancient Egypt. They were written by a Frenchman who is an Egyptologist and novelist. I bought the first three. They should arrive soon."

"That sounds like fun. Maybe I'll take a look."

I remembered Lin's reaction to the movie featuring Thor. "Just don't get mad if he isn't very accurate. I know he's an expert, but there is still a lot he couldn't possibly know."

"I know. I'll try to be understanding. I'm more patient than Lin."

"Hey!" Lin protested.

They both giggled like teenagers.

"Well, let's get started, shall we?" Agna said, still grinning. She lay herself along the sofa, just like Lin used to. Lin looked surprised, then a tad affronted. That was from her playbook. She flounced over to occupy an armchair.

I turned away to switch on the recorder so as to conceal my amusement.

Tape 20, Volume 2

I loved my time with the merpeople but their world was one of frivolity and gaiety. Not that there's anything wrong with that, but I'd known something different, so it wasn't enough. I'd miss the old king, but he wasn't the only god I'd known. While he was wise and knew more about the world above than his subjects, he still didn't have that much new to talk about. I needed a change.

I would go off exploring sometimes and take a long swim to look for shallow waters that might herald a shore. The oceans were quite dangerous for a mermaid on her own. There were sharks and other huge fish that could take me in one swallow. The whole of Midgard was down there, too, which provided plenty of obstacles and strange currents. It was quite useful, though, to have something to hide behind.

There was one town I visited often and got to know the streets and buildings intimately. I knew which doors were too small for a shark to get through and how to wind my way through alleys and paths too narrow for anything large to follow me with any speed.

The thing I dreaded most was the sea serpent. I'd heard it was big enough to circle the old earth and hungrier than a pack of starving wolves. I'd never seen it, though.

On one of my outings, I took a different direction, one I had not yet explored. It was a strange experience. Devoid of buildings and tree trunks, it must have been a desert. The seabed was sandy, with weeds undulating in the currents. It seemed lighter than other places I'd visited, perhaps because there was such a large, empty expanse.

Waves started to form, unusual this far down. That meant something huge was nearby, agitating the water. I looked around. There was nowhere to hide. I plucked some seaweed that had long spatulate leaves and draped it all over myself. I tried to stand straight and still, although the waves made it difficult to keep my balance.

Then I saw it, a huge triangular head with a tongue flickering in and out, slithering along the seabed. What I could see of its body gleamed like a thousand mirrors that reflected the greens and aquas of different seaweeds in all their hues. Its body was the circumference of ten tree trunks, and its tail was still out of sight. Those dreadful eyes—like basilisks, turning from side to side as it searched for prey.

When a whale passed above us, the serpent reared up, wrapping itself around the poor creature. The whale's cries were heartrending as it tried to wriggle free. Soon it went limp. The serpent opened its jaws and swallowed the whale. I watched, repulsed, as the whale passed through its body to form a huge lump somewhere in the middle. The head was still held high, as the whale's tail was not yet out of sight.

While the serpent was distracted, I moved very slowly backwards and swam, moving my tail gently so as not to attract attention. Once I reached darker waters, I swam as fast as I could in a straight line, terror making me heedless of other dangers that might lurk.

The shock of what I had witnessed must have addled my brain. Merpeople and gods don't need air, but whales do. I'd tried to get my head above water a few times on my outings, but the surface of the water seemed to rest on some sort of ceiling. Not hard, exactly, but impenetrably dense. I'd wondered if the long swim up there had weakened me, but that seemed unlikely. I'd never thought to question how the giant kelp survived or the fish I'd seen darting in and out of sunken dwellings and carts. There must have been some fresh currents to keep the water fresh. But I'd never seen anything as large as that whale, whose blowholes would demand access to the surface and air. I kept on swimming, looking for a way out.

I slowed down when I came to a line of rocks. The water was much lighter now. I could see the surface, like a mirror of sun and cloud. My heart lifted. Had the world awakened? I swam over and around the sharp, black rocks. Sure enough, my tail touched sand as my head rose above the water. I suddenly found myself gasping. I hadn't breathed air for centuries. I stood quite still and willed myself into my old self. My legs were unsteady as I stumbled through the gentle waves to the shore. After I'd trudged up the beach, I had to sit and rest.

I was happy to have survived the serpent's notice. But I felt deep sorrow for my brothers and sisters, the merpeople. And for my king, Njord. They would think I'd perished, so they needn't know I'd forsaken them without saying goodbye. It wasn't my fault—it was just the circumstances in which I had found myself. But I didn't feel good about it. They'd given me sanctuary when the nine worlds collapsed.

I looked around. This must be Earth. I got up wearily to see more of the place. A line of trees lined the beach and might offer cover and shade. The sun had become swelteringly hot. I walked through the woods until they opened up, and I found myself in a garden so full of flowers it was almost an assault on the senses. There were fruit trees with apples, pears, peaches, and all kinds of different colored plums hanging from them. The glorious sight lifted my spirits.

Voices. I lay flat in the tall grass. A man and a woman entered the garden. Both naked, they strolled hand in hand among the flowers. The woman plucked an apple and started to munch it. The man looked confused. I didn't understand their language, but they seemed to be arguing. She picked a peach and offered it to him. He turned it around and around, staring at it as if he didn't know what to do with it. The woman put it against his lips, and he licked it. When she mimed a bite, he bared his teeth and bore down. After that, he devoured the peach eagerly, juice dripping down his chin. The woman laughed, and they collapsed on the grass and started to make love. That was my cue to leave.

So, there were people. Now what? I had no idea where on Earth I was, but at least it was warm. I walked for a few hours until I found a deep cave. I made a bed of moss deep in the recesses and slept.

Voices woke me, many of them this time. I sidled to the entrance and found a group of dark-skinned humans coming my way, wearing clothes of some sort of soft, thin material. So, the place was inhabited by more than just those two I saw earlier. I looked down at myself and realized I should cover myself. I closed my eyes and willed my old clothes back. I looked different from these new people, but at least I was covered. I wove a protective shield around myself.

I stepped out of the cave. I suppose I looked strange to them because they were so frightened they threw a spear at me. My shield protected me, so the spear fell to the ground. That frightened them even more. They talked excitedly amongst themselves—I didn't understand a word—before beckoning me to accompany them. They took me to a settlement of rough huts, one much bigger than the others. I was guided inside. There they offered me bread and milk. I didn't need any sustenance but knew the people of Midgard regarded hospitality as a duty that must be respected by a guest. I wondered why they did not offer me fruit. It was still warm outside, so there must be plenty available.

I did not sleep that night but flew in the direction of the coast, looking for that splendid garden. I found the beach much eroded now. The trees were mostly there. Some now seemed to touch the moon, and others lay where they had fallen and rotted. Where the garden had been was overgrown with a tangle of underbrush. Some of the fruit trees were still alive, although old and gnarled. One or two bore a little fruit.

I knew, then, that I had slept for many, many years. I couldn't tell how many. Long enough for trees to grow as high as the sky, long enough for a garden to die, and long enough for a new generation of humans to populate the Earth.

I stayed with those people for a hundred years. They worshipped me. I taught them to clear that garden and grow crops. They were afraid of it at first. There was some sort of legend that it was inhabited by evil spirits. They called the place Ydun. I assured them there was nothing to worry about. They looked after the fruit trees and planted seeds from the fruit that were enjoyed by their grandchildren.

I became restless, wanting to see what else was happening in the world. I told them I must leave to help others like themselves. I told them I would always be with them in spirit. They prepared a feast, and the children sang songs and danced for me.

When night fell, I gave them my blessings and flew away. Looking back, I saw a sea of gaping faces watching my ascent. Some of them knelt and clasped their hands together. It was a showy exit. I'm sure their ancestors still talk about it.

"You are so naughty," Lin said, laughing. "You probably started a religion."

"Well, I helped them live better. And they were properly grateful."

"I wonder how many of today's religions started in some other way than is told," I said. "Although there was a god involved, just not the sort of god everyone thinks of now."

"Who knows?" Agna said. "Who knows?"

Agna propped herself up on one elbow. "I'll just summarize the way I skipped around. I believe Lin has recounted my stories about Tut?"

I nodded.

"Then we'll get to the last bit in Suez."

Suez?

I flew south. I wasn't in the mood for a cold climate. I still remembered the misery of the three-year winter before Ragnarok. Soon I came to a land of mountains and lakes, jungles and deserts. I came to rest in a lush, wooded area that reminded me a little of Ydun. I thought of resting on the grass under a tree when a mighty roar sounded not too far away. I'd heard tales about lions, and that might well be one. The undergrowth crackled, and the massive cat came into view. It looked at me with slitted eyes and licked its lips. I became invisible, whereby the poor cat paced in circles, sniffing and marking as it went. It soon wandered off to look for other opportunities.

I decided to look for somewhere a little more sheltered, like a cave. I soon found one and walked deep inside. Although I see well in the dark, I almost stepped into a shallow pit. A cluster of snakes writhed around each other in that pit in a ghastly dance. When one of them spotted me, it hissed and lunged, which encouraged the others to do likewise. I beat a hasty retreat and decided to seek out a more welcoming environment.

Days later, I flew over an island that looked pretty. Plenty of foliage, sand, and sea. That was Crete. The inhabitants were suspicious at first but came around when I showed how useful I could be. I made myself a little stone house, which astonished them. Then I set about learning about the wild herbs the old women collected for their remedies. I collected them, too, but added my own magic touch.

They indulged in one horrifying ritual each year. A vicious monster lived in a labyrinth deep underground. He demanded the sacrifice of young people every year, or he would wreak havoc on the community. It was supposed to be an honor to be chosen, but I don't think any of those unfortunates thought so as they were being eaten alive.

After a few years, I spoke their language well and learned about the pantheon of Greek gods. So much time had passed since Ragnarok that we had been supplanted. Humans craved their gods. And jealous gods, they turned out to be. After fifty years or so, they all began to talk about how I still looked the same as when I arrived. Some admired me for it, and some feared me. I'd never set myself up as a god in Crete, as they already had their own. Time to leave.

Next, I flew over a land that was lush and green with a long river that snaked into the distance. A strange object came into view—a gargantuan statue shaped like a lion, but with the head of a man, sat proudly in the middle of a swath of grass. Egypt. And there I lived for centuries, through dynasty after dynasty, wars, climate change, and religious upheavals. What had once been a verdant land became mostly desert except for a wide strip of land on either side of the Nile, whose annual flood fertilized the strip with its silt. Cities arose up and down the great river—Thebes, Memphis, Cairo, and Alexandria in the north. Egypt became my home. Now I have my London house, but Egypt is still my real home. I left Upper Egypt not long after my Pharoah

Tutankhamun's tomb was desecrated and his remains moved to Cairo. I have a house in a leafy section of the city where I sit in the garden meditating after dinner, hoping my boy will visit me once more.

Agna looked sad. "I know Lin has a special affinity for Egypt, too."

"Yes. You will soon meet Reema, the Syrian girl I told you about. She reminds me of my Reema sometimes. She's so busy I hardly ever see her. She's doing a medical residency in Philadelphia."

"I look forward to it," Agna said. "Now, let me finish up. Dredging up all these memories is disturbing—memories I once put under lock and key in my memory bank. Agna hugged herself, bending forward over her knees as if dizzy. After a few minutes, she slumped back and closed her eyes.

I lived in Cairo during World War II. It was a contentious time. Some favored supporting the Nazis as a way to rid themselves of British rule. But they were kidding themselves if they thought Nazi rule would be any better. Hitler probably despised Arabs as much as he did the Jews.

I think it was near the end of 1941 when I took a trip to the Suez Canal. I'd heard so much about it that I wanted to see it for myself. I knew British troops would be guarding it aggressively because of its crucial role in linking the Red Sea with the Mediterranean. Suez was a lovely, old town, ancient in parts. I stayed in a hotel that catered to foreigners and treated its guests like royalty.

A group of guests sat in the lounge most evenings, enjoying their after-dinner drinks. Sometimes there was a band in the ballroom, and both dinner and dancing took place there. I had danced with a gentleman called Kurt a couple of nights before, who told me he was Swedish. He didn't speak English like Swedes typically did because his pronunciation sounded more guttural. Anyway, I didn't think too much of it. The next night he came in late and sat next to me in the lounge.

"I saw you at dinner, and then you disappeared before the *Om Ali* was served," I said. "One of my favorites."

"What is that?" he asked.

"It's made with puff pastry, nuts, milk, and spices. Delicious."

"I do not care for these Arabic concoctions," he said.

"So, did you go for a walk?"

"I like to walk by the canal in the evenings."

Well, I knew he must have done it very stealthily because no one was allowed anywhere near the canal at night. It was hard enough to take a look during the day. I resolved to keep my eye on him.

The next evening, Kurt excused himself early again. I followed soon after, which caused some raised eyebrows from the ladies, and probably induced a juicy stream of gossip. When I got to the courtyard, I thought I'd lost him, but there he was, coming out of the foyer all dressed in black. He must have gone back to his room to change.

Invisibly, I followed him to the administrative building. He drew out a pistol and crept up to the window. What did he want? Plans, perhaps?

"What do you want here, Kurt?" I asked, visible once more.

He whipped around and leveled the pistol at me. "What do you want? Do you work for the British?"

"No. But I don't like Nazis, and that's what you are, aren't you? I know you people want to seize the canal."

"I am sorry, but I cannot allow you to prevent me from serving my **Führer**."

"If you shoot me, a whole lot of British soldiers will come running."

"Well then, we must do it quietly."

He moved toward me. I stopped him. He looked concerned, not understanding why he couldn't lift his feet or arms. I moved his right hand that held holding the pistol, until it rested against his temple.

"What are you?"

"I am someone you cannot overcome."

I moved his finger to the trigger. He turned pale.

"Please, no. Have pity." His thuggish tone had been replaced by a whine.

"Like your **Führer** had pity on all those Jews he murdered?"

I moved Kurt's finger to pull the trigger.

Invisible again, I watched as soldiers came running, rifles pointing at Kurt's body.

"He shot himself?" said one.

"Why on earth would he do it? Why here?"

Why indeed?

Agna sat up suddenly. "Teatime," she said. "I bought some thick English cream today, and Auntie made scones."

I was surprised by Agna's story, although I should have known not to be surprised by anything at this point. Magic plus a pistol. And she made him do it to himself. At least Kurt experienced fear, probably too scared to give a thought to the fear and pain that he and his Fuhrer must have caused others. Agna's actions were pretty cold-blooded, although one mustn't overlook that he was about to kill her. But ... that is war.

28

It was the beginning of August, and soon to be Rose's third birthday, which we decided to celebrate at the Bay. Lin loved the new house down there, and we visited often.

I was sad Auntie Peggy couldn't make it. Her best friend from school was visiting from Canada for a couple of weeks, which I knew would prove altogether too much. She'd gone back to her own house ... reluctantly. Lin told her to come back as soon as she was able. I'd gotten a good load of food in for Auntie, so at least she didn't have all that to carry. I dusted and made up the spare bed, too. Both she and her friend were vaccinated, but I was still uncomfortable with it.

Margareta was backpacking around Europe with friends, which I didn't think was such a good idea since COVID was still around, although not as bad as before.

Lin waved off my concerns. "She's a strong girl. I'm realizing more and more that she's almost like us."

Yes, but not quite. She was certainly extraordinarily strong and intelligent, but I'd never seen evidence of Lin's preternatural speed and hearing. Anyway, it was none of my business, and she was a tough cookie.

Sven would come down with us. It was fun to see how he doted on Rose, always taking her out for walks, playing with her, and teaching her to talk. Agna was still visiting, and Dr. Ayre came, too, toting her black medical bag she took everywhere. Agna would sleep on the pullout in Hunter's study on the third floor. Ayre was assigned Margareta's room next to Sven's on the second floor. As always, Rose and I shared the ground floor with Dora, which made life easier as the kitchen and washer/dryer were down there.

My little suite had a view of the Bay from my bedroom, a small bedroom for Rose, and a bathroom whose window looked out at the tree-lined creek on the side of the house. I loved it down there and often wished I could stay permanently.

Lin and I had bought lots of good things for our little party—cupcakes, potato chips, sodas—as well as things grownups would appreciate, like a crate of champagne, which Dora and Sven loaded into one of the SUVs. The big chocolate birthday cake would please everyone with its two fat pink candles. I was glad Rose was too young to want a party with friends, as this was much easier than tears, toilet mishaps, and the few parents who would invite themselves.

We arrived on a rainy afternoon, which made getting everything inside the house a challenge. Sven turned on the TV in the main living room for Rose to divert her attention from all the goodies and gifts being carried in. He seemed almost as entertained by *Sesame Street* as she was.

Fortunately, each of the three floors had a fridge, so we had plenty of space to stash everything. It took us an hour to put everything away, plug in the appliances, turn up the air conditioning, and flip the breaker for the hot water heater

Dora made iced tea with fresh mint from the pots of herbs along the back of the house and fresh lemon, and we finally sank down to sip our icy drinks. The house wasn't yet cool, so we'd all worked up a sweat. At least a breeze was coming in off the Bay, so Lin left the sliding glass doors open—which didn't seem to make much sense, although maybe the cooler air helped things along.

Rose yawned a couple of times, so Sven picked her up and put her down for a nap. He sat on the floor by the cot, reading until she fell asleep. Marvelous.

As soon as Rose woke up, she clamored to go down to the beach. 'Beetch, Mommy, please, beetch!" I dressed her in her new pale blue bathing suit that sported a fringe around the hips. She looked adorable with her blond curls caught up in a matching barrette.

When we got down to the shore, I unfolded her towel and set down her bucket and spade before rubbing sunscreen over her fair skin. To my surprise, Dr. Ayre seemed enchanted by her.

"She really is a lovely child, Mary. Rose, would you like to swim with me?" she said, her voice taking on that lilt I remembered from my labor. Rose gazed at her, eyes wide and wondering, as if mesmerized.

"Yus, I will swim wit you."

They cavorted in the water, which I noticed was getting a little choppy again.

I jumped when Agna laid a hand on my shoulder. I hadn't realized she was behind me.

"Don't worry," she said. "There are enough of us around that she won't come to any harm. I'll watch her."

That was reassuring, so I was able to relax. Hunter and Sven had set out all the chairs, so I selected a chaise, soon lying back and unwittingly falling into a snooze.

"Dinner's ready," woke me. I looked around, somewhat dazed. There were only three of us left on the beach—Rose, Sven, and me.

"Gosh, I hope Rose didn't catch too much sun," I told Sven.

"I put some more sunscreen on her an hour ago, so she should be all right," he replied. "Why don't you take her up to the house? I'll deal with the chairs."

"Thanks," I said. "You know, you really are a special kind of guy."

He blushed and busied himself with folding my chaise.

Rose didn't voice her usual protests when we left. She'd tired herself out.

I could smell the food before we crossed the road. Dora must have barbecued chicken.

I had to help Rose with her food. She fought the sandman valiantly but fell asleep in my lap as soon as I'd spooned the last morsel of strawberry ice cream into her mouth ... so much for the potty and toothbrush. Oh, well, that's what diapers were for. We'd been doing well on that front, but this was an exception. I'd put on her pajamas before dinner, so all I had to do was add the diapers.

When I laid her down and pulled down her pants, she woke up suddenly.

"Potty," she said.

I took her in there, and she peed.

"Good girl. Shall we just use the pull-ups tonight?"

"Yus."

She fell asleep as soon as I put her down. She looked like an angel. I guess every mother says that, but she really did.

As I turned to leave, I found Hunter in the doorway.

"Can I look at my angel?" he asked. "I've hardly touched her today."

"She's so lucky," I said. "Having all these people who love her."

Hunter leant down and kissed her forehead, gently brushing her curls aside.

"My angel," he said. "My angel." He put his arm around me while we admired our daughter.

"I'm pretty tired, too," I said. "I'll socialize for just a little while, then I must get an early night. There's going to be a lot of excitement tomorrow."

"I can't wait for her to open her gifts," Hunter said, his eyes gleaming as if he would be the one getting them. "She'll be so excited."

"I hope you haven't gone overboard. You know what too much excitement leads to."

"What?" he asked, puzzled.

"Tears. When they get overexcited, they can't always handle it. Then they cry."

"How odd."

Dear Hunter, so clueless in some ways. Surely his own children had meltdowns sometimes.

We joined the others. Dr. Ayre and Sven were doing a jigsaw puzzle. They invited me to join them, but when I saw the cover picture—a sea full of sailboats and a sky full of clouds—I knew I was too tired to focus. Agna and Ayre sat chatting in armchairs in one corner, clearly reminiscing from the snippets I could pick up—*do you remember when*, and *I never did like*, and *that was so unlike him*. Lin switched on the TV, and Hunter slipped in a DVD. More blood and guts, I supposed. But it was a British crime drama and rather well done. A good plot and no gunfights. To my surprise, I made it to the end.

I slept well that night. And Rose was dry in the morning. I took her to the bathroom so we could both wash our faces and so on. No need to shower until after the beach. I looked out the window and was surprised to see a large pine tree quite close to the house. Surely it hadn't been that close the last time I looked?

Trees don't get up and walk. I went to look out of the window in my room. Everything seemed normal—the water smooth and sparkling, showing none of the frenetic whitecaps of yesterday.

We went out to the living room and found only Dr. Ayre at the table with her tea and toast.

"Good morning. Mothers and doctors get up early," she said. "Did you sleep well, little Rose?"

"Yus. Rose dry."

"Well done! You are a big girl now. Two years old." Dr. Ayre gave her a big kiss. "Did you sleep well, Mary?"

"I did, thank you. Sun, sand, and sea can be exhausting. How about you?"

"I did. Not that anything makes much difference to us, you know."

"No, I guess not. I forget sometimes that you are all—different."

She laughed an undulating and captivating arpeggio. Her blond hair, hanging loose for once, was shiny and thick, just a shade darker than Lin's golden tresses.

"The fact that we seem normal to you most of the time is gratifying."

I thought it was more than that. "Alarming" sprang to mind. But comforting, too. The gods thought of me as family.

Dora put our breakfast in front of us—scrambled eggs and toast, tea for me, and orange juice for Rose. A bowl of fruit salad lay between us, which Rose dipped into with her left hand while spooning egg into her mouth with her right. She was quite dexterous. Not that I knew any other children to compare her with. I'd have to remedy that soon.

"Beetch! Beetch!" So down we went. None of the chairs were set up yet, so I sat on a towel while Rose tried to build a sandcastle. Sven had shown her how to fill the little bucket and turn it upside down to make the turrets. I had to remind her to use wet sand, as the first try with dry sand frustrated her almost to the point of a tantrum.

After an hour, Sven came down, pulling the chairs on a trolley. I stood up while he arranged them across the beach.

"It's going to be a hot one," he said. "I'd better get some umbrellas."

I turned as he started back to the shed beside the house and gasped. Several of the trees that used to line the creek were now within six feet of my bedroom wall.

"Sven. The trees."

"Bloody hell!" He sprinted to the house.

How much did he know about his parents' true identity? They'd decided not to tell him when they told Margareta. Maybe she told him. Well, it would have to come out soon.

Are we safe here? Safer at the house? But the trees were crowding the house, not the beach. I decided to stay well away. Fear gripped me.

Ayre soon joined me. "A little disturbance," she said.

"What's going on?"

"A few trees have dragged themselves up to the house, leaving huge trenches behind them. I think they've broken most of their roots. They'll probably die."

I gasped in horror. It had taken years for those trees to mature to their full splendor.

Rose fought her way out of my clutch. "What Mommy? Mommy sad?"

Ayre picked her up. "No, we're not sad. We just have to save some trees."

"What're they going to do?" I asked.

"Lin has sent Dora to see if she can deal with it."

"Dora? What on earth can Dora do?"

"Didn't you know she is a wood nymph? She can talk to trees. Lin can talk to trees, too, of course, but not on the same level. Dora can touch their souls."

"I did know that. I'd forgotten."

We moved to the edge of the beach, where the grasses gave way to the road, and watched Dora dance naked around the trees, running her hands over their trunks and sometimes embracing them. I heard the faint ring of a poignant song that seemed to draw on my deepest memories, memories that were not born of this life.

Rose stilled, too, leaning back against me, her eyes closed, lips moving as though in silent prayer. I don't know how long it went on, only that I stayed still, fearful of disturbing the haunting call.

The song stopped. Dora stood in front of the trees, her arms raised. The pines fell back with a mighty crash, birds and leaves flung out by the force.

"Poor trees, poor things. They were just tools," Dr. Ayre said.

"What do you mean?" I must say I felt like weeping at the loss of these pines that had persevered for so long through storms and drought. And the birds, too, although most of the chicks must have left by now.

"It must be Loki's doing. Curse him."

"You mean he's still around? I thought the snake swallowed him," I cried. "Rose is not safe here."

"We'll take care of you. Let's go up and find out what Dora has to say."

Dora had plenty to say ... once she got over her crying fit. Lin looked sad, too.

"My beauties, my beauties," Dora kept saying. "That Loki, he's a snake now. He crawled up them every day, whispering his poison, promising them eternal life. All they had to do was crush all of us, and our powers would enter them, granting them and their seeds eternal life. Lin told me lots of stories about him, the wicked things he's done. I told them all about him. I told them all about Lin and Hunter and the good things they've done. And Dr. Ayre. I told them they'd been tricked because Loki was the wicked one. They believed me because I'm one of them, and Loki isn't." She buried her face in her hands for a few minutes before continuing.

"The poor darlings broke their roots, dragging themselves like that. It was agony for them and all for nothing. They couldn't live or stand without their roots. They began to wither while I was talking to them, losing their leaves. They wept for their lives, the waste of it all. And then they gave up and died." She started to cry again.

We all listened in silence.

"Loki is bad," proclaimed Rose. I was surprised she'd picked that up from Dr. Ayre.

"Yes, darling, he is," I said, picking her up. I looked around. "What will he do next? Should we leave?"

Lin said, "Not until we've had the party. Then we'll talk about it. Let's have lunch."

"There isn't any," said Dora, annoyed. "I haven't had time."

Hunter chimed in. "We'll order pizza. It's a party day, after all."

I thought it best for Rose to nap after lunch, as there would be so much excitement. But she wasn't having it.

"All right," said Lin. "Let's do the birthday, then we can all go to the beach."

We all put our gifts on the table, and Sven brought the cake downstairs. Dora poured juice for Rose, and Hunter popped corks while Lin set out the flutes.

Rose sat on her little wooden rocking chair and gazed around her, bemused.

"What, Mommy? What dat?"

"It's your birthday, sweetheart. You're two years old. You get birthday cake and presents." I handed her my present. "This is for you. Shall I help you open it?"

"No. I will do it myself."

She pulled and ripped, squealing with delight when she saw the purple teddy bear. She held it tight and kissed the top of its head.

And so it went on. A dump truck from Hunter didn't get much reaction. He promised to show her how to use it at the beach. I thought it a strange gift until I realized how much fun she'd have scooping and dumping the sand. Dr. Ayre got her a full-length pink dress with puff sleeves and lots of frills. We had to call a halt to the proceedings as she insisted on trying it on right away. I was a little concerned about collisions with chocolate cake, but what could I do? She loved it, twirling this way and that to make the skirt swirl out.

Lin gave her a little tote full of plush baby animals. Dora shyly offered a glittery bag with drawstrings and was visibly relieved when Rose cuddled and kissed the handmade velvet squirrel it contained. Purple teddy and yellow squirrel were solemnly put to bed next to each other against a cushion in the corner of one of the sofas. A large piece of pink tissue paper served as their blanket.

Sven seemed to be holding back. "I didn't know what to get," he said. "I hope she likes it." More squeals of joy as she opened a fairytale castle that opened up to show little figures of a royal family and their dog. She immediately started moving the figures around, putting a baby princess to bed with the dog at her feet.

"Sam 'n' me," she said before giving him the kiss and "tanku" I'd insisted she bestow after opening each gift. Sven looked fit to burst, obviously not too traumatized by the morning's events.

I sat back, watching my babe playing with her new toys, happy and content—a miracle child, loving family, and the pleasant buzz of delicious bubbly.

"Time for cake," Lin announced.

Hunter picked up Rose, and we all crowded around the table. Rose's eyes grew wide when she saw the gorgeous confection whose dark sheen was dotted with crystallized roses and violets. Hunter lit three pink candles, and Lin started the happy birthday song, which we all joined in. Rose was confused until we got to the "dear Rose" part, when she pointed at herself and giggled. I tucked a napkin into her collar to try to protect the dress, making sure she didn't get too much of the outrageously rich cake. She ate a small slice and chewed a few floral garnishes, particularly enjoying the violets, which I didn't expect.

We were all ready for a nap after we'd more or less demolished the cake. But who can keep a determined child from the beach? After I got her into her swimsuit, Sven carried her down there, together with the dump truck, and we all followed, taking our topped-up glasses. Hunter held a bottle in each hand and Lin a small ice chest. We mostly flopped down under the umbrellas. It was getting a bit too hot for comfort—at least for those of us who were human.

Hunter and Rose dug up sand and deposited it on their growing mountain with a great deal of satisfaction. Hunter suggested starting a new mountain, but this one had to be even bigger. Hunter had looked a little downcast by his gift's cool reception, but it was clear now his choice was a success, which delighted him. He was having fun, too.

Soon, Rose started to yawn. I spread out a towel in a shady spot, and she fell asleep in no time. I worried about dropping off in case she woke first and got herself into trouble, but I'm afraid I did.

The roar of powerful bikes jolted me awake. Was it a dream? No, they still revved and rumbled. I took a quick look at Rose. Still asleep. The others were all on their feet. The looks on their faces worried me, so I got up to see what was going on. About fifteen leather-clad bikers strode down the path. They didn't look friendly.

"Sven and Mary, stay with Rose," said Hunter.

The gods lined up in front of the intruders.

"What do you want?" Hunter said, his voice almost a growl. "You are on private property."

"Are we now?" said the lead biker. His eyes looked Lin up and down and flashed yellow. I remembered Lin's stories. Loki had taken over this man's mind.

Dread consumed me. Rose stirred, so I picked her up.

The man turned to me. "Cute little girl," he said. "I wish I had one just like that."

My stomach knotted while my breath came in short bursts.

Agna moved in front of Hunter. "Hello, boys. How nice to see you."

"Who are you? Get out of the way. I have no business with you." His voice sounded oddly high-pitched.

"Ooh, sorry," Agna said before dissolving into a mist that evaporated immediately.

The leader was not fazed, but the other men gasped and started muttering amongst themselves.

"Is this better?" said Agna as she reappeared behind them.

They whipped around as if they'd heard a gunshot.

"Nice friend you've got there," said their fearless leader. "She doesn't scare me."

Lin had not uttered a word. She just stared at the man. Hunter had said nothing more. Rose was still sleepy, lying against my shoulder.

Sven muttered, "Oh, my god, oh, my god."

Quite so.

"You should be scared of me," Agna suddenly trilled before throwing up her arms and letting out the screech of a demented banshee.

The men flailed, their clothes puddling on the sand as their bodies shrank until they scampered out of pant legs and sleeves as ... rats. Rats the size of corgis.

Lin yelled, "In the name of the gods, why rats?"

"Oops, that came out wrong," said Agna. "Sorry."

Meanwhile, the rats went for us. One climbed up my leg, making for Rose's toes. Sven snatched her out of my arms, and the creature bit a chunk out of my arm instead. I couldn't help yelling in pain, which frightened Rose, who started to wail.

"Shit," yelled Sven as he punched off the rat, who'd tried again to reach Rose.

It scurried into the undergrowth.

"Shit," piped Rose. "Shit, shit."

"Sven, run to the house with her," I said.

"I can't leave you."

"Rose comes first."

He took off across the matted grasses and weeds, closely pursued by that rat, which persevered, despite its limp. Sven stopped, turned, waited, and kicked even harder this time. He dashed into the house and slammed the door.

Several ganged up on Hunter, who punched, kicked, and stomped until he'd dispatched four or five. They obviously meant to separate him from Lin, whom Loki attacked in a frenzy, his teeth bared and yellow eyes flashing like a beacon. She punched and kicked, but he moved back in after each setback, seizing every opportunity to take a bite out of her. They moved so fast I could barely make out what was going on in the blurred pinwheel.

"Do something, Agna," Lin screamed as she danced and spun in an effort to shake off the beast. Hunter tried to help, but Loki managed to dodge his efforts, resulting in Hunter landing a hefty punch on Lin's shoulder instead.

She fell, and Loki jumped on her head. She sprang up and threw him into the sea. The tide carried him out a little way, but he rode the next wave back far enough to bring him to shore again. He ran at Lin, who managed to land a kick worthy of a prima ballerina, stunning him momentarily.

Another screech pierced the air. Rats squeaked and tumbled as their fur fell away to reveal scales, their voices stilled, and their legs spread into fins. I was still shaking with fright and pain, but this latest development calmed me a little. The biggest fish, its mouth gaping and yellow eyes staring, flapped at Lin's feet.

"Agna, that's brilliant," she cried. "You've outdone yourself."

"About time," Hunter muttered.

The screech of seagulls as they flocked to the beach became deafening. A couple of ospreys got first pick as they'd been watching from their platform just offshore. I was surprised they were still there. It was high time they began their trek to South America. Soon all the fish had been taken except one: Loki. He was huge and thrashing furiously, too much for even the ospreys to handle.

An eagle swept in, no doubt alerted by the commotion. It grabbed Loki in its huge talons and started tearing away at him right there and then.

I turned aside. That had once been a man, after all, even if Loki had invaded him.

"All done," said Lin. "Perhaps now we can relax."

Only the middle section of the fish remained after the eagle flew off, its denuded backbone somehow obscene. I shaded my eyes and watched the bird soar. Suddenly it spiraled and somersaulted, careened sideways, rose up and up until it levelled off, turned, and dive-bombed Lin. She jumped aside and smashed her fist into it. It tumbled to shore, where Hunter stamped on its head. He picked the magnificent raptor up by a foot and laid it at Lin's feet.

"Burn it," she said. "You can get into a lot of trouble for killing an eagle."

"What will the neighbors say about all this?" I asked.

Lin replied, "The windows in the house next door don't look out on this beach. And it's a weekday. I don't think anyone saw. Anyway, who'd believe them?"

I wasn't sure I believed it myself.

"I need a nap," said Agna, limping up the path. "I'll see to the bikes later." I remembered how casting spells took it out of her. I hoped she'd make it upstairs to her bed.

"Mom, Dad, I need a word with you," said Sven, who'd just come back down. He must have left Rose with Dora.

"Yes, well, go and get me some matches first," said Hunter, glancing nervously at Lin. "Anyway, I have a lot of wood to chop. You'll have to help."

"Of course, Sven dear, we'll have a little talk after dinner," said Lin, patting her son's arm as if she planned to tell him a bedtime story. Some bedtime story.

Thank goodness Dr. Ayre hadn't stayed long at the beach. She'd be able to patch us all up. I hoped I hadn't caught a nasty disease from those teeth.

Lin needed help more than me, special powers or not. She had multiple bites that oozed white milky fluid.

"Come on, Lin," I said. "We need to get Dr. Ayre to see to our bites." Mine stung badly.

"You go," she said. "There's a little more to do here."

Dr. Ayre took one look at my bite and ordered me upstairs to her bedroom.

"No, no, no," shouted Rose as I began to walk away. "More beetch. Shit."

I was too tired to deal with a meltdown and the language. "All right, wait just a little longer. We'll take a walk and see if we can find some shells. Mummy has a hurt that Dr. Ayre is going to fix."

She seemed to understand and sat on the sofa with the purple teddy perched on her lap, the orange squirrel sitting between the teddy's legs.

Dr. Ayre didn't even wash the bite, instead smothering it in some thick salve that smelled of jasmine.

"I'll bandage it to keep the ointment in place," she said, wrapping it tightly with snow-white gauze.

"Thank you, Dr. Ayre. That hurt a lot."

"Does it still?"

"Well, actually, no." *What the hell is in that stuff?*

Rose and I walked down to the beach with Sven, who had finally found the matches. If I'd thought about it, I could have told him they were on the mantlepiece behind a wooden goose, out of Rose's reach. Buzzing with pain and shock, I hadn't been thinking straight.

The remains of the bird lay still as Lin and Hunter stood quietly, embracing each other. To my surprise, the green-eyed monster stayed in his lair. It was as it should be after such a fierce battle. Lin needed comfort.

"What dat?" Rose said, pointing to the decimated bird.

"Just a little accident," I said. "Nothing to worry about."

She seemed to accept this.

I took her up to the concrete drums that bordered the property. Rose found lots of very ordinary shells, which I obligingly stashed in the pockets of my cotton robe. I smelled what must be burning feathers and couldn't help turning around. Sven trudged back up the path while Hunter knelt over the eagle's carcass, striking matches to light feathers all the way along its body. He'd even spread the wings to burn those.

I was suddenly struck with the horror of what I'd witnessed and the ensuing deaths. But if it hadn't been them, it would have been us. I had no doubt about that.

Hunter had a fair blaze going now.

"Would you like a snack, darling?" I asked Rose. "You can show Sven your new shells. He loves shells."

She didn't protest this time. "Cake?" was all she said.

"I think it's all gone," I said. If there was a smidgeon left, she could have it. My baby deserved all the good things life could offer.

I looked out to sea before going in. A couple of sailboats forged their way back to safe harbor at Solomons Island. Outlined against the horizon, a container ship, stacked like a child's castle of blocks, headed up toward Baltimore.

A day almost done.

29

A shadow slunk through the undergrowth toward the shore. A red fox peered out of the tall grasses along the sand, sniffing to locate the new delicious scent. She scurried across the beach to the carcass. Her kits had devoured every bit of the rabbit she'd caught earlier. Now it was her turn.

The feathers were not entirely gone, but nothing her teeth couldn't handle. The fire hadn't done much damage, only cooked the meat. She tore into it, crunching the bones with relish. She'd been hungry for a couple of days now. Now she felt fine. Finer than fine. Strong and fiery, her blood fizzed. Time to move on. The kits would leave soon, anyway.

She trotted up the path, not bothering to hide—it was her territory. Maybe she wouldn't feed the kits tomorrow. It was about time they fended for themselves. She was sick of the endless cycle of hunting and dragging the food back to their den under the garden shed. *Enough.*

She usually taught them how to hunt before they left. Not this time. *Enough*.

She must see what lay beyond the woods. Humans came from there. But this was where she was supposed to be, something she had to do. Never mind, she could come back. Somehow she knew she must come back.

She stopped outside the shed, suddenly feeling dizzy and weak. Not right. What were these feelings? Strong, but ... what?

Energy bubbled up, firing her legs. Kill something. Anything. She streaked into the woods behind the house.

Kill.

Book Club Questions

1. *How is Mary's outlook changing as a result of living with Lin and Hunter?*
2. *Is Lin or Hunter's outlook changing as a result of living with Mary?*
3. *What is Auntie Peggy's attitude regarding Mary's situation? Why do you think she takes Mary's revelations so calmly?*
4. *Why is Lin so attached to Agna?*
5. *Were the actions Lin took to save her daughter from Loki reasonable? Were there alternatives?*
6. *What do you think about how religious issues are dealt with in the book?*
7. *What did you recognize in the book as being inspired by well-known myths?*
8. *What did you recognize in the book as being real places and situations?*
9. *Do you think Lin was exploiting the prostitutes in Bruges, or was she just making the best of a bad situation?*
10. *Will Rose run into issues when she starts to make friends her own age?*
11. *Is Loki indestructible?*

Author Bio

D. A. Spruzen grew up near London, U.K., graduated from the London College of Dance and Drama Education, and earned an MFA in Creative Writing from Queens University of Charlotte; she teaches creative writing in Northern Virginia when not seeking her own muse. The *Witch of Tut* is the second book in her series, "*Sleuthing With Mortals*." The first, published in September, 2023 is The Turkish Connection. Other publications include an historical novel *The Blitz Business*, and a poetry collection, *Long in the Tooth*. Her poems and short stories have appeared in many online and print publications. She resides in Northern Virginia and Southern Maryland.

More books from 4 Horsemen Publications

Crime, Detective, and Noir

A.K. Ramirez
Secrets & Photographs

Joe Davison
Journey to Hell

Mark Atley
Too Late to Say Goodbye
Trouble Weighs a Ton

Paranormal & Urban Fantasy

Amanda Fasciano
Waking Up Dead
Dead Vessel

Beau Lake
The Beast Beside Me
The Beast Within Me
Taming the Beast: Novella
The Beast After Me
Charming the Beast
The Beast Like Me
An Eye for Emeralds
Swimming in Sapphires
Pining for Pearls

Chelsea Burton Dunn
By Moonlight

J.M. Paquette
Call Me Forth
Invite Me In
Keep Me Close

Kait Disney-Leugers
Antique Magic

Lyra R. Saenz
Prelude
Falsetto in the Woods: Novella
Ragtime Swing
Sonata
Song of the Sea
The Devil's Trill
Bercuese
To Heal a Songbird
Ghost March
Nocturne

Megan Mackie
The Saint of Liars
The Devil's Day
The Finder of the Lucky Devil

Paige Lavoie
I'm in Love with Mothman

Robert J. Lewis
Shadow Guardian and the Three Bears

Valerie Willis
Cedric: The Demonic Knight
Romasanta: Father of Werewolves
The Oracle: Keeper of the Gaea's Gate
Artemis: Eye of Gaea
King Incubus: A New Reign

Fantasy

D.A. Spruzen
Turkish Connection

D. Lambert
To Walk into the Sands
Rydan
Celebrant
Northlander
Esparan
King
Traitor
His Last Name

Danielle Orsino
Locked Out of Heaven
Thine Eyes of Mercy
From the Ashes
Kingdom Come
Fire, Ice, Acid, & Heart
A Fae is Done

J.M. Paquette
Klauden's Ring
Solyn's Body
The Inbetween
Hannah's Heart

Lou Kemp
The Violins Played Before Junstan
Music Shall Untune the Sky

R.J. Young
Challenges of Tawa

Sydney Wilder
Daughter of Serpents

Valerie Willis
Cedric: The Demonic Knight
Romasanta: Father of Werewolves
The Oracle: Keeper of the Gaea's Gate
Artemis: Eye of Gaea
King Incubus: A New Reign

Kyle Sorrell
Munderworld

**Discover more at
4HorsemenPublications.com**

www.ingramcontent.com/pod-product-compliance
Lightning Source LLC
Chambersburg PA
CBHW020504310726
48979CB00016B/2772/J

* 9 7 9 8 8 2 3 2 0 2 1 3 8 *